Also by Ian Laver

Novels –
CRUCIAL STEP
UNEASY

Short story collection –
DEADLY SINS

Other collections and anthologies -
Coolum Wave writers-
BRAINWAVES
COASTERS
UNDERCURRENTS

Short stories and Haiku - numerous

HARD HITS

by

IAN LAVER

HARD HITS
First published in Australia by Ian Laver 2025
https://www.ianlaver.net

A catalogue record for this
book is available from the
National Library of Australia

ISBN: 978-0-6451887-6-9 (pbk)
ISBN: 978-0-6451887-7-6 (ebk)

Cover design by Jan Forbes © 2025
Typesetting and design by Publicious Book Publishing
Published in collaboration with Publicious Book Publishing
www.publicious.com.au

Disclaimer
These stories are works of fiction, some are based on real events but all characters are fictitious and any resemblance to actual persons, living or dead is entirely coincidental. Some geographical locations exist but some are invented.

PRAISE for CRUCIAL STEP ...

What a glorious read! Wow! What a journey! Your vivid descriptions paint a picture more than any postcard or photo could do. Wonderful. I really loved your well-drawn characters – particularly Theo, Jack, Biru, Eric and Franka. Your art with the dialogue was very well done and blended in perfectly for the characters both Asian and Swedish (and, of course Australian!). The tension ebbed and flowed nicely and kept me totally engaged.
BOB GOODWIN, *author of Ezekiel, and the Max Justice trilogy*

Crucial Step, with its well-drawn characters and action-packed story taking place in exotic Asia, will keep you in suspense all the way through.
ROBIN STOREY, *author of Murder Undone and Secret Kill*

Crucial Step builds its tangled web of foreign intrigue as a young man battles the demons of his past and those who stand in the way of the truth. Once caught in the web the reader is there to the end. A good read.
KEN FISHER, *author of Beach Spinifex*

PRAISE for UNEASY...

"Uneasy" is an excellent, fast-paced police drama with a gritty authenticity that transports the reader to South East Queensland in the late 90s. The main characters are flawed but likable, the language is believable and the story is gripping from the first page. Great read, and looking forward to more from this series.
COLIN HOLLOWAY, *goodreads.com.au*

...a well-crafted interwoven story line. Captures the imagination from page one... great stuff!
BRIAN PURDEY, *author of Mindfulness Decoded*

I just finished your book Uneasy. Just terrific! Well done! A crushing finale, worth reading right to the end.
ALISON QUIGLEY, *Sunshine Coast author*

PRAISE for IAN'S SHORT STORIES ...

Australian Literary Review ...people on the fringes of society... a confrontation between characters in Ian Laver's Rough Justice...
Peter Cowan Short Story Competition ...Hellfire Pass – taut and unsparing, this portrait of memory and mateships gifted an ending of courageous sorrow as good as the best literature.

Author's Note

HARD HITS is my latest collection of short stories, many with a sinister edge, but all with a hard-hitting message. Some of the characters perpetrate terrible acts and some are unfortunate enough to be placed in dire circumstances. Others just cannot help themselves either because they are opportunistic, weak, criminal, or somewhere in between.

Each story places someone in a position where they must make a decision. All of them face moral and ethical choices, often impacting others. Some of the characters have good intent, others purely evil.

Where do you fit in the scheme of things? What decisions would you make if forced into a corner?

Some of these stories were written twenty years ago or more, as a result of prompts selected by members of various writing groups I have been privileged to be part of in my writing journey. Many are based on actual events and seven of these stories have won awards in various writing competitions.

I hope you enjoy this collection because although you may feel challenged by some of the characters and their actions, the stories are about people around us, maybe even people you know.

Ian Laver

Foreword

Many years ago, Ian Laver, a long-term friend, confessed to me that he wanted to be a writer. Having had some experience in this area myself, I thought, 'Good luck!' Over the ensuing years, he has shown his enduring passion for writing, and I have watched him grow in his pursuit of his dream.

In typical Ian fashion, he has not only connected to others on this path but has also shown leadership skills and a willingness to put in time and effort. Combined with these qualities is a humility and eagerness to learn and share his own acquired knowledge, learning from others in the process. As a consequence, his literary output is not only impressive but also progressive. His community spirit and keenness to share has made a name for him on the Sunshine Coast particularly.

If 'Crucial Step', 'Uneasy' and his last book of short stories 'Deadly Sins' are anything to go by, 'Hard Hits' will indeed deliver what it promises. Stick with this writer, dear reader, and not only will you see him go far but you will also be generously included in his journey. For that is how I would describe the person and his fiction – generous: of characters, plots, twists and turns, surprises and just plain feel-good outcomes (but not always).

You could describe all of Ian's books as hard hitting in one way or another. So, sit down with the latest, aptly titled 'Hard Hits', dip in and out, page turn, marvel at the storytelling and characters, try to guess where the story is going, enjoy the prose, be an active reader. It will be impossible not to be with this engaging writer! If this is the book you start with, you will want to rewind and read the others. I see more awards coming his way.

Andrea Rankin, nationally accredited professional editor (IPEd), non-fiction writer

Contents

In the modern world

Hot issues

May be solved with the touch of a button

Accused

'Mr Mosley?'

Dennis Mosley turned. 'Yes?' He knew the rules and was reluctant to engage with a 16-year-old female student without another person in the room. There was nothing he could do about it now. After all, he had asked her to see him sometime during the day and lunch break was nearly over; he had expected someone else to be around.

Tayla Murphy crossed one tanned leg over the other and swished her long, blonde hair behind her shoulder. He tried to look away but could not. Fragrant air filled the space.

'Tayla, I ... er ... wanted to speak with you in relation to your exam results.'

'My exam results ... *Sir?*' She cooed and breathed in, expanding her developing breasts.

Mosley stroked his three-day designer stubble to give him time to claw back the upper hand. Trying to sound firm he said, 'Tayla, you failed.'

Blue eyes glinted as she inclined her head. Her gaze still had him nailed. The trace of a smile tickled the corners of her mouth, and she ran the tip of a red tongue across almost milk teeth.

Mosley stumbled on, better to talk than ... 'Tayla, you have to knuckle down and take this seriously. You don't do your homework; you wag school and don't seem to study. You need a High School Certificate to get anywhere in the world ...'

She pouted in a husky whisper, 'Will you pass me … Sir?' Her gaze did not waver.

Mosley had not moved on from wondering why a 16-year-old girl wore lipstick to school, and makeup.

Tayla leaned back in the seat and slowly lifted her school tunic to show her upper thighs.

'*Stop this!*' he hissed. 'Stop … stop this nonsense … or I'll take you straight up to the Deputy Principal's office *now!*'

Tayla Murphy did not even blink and the slightest of smiles remained. She stared at him; insolence balanced with confidence. She lifted her chin. 'No, I don't think you will, *Sir*, or I will say you touched me inappropriately.'

Mosley! For God's sake get a grip on this, man!

He was so shocked it inadvertently allowed him to break the locked, staring contest. He looked past her for a piano-wire moment and then struggled to re-engage eye contact. *You are the adult here, Mosley.*

'*What* did you say?' His forehead tightened.

'I'll tell on yooooo, I know you want to touch me …' the voice was breathy and the action of gently rolling her head was classic Marilyn Monroe. She snuck her tunic higher, showing white panties.

'Stop this … *now!*' he barked, louder and remonstrated, pointing his finger heaven wise. 'Stop this, you will get *expelled!*' He almost added, *and I'll end up in bloody jail!*

∞

The bell rang to signal the end of last lesson and the end of the school day. It could not come soon enough for Dennis Mosley, but it was not over for him, or maybe it was.

He nodded towards Tayla who had taken her time packing up. The class shuffled out in a rumbling, noisy shamble as she ambled over and sat down in the chair he had positioned for her.

It was the same again. Leg crossed over, hair behind the shoulder, pouty, red, shiny lips, white-on-white teeth, blue sparkling eyes. The air filled with mint and frangipani. 'You wanted to see me again … *Sir?*'

He took a deep breath; this time he was more in control ... but not much. He raised both hands in a stop gesture. 'Tayla, look, you must realise this is very serious. I cannot pass students for bribes or doing favours.'

Same confident manner again. She almost kissed the words, 'Why not, Sir?' She leaned back, this time showing lacey red panties.

Mosley, for God's sake, man!

She winked, 'I changed them in class, just a few minutes ago. I was looking at you when I did, you were looking at me ...'

'*Stop it!*' he almost yelled, 'I can't pass you and I am going to report this!'

Tayla looked around, maybe to see if anyone else was around. 'I'm going to say you put your hand up my *dress!*' Her demeanour changed from seduction to black and cruel.

He forced his teacher voice. 'You know that is not true.'

She became Marilyn again. '*We* know that, that is our secret but ...'

'You can't do this, Tayla.'

A knock on the door arrested the moment. 'Is this a convenient time?' said Emilie Doxie.

Tayla turned and said in a harsh tone, 'Miss Doxie, Mr Mosley put his hand up my ...'

'That will do, Tayla Murphy,' snapped the Deputy Principal as she placed her laptop computer on the desk. She pressed a button. 'Look at this!'

The screen showed the Skyped interaction between Mosley and Murphy, audio distant at times but clear enough. They listened for a couple of minutes.

Tayla looked at Mosley, eyes bulging. He pointed to his laptop facing her and then back at Ms Doxie's computer, still showing the recording reduced screen in the corner.

He said, 'It's all there, screen off but Skype camera on, still going. Ms Doxie was watching all of this in her office. You are in big trouble, Tayla,'

'Right,' interjected the Deputy Principal, 'let's go to the office and get your mother down here, she knows the way by now.'

'*My mother?*' yelped Tayla, 'but ... but ...'

'She may be the least of your problems because you may have to face criminal charges; and it's Ms Doxie, not Miss, alright, let's go.'

As Tayla walked toward the door she turned. Her face was white, and crystals crowded her eyes. She looked very much the 16-year-old schoolgirl she was.

Mosley was internally shaking as he cradled his head in his hands. Many thoughts scrolled through his crowded brain. *What if…?*

The End

A time will come

When we must stand up -

Will you be ready?

Honour Has a Price

Walter Morris just managed to slip the phone into the gauze pocket of his bulletproof vest as he observed Sergeant Raglan, closely followed by his shadow, Corporal Taggard, almost upon him.

'Ah, the Rag-Tag Team,' mumbled Walter to himself.

A gust of dry, desert wind pushed a cloud of forty-five-degree dust high into the air.

'Hey, where's Wally?' quipped Taggard, lighting up a cigarette, head swivelling like a prairie-dog, glancing the full three-sixty.

'Funny man, Tag, not very original, why don't you try another one?' The dislike was clear in Walter's voice.

Sergeant Raglan's glistening gaze penetrated like the heat of the day. 'Hand over your helmet-cam, soldier.' A command, not a question.

Walter just stared for a long minute. 'And why would you want my cam, *sir*?'

'Stop fucking with me, dick-wit. Helmet-cam! Now, Corporal Morris, that's an order!'

Walter slowly unclipped the camera from his helmet and handed it over, making a show of defiance. At the same time, he pretended to adjust the chest strap on his bulletproof vest, touching his phone. He said loudly, 'I asked you why you wanted my helmet-cam, sir? Just curious.'

'Shut your gob,' offered Taggard, show some respect to your superior ...'

'Back off Taggard. Remember, you are the same rank as me, at least last time I looked, right?' Taggard puffed out his weedy chest, pretending the tough nut.

Sergeant Raglan nudged Taggard, 'Hey, look at this? Oh heck, oh, woops, I just accidently deleted this morning's footage, gee willikers, sorry. Heavens, gee, Morris, sorry mate. Tough luck, you can just document it as cam failure, the admin morons don't give a fuck, they don't check it anyway.'

Morris piped up in a clear voice, 'Sir, why did you delete that? Wouldn't have anything to do with you shooting an unarmed man and not wanting to have any record of it, would it? I'd be guessing right that you and knucklehead have already deleted your footage?'

'Hey, dick sack! Watch your mouth. You don't speak to me like that, right! Remember you are speaking to your superior officer,' replied the sergeant, rocking around on his toes and rubbing his nose, clearly annoyed.

Morris kept trying to bait him. It was clear the sergeant had just had a line of speed. 'Sergeant Raglan, you shot an unarmed man with his hands up. You are a disgrace to the Armed Forces.'

Raglan kept moving on his feet, an almost punch-drunk stance. 'Fuck you Morris, so what if I did shoot a fucking raghead, one less in the world. Watch who you're speaking to, I'm the sergeant 'round here and you are a corporal, right?'

Taggard with his bulging Marty Feldman eyes, glanced in all directions and began to giggle in a demented way.

Morris had to keep focussed. '*Sir*, you killed an unarmed man. He was a human being, a local farmer and he had his hands up, but now, thanks to you deleting the incident, we have no record. But I just want you to know that I know, alright?'

The sergeant's eyes shone. 'Where do you get off, dick-wit? Eh? Sure, I shot the cunt, yeah, he was unarmed and fucking A one, yeah, he had his hands up but get this?' He pulled out an old revolver and dangled it by the trigger guard. 'For the record, I confiscated this off the bastard, didn't I Corporal Taggard?'

'Absolutely, sir, two witnesses against one, definitely armed.'

The sergeant was not finished, his cockiness and arrogance could not be contained. 'And you, Corporal fucking Morris, had better watch your back cos from now on, you might just get a bullet in the back – from this gun.' His swagger slowed but his eyes glistened. 'So, if I was you, I'd play along and keep your gob shut.' He threw the helmet-cam back to Morris.

'If you say so, sir, I'll do my best.'

That answer stirred up Taggard again. He stepped closer. Morris knew the revolver was probably taken off a Taliban fighter ages ago and had been stolen from the storeroom back at base.

Taggard made a pretend gun with his hand, sighted down his index finger and said, 'Bang, matey boy. Keep looking over your shoulder. You're a gonner, prick.'

They both turned, leaving Morris sitting in the shade of the olive tree. The shade was only by dictionary definition; it did not seem to make any difference. Sweat trapped under his heavy clothing felt like a sauna. When the other two were some distance away he pulled the mobile phone out of his pocket and pressed the button to stop the recording.

'Gotcha, you bastard,' he said.

He quickly pressed send. Colonel Miles at CII, Central Internal Investigations, would be pleased with the earlier text as well, a copy of the film footage showing the murder of an unarmed farmer. He had just managed to insert the memory card before the camera was confiscated and the footage deleted. They had been trying to get evidence on Sergeant Raglan and his mate, Taggard, for some time. They were both out of control.

Corporal Walter Morris felt good about what he had done and felt a pang of pride. On the other hand, he had a strong feeling of uneasiness too, as those two psychos were certainly capable of murdering him as well.

There was a huddle and a stir of noise at the end of the wall. The men were preparing to go. Morris gathered his things and moved in their direction.

Sergeant Raglan whispered at combat volume, 'Okay you pin-heads, listen up, let's move out, down the end, past the buildings and through the field. Normal formation fellers, but, hey, Morris?' He pretended to consider a request, or a favour. 'Um, I heard you mention you wanted to take the lead? Here's your chance, way you go.'

Sergeant Raglan sneered and held a long stare, then began chuckling. Corporal Taggard sniggered, prairie-dog head jerking around, eyes bulging.

It became even hotter inside Walter Morris's flack-jacket.

The End

Feeling lucky?

Sometimes a change makes sense -

When you are ahead

Chance Encounter

'Fish net? Naah, black stockings, yeah, they'll do,' Jewel said to the mirror.

You did not use your real name on the game. She pouted full lips at the mirror, applied a smear of red lipstick and performed a rolling mmmmm to spread the colour. She took a drag on her cigarette and placed it in the ashtray. A red circle decorated the filter.

Tonight, she would try another hunting ground. It was becoming harder to attract punters in the city and the Valley because the police had cracked down. Also, over the last six months, one woman had been murdered and three had disappeared in town. All four were believed to be prostitutes. The word around was that maybe the murdered woman was just unlucky, or a jealous partner had taken her out, and the other three could have gone back to where they came from. The Nest Strip Club did not pay much but did help pay the bills when she was desperate.

In the city she had been picked up by police before and put in jail or dropped at a rehabilitation facility overnight. She did not want that. Jewel was not ready to drop her habits, not yet anyway. She looked down at her arms and smiled. She managed to find a vein in a different spot each time. Her habit was not too bad, she would give up soon.

Tonight, she thought she would set herself up along Brunswick Street, near the Crystal Encounter Wine Bar. She had worked all the pubs along the main drags everywhere in Brisbane until eventually bar staff began to recognise her and that was that. Anyway, tonight she was going to work the street around the wine bar.

Her only problem was Morgan Crowhurst, who ran the girls in the area towards the Valley. Gaynor, one of his charges, had dobbed her in about three months ago for snaring punters.

Jewel dabbed deodorant under her arms and then from her bellybutton down to her bush. She poured a stiff Vodka, downed it and poured another. *Careful baby, not too much, hey.* She recalled what Crowey did to her. He punched her in the stomach and told her in no uncertain terms to disappear. That was a while ago and word on the street had it that Crowey had been banned for soliciting near the wine bar, so if she hung around there things should be alright.

∞

Jewel made a visit to her dealer. He was not happy about it but allowed her to hit up there. She took a taxi up to Brunswick Street, aware such a luxury ate into her budget, but she felt lucky.

Down the lane from the Crystal Encounter, the carpark was almost full, and all the vehicles were shiny new. She had been booted out of the wine bar six months ago and on the two occasions she had been back to chat up punters, she had been escorted to the door.

It was a good location because there were several recessed doorways to flatten into if the police or an enemy cruised around. Also, a carport open to the street, sheltered by a bushy garden, gave her a perfect spot to service clients. Jewel was ever wary of Crowhurst, but a stroll 30 meters or so down Brunswick Street put her mind at rest. She could see one of his girls way down towards the Valley end.

She was in luck. A snappy suited punter with a bald head gave a nod and she fixed him up in a doorway. His excitement level played to her advantage and he was soon on his way in a flash SAAB.

Fortune favoured Jewel again and she could almost feel her bank balance going up. She hoped the big man was not due for a heart attack as he puffed and panted and almost collapsed on her. He gave her a generous tip and a slap on the bottom.

A cold westerly came up and she wished she had a cardigan. An hour passed so she ambled to the park above the Story Bridge. She had to sniff a line, not easy in the wind, but she could not risk doing the needle thing. She took a long tug on the vodka flask.

Back to the wine bar precinct. Business was slow. Down to Brunswick Street again and a casual wander, making herself sexy and available to the prowlers and invisible to the police - and Crowey's spies.

In luck again, a tradie in a work ute, dressed rough but with a friendly face pulled up next to her. She poked her head through the open window, rubbed thumb and forefinger together. He fanned fifties. She jumped in, they went around the corner, quick service, money in hand and back on the street again.

A black Landcruiser sidled up. She had to stand her full height to see in. Cute bloke, winning smile. He fluttered crisp hundreds. Mid-thirties, Clark Gable wink, slightly worn face and a small scar across an eyebrow. Football injury, fight? Rugged look. Strange eyes. Don't care, anything to get out of the wind. Also, three hundred, way above the rate.

Jewel reached for the door handle.

'*Oi! Eh you, fucking bitch! You!*' came a bellow from down the street.

Oh no! Crowey! 'Sorry mate,' she yelled in the direction of the punter. Jewel whipped off her high heels and sprinted across the main road, narrowly missing a taxi.

Crowhurst waved his ham-like arms and wobbled his weight towards her, but she was well away. He only caught her last time because she tripped in her high heels. He was no match for her as she pelted down Kent Street.

∞

Saturday morning Jewel rolled out of bed. Cup of tea and cigarette in hand she clicked on the television.

News flash. *Serial killer arrested!* On the screen was the face of the punter in the Landcruiser. Cute bloke, Gable wink, strange eyes, scar through an eyebrow.

'Christ Almighty,' she whispered, voice husky with smoke, 'Honey, it's time to find a new job.'

The End

Some people should not be -

Reason cannot win -

There is only one solution

Pruning

'I'm sorry Ms Stanthorpe, naturally we'll do all we can, and everythink, but it's bloody unlikely anyone will hand it in.'

'Okay, thanks for your help, sergeant.'

Blanche hung up and took another sip of wine. She was not too worried because the leather carry-all, although not an el-cheapo, did not contain anything of real value. But still, she knew she had been careless.

'Lucky me,' she sang, Marilyn Monroe style and topped up her glass. She was lucky indeed, because in her small shoulder bag was her passport, Indian visa, wallet, and mobile phone. She had almost put them in the leather carry-all under her feet. How could she not have even felt it disappear? No recollection of anyone in the seat behind let alone a hand reaching under and pinching it. The creak, groan, and sway of the railway carriage as well as clickety clack, lulled her. The parade of stations and the blurred faces of beings she had no need to know anything about, zipped by. Almost like a sedative. With all the dramas of finishing work three days before, her head buzzed with things to do in preparation for the overseas trip in two weeks' time. She had reported the loss of the bag at the station master's office.

'Yep, no worries,' mumbled the *all about me* rosy-cheeked trainee, scratching his neck, obviously more concerned with the itchy label on the inside of his shirt. A fuzzy platform announcement in the background pretended efficiency and order. 'I'll make a note of it in the ledger. Here, fill this out, will ya?'

She shook her head free of the station hustle and half closed her eyes. So much for someone happy in their work.

The next morning Blanche spent nailing down insurance and accommodation details with the travel agent. After coffee with Gloria, she ticked off a few other commitments on the list of things to do. Planets were lining up because she had sold her car to Gloria who was kind enough to allow her to use it until the day she left. She was even more grateful to Gloria because she had not known her long. The loss of the bag though felt like a grain of rice in her shoe, no chance of dismissing it. She compromised her irritation with the practical reminder to be more careful and tuned in to more immediate things. Especially travelling overseas.

She'd had enough of Sydney and the trip to India was the break she needed before taking up a job in London later in the year. She had told Gloria there were no plans beyond the job in London and if any of that did not work out, she was happy enough to go with whatever might pop up. There was no desire to return to Australia for a year or two, and when she did, it would probably be her hometown Brisbane. The marriage to Nick was okay for about a year and then seemed to go nowhere for the next two. The separation was easy because they both had separate bank accounts and he was offered a temporary job up the coast. Both realised the whole thing was a simple case of two inexperienced people colliding. At no stage did the subject of children really get discussed seriously. She was thankful for that because some of her friends had bitter custody battles over children, money, and property. They had been separated for over a year and, surprisingly, were very good friends. Too right, she thought, she was ready for a change if not an adventure.

∞

'Blanche? Blanche Stanthorpe?'

'Yes, speaking.'

A short silence.

'I believe you lost a bag on the train yesterday?'

'Yes, that's right, umm, who is this?' She pushed her blonde hair away from each ear, changing hands with the phone. The action reminded her to have it cut before going away.

'Name's Gill, I've got your bag here.' A *bright have a nice day* voice.

'Great. How did you …?'

'Oh, someone handed it in. Of course, we can't guarantee everything is inside, but at least you get your bag back.'

'Ah, you're from the railways?'

'Yep, cleaner, well supervisor really, anyway, one of our custodians handed it in.'

'That's great; I might call in at the station master's office later today and pick it up.'

'Yeah, ya can but it's not necessary, I can drop it off at your place, I only live at Sutherland.'

'It's okay, I can go to the …'

'No problem.'

'Do you know where I *live*?'

'Live? Oh yeah, Griffo, at the master's office told me when I reported it to him. We often help each other; things get handed in all the time. He said it was okay to …'

'Fair enough, thanks.'

'I'm off duty now, see you in about half an hour. If that's convenient, of course?'

'Er … okay, that's fine.'

Blanche was too preoccupied with packing appropriate clothing for Kerala to wonder anything.

∞

'Gilbert Oakley, people call me Gill.' A strong arm held out the bag. A wiry athletic build, medium height, couple of inches taller than her.

Blanche nodded, 'Right, thanks Gill, I'd like to give you some sort of reward.'

'No, not necessary, we're not supposed to accept any remuneration you know, government employees and all that.'

Blanche pulled out a fifty. 'Here.'

'No, can't take it, it's just a pleasure to be of service. No, that's okay, really.' He looked down at his brand-name sneakers. A sour unwashed odour emanated from him.

He made no effort to take the money, so she poked it back in the purse. She looked up, feeling slightly uncomfortable and tried to look past him at the golden cane palms but his demeanour demanded presence.

'Right … well thanks Gill, she smiled, must be going, I'm in a bit of a hurry.'

'You could invite me in for a few drinks or something.' His glance drifted upwards and made a point of levelling at her breasts. His mouth formed a line, the slightest indication of a smile.

The dead fetid air hung. A yapping terrier, down the road, started barking. She frowned. 'Um … no, sorry but I have things to do … and I'm going out soon.'

'Okay, no harm done.' His voice shifted to gritty and his glare sharpened. His cat's eyes zeroed in on hers. 'See you soon.' It was almost a taunt.

He slowly turned and walked off taking purposeful steps. The halo of body odour remained behind in the air, forcing her to close the door with purpose.

Blanche leaned against the inside of the door, slightly panting as if she had just returned from a run. She stood motionless for a couple of minutes. What she had just experienced gave her the shivers. She shook her head to try to clear it all and then checked the bag. Everything appeared to be in order.

∞

Next morning, just walking out the door, the landline rang.

'Hello?'

'G'day, Blanchie, Gill here.'

Silence. Ice tinkled down her vertebrae for a second.

'What … do you want?'

'How about having dinner with me tonight?'

'What? No, sorry er … I … I hardly know you, Gill. Besides, I'm already doing something tonight.' Her forehead felt like it had contracted and her ear against the phone was warm and moist.

'Well, well. That's not a very nice thing to do to someone who did you a really good turn, now is it, hey?' A sing-song voice.

'Gill? What is …? This is most inappropriate, I mean …'

His voice hardened like gravel, sounded like it came from a dungeon. 'Don't get uppity and bitchy with me, right? I went out of my way to …'

'Your … your behaviour is outrageous! This conversation is over!' She slammed the phone down. '*Bastard!*' Her spine tingled. A bead of sweat trickled down her back as she leant against the kitchen bench. Moments passed before her breathing returned to normal.

The phone shrilled causing her to knock over a cup. 'Bugger you, *mate!*' she barked and let the answering machine kick in.

'Hello? Miss Stanthorpe? This is the station master's office 'ere. We jess got a bag handed in which matches the description you gave us. No I.D. though.'

Blanche snatched up the handpiece. 'Hi, sorry, I was out in the yard. Er … you say you have a bag handed in …?'

'Yeah. Could be yours, ya know, had to check.'

'That's strange, a bloke by the name of Gill Oakley, railways' cleaner supervisor dropped off my bag yesterday …'

'Railways' cleaner? Gill Oakley, you say? Nup, never heard of him, besides, we got private contractors who do the cleaning. So, you got your bag? Coulda let us know, right?'

'Well, I only just … never mind.' She controlled her sigh. 'Thanks anyway.'

'Yeah, righto, I'll mark it mark it off the register then, orright?'

Blanche went to the shopping centre and chemist to sort out the last of her travel needs. In her haste earlier, she had forgotten some key paperwork for the bank and had to return home again. A quick search located the paperwork and as she turned from locking the front door, she felt a weight. That smell again. Feral body odour. There he was!

'Hi Blanchie, didn't startle you, did I?'

Her body froze for a second but then her insides shimmered. 'What? What are you …?'

'Now, now, Blanchie, don't be rude to a friend.' That sing-song voice again. 'I just wanted to talk to you, thought you might have changed your mind about tonight, eh?'

Her scalp tightened. He was so close; the almost corpse-like animal reek invaded her nostrils. Blanche wanted to back away but knew you did not do that with wild animals. She knew she had to make a move, could not go backwards, the only chance was towards the car. She was agile from playing sport. She sidestepped. He was faster though and put his arm across to the verandah post, blocking the exit. He brushed her jaw with a gentle elbow, a menacing passive show of power. She felt as if sugar-ants were crawling all over her back.

'Blanchie baby, don't treat me this way.' He looked at her, green almost cat's eyes. Still the sing-song voice.

Her stomach clenched. Her clock almost stopped again; the internal shaking continued. She knew he could sense it.

'*Hello Blanche!*' yelled Mrs Hartwell, who was walking her dog along the footpath, only a tennis court width away.

A mower started up down the road. The moment begged. Blanche ducked under his arm.

His voice turned to gravel and followed her like his smell. 'You've done it now, you fucking bitch, oh yeah,' he growled, left standing alone on the verandah, knowing he could not make a scene in front of the neighbour. 'You'll end up like Candy and Francy,' he mumbled almost to himself.

She composed herself and talked with the older woman. Eva Hartwell was quite hard of hearing and did not seem to have noticed Blanche's predicament. A fraction of a second later, Blanche looked back towards the front verandah. The westerly afternoon sun bounced off the front window. No one there! Eva continued on her way and Blanche dashed over to the car. She hit the door locks, reversed out and drove in the direction of Gloria's. Before she pulled onto the main road, she forced yoga breaths to stop shaking and ease the tension from splitting her body. Her insides wanted to let go. A minute later it occurred to her to make sure no one was following. Cars swerved around her, some angry toots.

∞

'You need more than a cuppa,' frowned Gloria, playing with a delicate gold chain around her elegant, tanned neck. 'He sounds like a bastard best to keep clear of. Do you want to stay here tonight?'

'I really don't know Glor. I just don't know. This sort of thing has never happened to me before. He really frightened the life out of me. Just looked straight through me as if I wasn't there, his eyes, like Rosemary's Baby's eyes. *God!*' Her hands still quivered as she patted Fritz, the schnauzer. 'He's nuts, maybe I should ring the cops.'

Gloria slowly shook her head, 'No, I don't think so. I don't think they can do much.' She stuck up her index finger. 'I've got an idea. My cousin works at the Women's Shelter, maybe she can help.'

'Women's Shelter? Ease up, Glor, I'm not an abused housewife, anyway, I leave in about a week.'

'There must be a way to handle this situation. After all, you do have to go home at the very least to pick up your gear and clear out your furniture. Look, Blanche, I … er … was in an abusive relationship years ago.' She pulled down the hem of her top, displaying a string of five-cent pieces - scars just above her breasts. 'See these? The bastard burnt me with a cigarette because he thought I was seeing someone else – which I wasn't.'

'Good Lord!'

They looked at each other, listening to the silence.

'What happened, I mean …'

'He went to Perth as far as I know. Fortunately, he decided he didn't want to live here … anywhere near me. Right, so, how about I make a phone call? No harm in a phone call.'

'Yeah, I suppose you're right. Okay, where's the wine?' said Blanche, just to hide her nervousness. 'Naaah, how about a double something? Got any … whisky, bourbon? How about G and T?'

'That's the idea, Blanche, get one for me, too. I'll make a call.'
Gloria eased her lithe frame off the stool and grabbed the phone.

After, they talked about Gloria's cousin Sophie at the Women's
Shelter. Two drinks later, the phone rang.

'Ms Faulkner? Ramsay Woodward here, Ramwood Investigations.
Sophie told me to give you a bell, maybe I can help you.'

'Well, it's not me who needs help, it's Blanche and she's here now.'

'I'm free at the moment, should I come around?'

Gloria gave him the address. The conversation sounded stilted.

Not long after, Fritz started barking. Gloria opened the door to a
six-foot, and more, rugby frame with a blond number-two buzz cut,
and a re-arranged nose.

'G'day, I'm Ramsay but everyone calls me Ramso,' the young
man said.

Blanche noticed Gloria look at him, almost as if she knew him.
They sat down in the lounge and he gave a quick rundown of the
things he did and the connection with the Women's Shelter.

'Yeah, my cousin works there. She said you may be able to help
us ... er Blanche, I mean,' said Gloria.

Blanche noticed that look again.

'Right, how can I help?'

Blanche explained her situation; he intervened every now and
then and scribbled notes on a small, curly wired notepad.

'I get the picture,' said the big man, twirling a small gold earring
in his right ear. 'First up, we need to talk about fees.' He handed
Blanche, a sheet of paper. Read that. Rates are based on 24 hours
or part thereof plus expenses, of course.' He turned to Gloria. 'Any
chance of a cup of coffee?' That look again.

Blanche read the schedule, wondering for a moment if she should
spend the money. She came to a decision and put the paper on the
table. 'Um, yes, that seems okay.'

He ran a large paw over his close-cropped number two. 'Just had
it cut,' he smiled but the smile hardened slightly as he continued, 'I
don't see any major problems here, we should be able to get this prick
off your back reasonably quickly and I can't see it costing you too
much. However, there may be decisions that I have to make during

this process, but we will get to them as we go.' He nodded and smiled briefly at Gloria as she handed him a mug of coffee.

'Thanks. Now, as you probably know there is no shortage of bastards like him out there. These character types vary from harmless idiots to extremely dangerous people. I know a bit about it because I did a couple of years of a psychiatry degree. Firstly, we must establish a rating which will allow us to deal with this person in the appropriate way. The way the law works, it is difficult for the police to do anything until there's been an action. Unfortunately, then, in many cases, it is too late. Just from what you've told me; my experience tells me that this crawler is not at the lower end of the scale. It's one thing to make stalking phone calls; it's a whole new bucket of chips to actually confront someone, which has happened in your case. He needs to be stopped.'

Blanche butted in, frowning. 'How *do* you stop these sorts of people?'

He held up his hand. 'We'll get to that later, but there's a range of methods at our disposal. Trust me. Now, in almost all cases, these people have a paper trail or, if not, a history someone knows about.'

Blanche was about to ask him again what he intended to do when he continued. 'We have resources to find out information and whilst that is happening, we'll hover around your house. Even money he will be hanging around there too. We will pretend to work near your place and then we'll follow him, find out where he lives and anything else.'

'You say, *we* quite often.'

'Yes, like I say, we have resources, and I know people, we help each other.' Blanche nodded. He added, 'Do I look like a gardener?' his smile was softer.

That question eased the lid off tension in the room.

'Blanche, will you be staying here with Gloria?'

She looked at Gloria and they nodded.

'Now, I have Gloria's landline number and I would like both of your mobile numbers in case I have to contact you in a hurry. You can relax, I doubt we'll have anything for you tonight, but I will contact you tomorrow, okay? Here's my card.'

∞

Blanche was up early and already had the coffee on when Gloria wandered in rubbing her eyes. Butcherbirds warbled outside in the stand of gums.

'How did you sleep, Blanche?'

'I confess, not very well. I was aware of every little noise throughout the whole night.'

'Well, my dear, no one would get anywhere near the house with Fritz sleeping in the passage. He probably would be a pushover in a confrontation, but his barking would have the neighbours complaining, yet again. They don't understand the responsibilities of owning a dog.' She rolled her eyes. 'How would you like to be locked up all day in …'

'Of course, you are right, but it's not every day I have someone stalking me and I have to say, this bastard has unnerved me more than I thought it would. Um, Glor?'

'Yep?'

'I … er have to ask, do you know Ramso … er I mean, have you met him before?'

'What? Oh, yes, slightly …'

When she did not go on and busied herself at the sink, Blanche couldn't help herself. 'And?'

'Nothing really, he just helped out a friend, once.' It was clear she did not want to talk about it. 'Righto, now, today at least you don't have to go to work. Fortunately, I do not have to be in until ten today either, but I hope we hear something before I …'

The landline tinkled. 'Yeah hi, look it's best you speak with Blanche. Here …' She handed the phone to Blanche and indicated the speakerphone button.

'Ramso here, we've managed to put together a colourful history of this mongrel. I will not tell you over the phone, I'm on my way. See you soon. Er, any chance of a coffee?'

It was a fight for the shower.

∞

Fritz started barking.

'Coffee?' asked Gloria, beaming.

'Yeah, too right, been a big night.' He stretched and yawned. 'Now, our Mr Gilbert Oakley turns out to be Gilbert Oaklands. These idiots can't help themselves; they never seem to get too far away their real names. We're certain it's the same person. We saw him sleeking around your place, not very professional either may I add. You were right doing something about him because you were in danger.' He took a gulp of coffee. 'Mister Oaklands has quite an award-winning stalking and rape history.'

'Rape?' Both women looked at each other, eyebrows up.

'Yep. I got a mate of mine, let's just say *in the know*, to check up on the two names you gave me, remember? Candy, turns out to be a Candice Woods, raped by our very own Mister Oaklands. He pleaded diminished responsibility and all that shit that the lawyers love to wheel out so that the system allows these pricks like him to continue doing what they do. Anyway, she had a mental breakdown and changed her name and eventually left the state. Don't know where she is now. Francy? The Francesca Elviras case never got to court, she committed suicide, seemed she couldn't face it all. He walked away from that one, free as.

'Prior to that there was a 14-year-old girl when he was 17. She was saved from being raped by a bunch of kids looking for a cricket ball. He was caught though, but that was thrown out because there wasn't enough evidence, and his age. He claimed that she let him. Let him? She had severe bruising around her face, and almost lost the sight of one eye. You should see the pictures. He got three months community service with no conviction recorded. Christ. Anyway, we can only wonder about a society that allows people like him to walk the streets.

'He has a long list of stalking and making nuisance phone calls from a very early age. Most of these types of cases, the system just seems to spit these toads back onto the street. We managed to get some good shots of him yesterday arvo. Positive identification, Gilbert Oaklands is our man. There.'

'What can we ... what can I do?' enquired Blanche.

'You can report it to the police, they can't do much, not the way the system is set up.' He leant back in the chair and stretched again.

'More coffee? How about something to eat?' said Gloria grabbing his cup.

'Coffee, yes, but I've just eaten, thanks.' He turned to Blanche. 'Can I speak with you outside for a moment?'

'Umm, yeah, sure.'

He stood up. 'Gloria, I need to speak to Blanche in private, outside, no offence, alright?'

'Er ... yeah, of course, I understand.'

Blanche noticed that look of familiarity passed between them again as she followed him across the weather etched, floorboards on the back verandah, down the rickety steps and on to the mown weed lawn. He turned to face her.

'What I have to say to you is in the strictest confidence, that's why I asked to speak to you in private, okay? A taboo subject.'

'I think I understand.'

'The Sisters in the Women's Shelter have a, well, we'll call it a network. At various times, they consider it necessary to prune out certain serial offenders. If you could see some of the cases I deal with on their behalf, you wouldn't believe it.' He looked into her eyes.

'Oh, I am starting to think I would,' she replied, probably quicker than she intended.

He looked down and gently kicked a dog's bone. 'Blokes. Blokes who sleek and crawl and stalk. Blokes who abuse and rape and kill women. They are out there, and the system is unable to deal with them. Now, what I have to say is serious stuff, right?' He looked at her again.

'Yes.'

'The Sisters will have a good look at this bloke, and chances are he will be dealt with. It is not your decision, nor mine either, for that matter, but I had to tell you.'

Blanche stood there and looked at him. Her forehead felt hot. They were in their own silence; the traffic hummed and tooted in the distance and small birds twittered in the native bottlebrush.

'Um, what do you mean by ... prune out?'

'Okay. Sometimes the slug is dumped out at sea, hugging a tractor rim, or an accident is arranged. This is not revenge, it's just necessary. The system can't handle people like this. The focus is on the perpetrator, not the victim. The do-gooders think it's more important to rehabilitate the criminal than carry out justice.'

'What ... what is your interest, your involvement, why are you so ... so committed?'

Ramso looked away into the bush for a moment and then his attention returned to her. 'My thirteen-year-old daughter was raped and murdered by one of these cockroaches. My wife would have died of a broken heart if she hadn't overdosed beforehand. He was found guilty of the lesser charge - manslaughter - and he was out in 23 months for good behaviour. 23 months!' His eyes shone; forehead tight. 'There is a group, a network, a secret cell. We call ourselves, Sisters and Brothers, S and B.'

It was her turn to look away for a moment. When she looked back, he was looking at her. She could not speak.

He took her hands gently in his. 'I'll ask you not to say anything to Gloria, we just had a chat out here, that's all. It's for her protection. I'll tell her we will be putting the matter into the hands of the police, and a bit of other jargon as well. The walls always have ears and despite best intentions, loose lips are very dangerous. If any of this comes up at any time, I will deny it. I was never here. You understand? Taboo subject, right?' His face showed no emotion.

They stood in silence for another moment looking directly into each other's eyes.

'Yes, I understand.'

Gloria stepped out the door, raised her hand and frowned. 'What are you two doing? Come on, coffee's ready.'

The End.

Sometimes things

Are not meant to be -

We should accept the umpire's decision

Rightfully Mine

'Leave me alone!' screeched Linda.

The room stopped. Gordon stepped back. She had not clouted him but may as well have. His hands went up, fingers out, an unarmed position. Then he slowly shook his head, eyebrows horizontal in bewilderment.

'What ...? I didn't ...'

'Stop! Go away!' Fury spun; she stormed off.

'But I ... yeah, sure. I ...' He turned to those nearby remonstrating helplessly. 'Look, I didn't do anything ... I mean ...?' Gawks and shocked stares tracked him, 'What in the hell's wrong with her?'

People shrugged, keen not to be part of it. They returned to their desks. Damage done.

∞

About a week earlier in the office, Linda beckoned Danielle over. She pointed to a business card on the desk, 'Look at this, he keeps doing these sorts of things to me. Last week, it was a ruler with his name on. On-my-desk!'

Dani's brow migrated to the middle and then held up the card into better light. 'Mmmm. Gordon McMasters - Rural Investments.'

Linda forced on, 'Yeah, well he keeps harassing me. I'm getting sick of it. He eyes me when I get in and out of the lift too. The bastard often organises it so he can open a door for me, too.'

'Um … what's wrong with that?' ventured Dani. 'He's probably just trying to be nice.'

'But that's the thing, I don't want him to be nice, I don't want him near me – I tell ya, he is a really creepy bloke. I wish he'd leave me alone.' She hugged herself in an angry shiver.

The office supervisor ambled past. The girls quickly switched to admin jargon until he was out of earshot.

Linda glanced quickly, darkness crowding her aura, eyebrows hard, 'Yesterday, after the awards presentation, he was under the stairs. I didn't see him until I reached the landing. The dirty bastard was looking up my dress.'

Dani nodded.

'He was doing that sort of thing before he was promoted too, in fact, ever since he started six months ago. Just the odd wink here and there but still. Creep.'

'Have you told your boss?'

'No. Not yet, but I was hoping he'd lay off, I mean, I don't encourage him, and I glare at him when he does those sorts of things. I've told him to leave me alone numerous times. The bastard just smiles. Oooooooooh yuk! I can't stand him.'

∞

Several days later, Linda cornered Dani near the female toilets.

'I don't want to bring it up, but that sleazy bastard touched me on the bum when I walked out of the lift. He was waiting on the eighth floor, and when the other person got out, he got in. The bastard smirked at me and said, *Aaaaah, alone, at last.* I couldn't get out. Fortunately, someone else jumped in at the last minute, I was packing it I tell ya, his eyes were all over me. When the doors opened, I got out quick - that's when he gave my bum a tap – sleazy mongrel.'

∞

The present.

Gordon sat down gingerly; he hoped no one had noticed him shaking. *What was wrong with Linda? That outburst a few minutes ago, 'Leave me alone!' Hell, I wasn't even near her. She's mental.* He glanced around, other staff kept their eyes down, feigning work.

Marlene, from Central Records, had witnessed the scene, fancy Gordon touching up Linda? It did not make sense; he was such a shy bloke, polite, easy going, but still? Nah, not Gordon. She had been on the panel interviewing applicants for the Rural Investments job. There were some well-qualified people who had put in for it, but she, and the other panel members had been impressed by Gordon's qualifications. And his overall attitude too. Marlene thought that it was always possible anyone could get a bit cocky because they won a job or a promotion, but she thought he did not seem like that. Of course, Linda was a good candidate too but had nowhere near the experience of Gordon. Why would he try to touch Linda? Aaaaaaah well, she knew blokes were strange creatures from another planet. But still, Gordon? She had trouble fitting him into that category.

Later that day, after a gruelling meeting, Gordon McMasters returned to his desk. He had been called into the Senior Clerk's office and had been informed that a complaint had been made against him by Linda Erinbermer. As he sat, head down, he knew he was the magnet for every eye in the room. *Hell, what a bitch!* He had been polite to her, considerate – he was sensitive enough to notice she had been disappointed at not getting the job; he tried to be nice to her, hell. He wondered why she was making these outrageous accusations against him?

∞

Next morning as Marlene entered the cafeteria, she zeroed in on Danielle sitting on her own in the corner.

'Ah, how's it going Dani, haven't seen you for ages, even though we work in the same building.'

'Yeah, it's easy to drift apart - grab a seat.'

They were work colleagues but had been out together socially too.

'How's all this business about Linda and Gordon?' ventured Dani in an easy probe.

'Yeah, she says he's been harassing her for ages, bit sleazy, although I must say I'm a little surprised, he doesn't really seem like the sort of bloke who would do that. She said he was standing under the stairs, just after the Awards and he looked up her dress.'

'Mmmmmmm.'

'Anyway, Marl, we managed to get some photos from the Awards Luncheon in the magazine. Here, have a look, I know you're not in them, but I am.' Dani smiled proudly.

'You get it easy, free lunch and all that.'

'Here, keep the mag, I've got another in my office anyway, but look, I have to go, I've got a meeting in a couple of minutes. Got to go, see ya.' Danielle stood up and grabbed her bag.

'Yeah, hey, we must catch up some time, it's been a while,' suggested Marlene.

'Sure thing, bye.'

Marlene sat there for some minutes, deep in thought. The Senior Clerk, Fred Goldman, who she knew quite well, had asked if she could find out any information about the allegations by listening to office gossip. In conversation, she had found out that on the day of the alleged touching-up, Mathew and Mark from Personnel had been near Linda when she yelled, and they were certain Gordon was several feet away. Also, Linda had accused Gordon of placing his business card on her desk. Maxine McNaught from the typing pool, thought she saw Linda take something out of Gordon's desk and put it on *her own* desk - she said it looked like a card.

Marlene knew something was not right. She stared at the photo in the magazine of the group of award winners, all smiling. Suddenly her eyebrows shot up. She noticed that Linda was wearing a smartly pressed pair of slacks. She had slacks on that day, not a dress!

In another part of the office, Linda sat at her desk, the reflection from the computer screen made her look like she was under water.

'No worries,' she spat through gritted teeth, 'No two ways about it, I am going to fix that fat bastard McMasters, what a prick. That job was rightfully mine. When they give him the boot, it will be mine, Officer in Charge Rural Investments. Yeah, mine - mine - mine. Bloody right. No worries, that'll teach him a lesson he won't forget.'

The End

Sometimes we make assumptions

Or act on impulse -

Can you hold your head up?

Rough Justice

'The news is not good, mate.' Doctor Stevenson had been his doctor for over 40 years, and there was a familiarity between them. Sometimes in fact, Chesty felt as if he had counselled the good doctor, who, it was rumoured, had a slight morphine habit.

The doctor informed Chesty that the tests confirmed cancer, and it was of the aggressive kind.

'How ... how long have I got Doc?'

'Well, mate, at least six months.'

'I guess I've had a good innings, I mean, I'll be 76 in a couple of weeks.'

'Look, Chesty, it's not all over with until it's all over, alright? If you look after yourself, you might squeeze a couple of extra months out of it.' The doctor looked away as he said the last few words.

'Doc, can you, I mean, when the pain gets really bad, can you slip me some ...'

'Yes, of course, mate, that goes without saying.'

They had discussed hypotheticals, and Barbara, on several occasions in the past, in happier times.

∞

The next day Chesty sat on the verandah of his place which was one of the last remaining beach houses along the river. Admittedly, there was a road between his house and the water, but he liked it.

Chesty was a realist and had known that he did not have many years left even before he received the news. Hell, he was even pretty sure that it was going to be lung cancer after all the years of puffing away. When he gave up 10 years ago, he joked that his body would react negatively when he withdrew tobacco. And what about his liver? After all those years of drinking and what about his kidneys, and the rest.

Barbara died two years ago. At the time he just felt like letting go. After more than 50 years of being together, she came home one day and declared that she was not well. She died three months later, with the help of their mutual friend, Dr Stevenson, her dignity only just intact.

She was allowed to choose her time, just at the point where it got too bad. He felt strong enough now and he hoped he had the courage to take steps to not be a burden when the time came.

He looked out at the shining brilliant water. The river was a blue two-pack mirror finish, like it was most mornings before the wind got to it. Those bloody developers, they had tried all sorts of tricks to get him to sell, but he wanted to spend the last years of his life here.

The developers were the worst kind of thugs because they had lawyers and bankers behind them. All they wanted was more money; they did not give a stuff about things that really mattered. Standard of living was not quality of life. The modern world was full of that thirst for more, and more, and more. Among that breed of people there did not seem to be anyone who could see or care that what they were doing was destroying the very thing that was the attraction. He figured that these faceless people must have children or grandchildren. What sort of world would they leave to them? If they thought deeply about that then they could not do what they did. He knew that greed was bigger than love.

He was going to join Babs soon, and although there was joy, there was sadness too.

Stan, his next-door neighbour had been over earlier. A couple of months ago, his daughter had been raped by a bunch of thugs who lived in the area. They had cornered her at the bus stop just up the road as she waited to catch the bus one night. They dragged her by the hair into the vacant block, bashed and raped her. Five males, bashed and raped her. They were found guilty. However, the lenient judge gave each of them a suspended sentence, allowing for time served, a bond and community service. What could one person say against five witnesses? They said she consented. Consensual sex? Chesty felt heat behind his eyes, how could any male do that to someone, particularly a young girl?

Chesty was not disappointed that he had his ticket out. There was no God. You lived; you died. Belief in God was just a way to handle how tough life could be if you let it get to you. He had the good times to think about, and Barbara.

∞

About 1 a.m. the next morning he heard noises outside. Sleep had been hard to find lately, and it was not uncommon to hear voices out the front after midnight. He walked out through the French doors that opened onto the deck. The sea looked like splintered glass in the light from the half-moon. Drunken louts were doing their usual, chucking bottles onto the concrete path. He had given up picking up the broken glass some time ago.

Chesty and his neighbours had rung the police on many occasions, but in recent times they did not even bother turning up, or if they did, it was hours after the event. A mate of theirs who knew a cop said they could not do much anyway, because the young people were from the margins of society – there was too much paperwork and too little consequence. Even when they got them to court, they could not pay the fines; their parents were non-existent or did not care. The police were understaffed and nailed down to quotas; sitting under a tree during the day pointing a radar gun at speeding motorists was a much-preferred pastime.

The world was moving too quickly for Chesty, there were too many people. People wanted more and more and expected more, and Chesty wondered if these cocky spoilt little bastards were any worse than the CEOs of the development companies. He doubted it. They were all the same. Criminals. Greedy bastards with no sense of decency; humans were the worst cancer.

He accidently knocked an empty cup off the table. Someone in the chip-on-the-shoulder mob down at the road heard it. 'Hey, you!' screeched some pimple-face voice. 'What are you lookin' at? We know you're up there.'

Someone threw a bottle that smashed in the gutter. Other dark shapes grabbed the fence wire and started rocking it backwards and forwards. It gave way. Someone wrenched the letterbox out of the ground and bashed it up and down on the driveway.

'Hey prick - hey buddy? Who do you think you are, you rich bastard? I'll bet you haven't got the fucking guts to come down here.'

Some other rusty-tin voice yelled, 'We got community service.'

The others laughed and whooped.

Chesty made a decision. Surefooted, quick, and silent from hunting days, he padded to the bedroom closet, and then the filing cabinet to get the bullets. He was used to working in the dark. The magazine clicked in, and he sleeked to the edge of the verandah.

'Hey, you,' he said, voice full of menace. 'Are you the boss around here?'

They could not see him, but he could see them. There was only the moon; he knew how to use it to advantage.

'You, I'm talking to you. You smashed my letterbox, mate.'

'Get fucked, dickhead!'

Three of them ran over and mounted the stairs.

He shot the first one straight through the head. The next two he hit in the heart. The shots fizzed out easily. A lifetime ago he had been in combat and in more recent times had shot many feral animals, but shooting close-up targets like this was a snack. A .22 is not a heavy gun, but any gun can kill. Three butterfly touches on the trigger, easy as.

The other two louts on the footpath stood stock still for about five seconds with ears sharp and upright, and then took off. He swivelled and trained the rifle on their disappearing backs. His finger rested in the air gap between the trigger and the guard. There was no need for vengeance; he had never shot anyone running away. The ones on the stairs who had trespassed did not even groan. Experience told him to check; army mantra, *enough gun*. They were dead.

Everything was quiet. He placed the rifle on the table and slowly picked up the phone lying on the chair and dialled 000. The person on the emergency line was not good at English. 'Where's Maroochydore?' He gave the address again and eased the handpiece onto the cradle.

The night was not cold but his hand shook. No writhing, wriggling, wounded animals … easy prey. He did not feel any remorse. Somehow, he thought he had contributed to something greater.

In a strange way, he felt at peace. A calm slowly washed over him. Chesty didn't know how long it would take for the police to arrive; he didn't care. He turned the light on so they would be able to recognize the place. His hand was not shaking now. He absent-mindedly picked up the day's mail that he had placed on the table earlier. Bills, he smiled, bloody bills.

Fancy that, killing three animals, and then sitting down and opening the mail.

He opened the first letter, his brow furrowed, phrases and words raced by. 'Testing Laboratory … sorry sir … mistake has been made … inadvertent error … mixed up with someone else …'

It was then that he remembered the message on the answering machine from the doctor to ring him back urgently. They had got his blood and X-rays mixed up with someone else's. He was not going to die, at least not now, from the ravages of cancer.

He heard the sirens in the distance, a few lights popped on around. He looked at the rifle; he knew there were two bullets in the magazine.

The End

When it needs to be done –

The best of us do it

Without thinking

R.I.P.

'Simms! Pay attention.' Mr McKerley closed his eyes for a moment. 'You might not care if you don't pass, but I do. Alright?'

'Er … why is that sir?'

'What? Because … um, two reasons.' He rolled both hands and arms, then held up an index finger. 'One, I do my best to make sure students in my class learn something, and even if they don't learn much, at least pass. Secondly, Simms, *you* may think you're a smart alec mucking around in class, but I don't want to see you end up being a labourer or … or ending up in jail. If you continue in the direction you insist on going, then you will be a no hoper.' He stressed the last three words. 'Alright? Now, pay attention, let us continue.'

It was Friday afternoon, and all Jack Simms could think about was having a cigarette and going fishing. At lunch time Dickie Drummond had pinched a packet of cigarettes from the corner shop whilst he and John *Bat* Masterson had kept Mrs Dunsmuir busy.

He could not wait to be down behind the fish shop to have a few smokes with his mates. They often took the afternoon off from school. Bat had been to reform school for a break-and-enter at the local tennis club as well as trying to sell a stolen bike. Drummond was on his last warning from the police.

So far, Simms had managed to keep a low profile with the authorities; although he had worn a track to the office of Mr

39

Mitchellmore, the deputy principal. He had returned to class many times with a sore behind.

Simms slumped his big frame on the uncomfortable, Department of Education issue, wooden chair and quickly forgot about the ongoing lesson. He glanced longingly at Annie Sloggett who sat diagonally in front of him. She felt him looking, raised her eyes and fiddled her skirt hem down over her slender, brown knees.

He sighed loudly. Mr McKerley stopped in the middle of a sentence. Submerged laughter bubbled to the surface.

'We are all glad you have woken up, *Mister* Jack Simms, because it's now almost time to go, wouldn't want you to spend the whole weekend here asleep, would we?'

Gentle laughter washed through the room as students packed up.

Mr McKerley held up his hand. 'Now everybody, I want you to finish those assignments because they must be in by Monday morning. Did you hear that, *Mister* Simms?'

'Er … yes sir.'

The bell jangled, and the class dismissed in a confusion of scraping chairs and babble. The teacher glanced towards Simms, shook his head, tucked a book under his arm and ambled out.

When Simms arrived behind the fish shop, Masterson and Drummond were into their second cigarette.

'Where you been, Simmo? coughed Bat, attempting to stand as he unravelled his pre-adult growth rings.

'Where do ya think? In church?'

'Ha bloody ha ha,' Drummond looked through a Milky Way of freckles, voice on the break.

Simms laughed. 'Nuts dropped, eh Drummer? Give us a cigarette, face-ache,' he continued, bouncing like a big rubber man.

'Hey, listen fellers.' Bat was keen to deflect. 'It's almost a king tide today *and* about to run out in an hour or so.' He did the drawback, and coughing took over for a second and then erupted.

'You should give up smoking, stunts your growth,' mocked Simms.

They all laughed and heckled each other about who was better at smoking.

'Anyway, a bit of angling of the dangling, whadya reckon, eh?' Bat liked to make potentially obscene comments.

They laughed again.

'Yeah, suits me. What do ya reckon?' Drummond turned to Simms.

'Can't see any reason why not.' Simms did a greedy drawback. He tried not to cough and succeeded in getting away with three or four sharp jabs. He knew his father would be down the pub until six and then out with his mates until late, if he came home at all. No mum anymore.

'Let's go then fellers.' Bat waved his arm. 'I've got two rods of mine and another one. You know, the one you kinda er ... borrowed from that pinhead kid down at the bridge last week?' He looked at Simms.

'Yeah, forgot about that. He was just a rich spoilt little prick anyway.' Simms lit another cigarette off the butt of the one he was smoking.

Bat's place was not far from the spit, so they hopped on their bikes and pedalled in that direction, smoking cigarettes, riding on the wrong side of the road and kidding each other on.

When they arrived at the Noosa Spit the tide was running in and approaching the top. At high tide there was always a time of complete calm, right at the mathematical top. Once it turned, a huge volume of water rushed out to the sea quickly for about half an hour and with it the chance of catching a few fish. The fast-flowing water stirred up nutrients as well as the tiny creatures fish feed on.

The boys sat back smoking, bullshitting on, sometimes farting or burping. And waiting. Their experience told them there was no point in throwing a line in until just after the turn of the tide. It was late afternoon in spring and the days had begun to stretch and gather some warmth. A few boaties speckled the glistening river mouth. The waves out on the bar, that had meshed and crashed when they arrived, were now calming considerably at the approaching high tide.

About twenty yards away a man in a red T-shirt sat on the bank watching a blonde woman and two toddlers playing in the shallows.

Simms looked out to sea and then back. 'I'm going to have to get a job.'

'Job? You aren't sixteen yet.' Bat continued chopping up fowl's entrails on a piece of wood.

'Doesn't matter. I'm not going to pass this year.'

'Who gives a stuff?' declared Drummond. 'My old man reckons I can start my apprenticeship with him soon's I turn sixteen. Hey, wish we had some jail-bait instead of chooks guts, eh.'

Reference to young females always cranked up laughter.

The young woman with the blond hair looked up.

'Hey, tide's just movin'.' Bat snatched his rod. 'Who's last to catch a fish has to get the next packet of fags, right?'

'Get nicked,' laughed Simms, 'It'll be you, anyway, you moron.'

The tide idled up, sat as still as a hunting cat, then slowly eased out, gathering momentum.

The lads chucked their lines in. Quick splashes from casts indicated action.

'Godda bite!' whooped Drummond, fumbling with the fizzing reel.

The young family looked over. The pace of the water increased.

'Whattaya got?' yelled Bat.

Just then the woman with the blond hair screamed. The man in the red T-shirt yelled something. Bat and Simms looked over, Drummond was too busy dealing with burning fingers and fizzing reel. One of the children was gently sucked away from the bank by the slowly swirling water.

Simms dropped the rod, kicked off his sandshoes and launched himself into the outgoing water. The child disappeared. The water swirled. Simms took three long strokes and went under as well.

He bobbed up ten feet further down clutching the boy by the arm. The speed of the water increased, and he did his best to swim diagonally across back to the bank.

The woman screamed again. The man waved his arms.

Simms made headway in the swirling and strong flowing current and eventually he managed to embrace the bank nearer the sea.

A woman fishing further down heard the commotion, dropped her beer bottle, and grabbed the child just as Simms was ripped back into the now boiling turbulence. He struggled, tried weak semaphore signals, gasped, and bobbed several times. Then he disappeared.

∞

As they lowered Simms's coffin into the ground, Mr Mitchellmore, the deputy principal nudged Mr McKerley and whispered, 'The only time he ever went with the tide it cost him his life. I've seen plenty of 'em. It's a pity lads like Simms never reach their potential.'

Mr McKerley took a moment before replying. 'Well, you know, I think maybe in the end, he did.'

The End

Some people

Have good hearts –

Others don't

Repeat

My name is Brenda. Now here is a story, true too. I didn't plan any of it. No-one could plan something like this.

I met Wayne at a trials motorbike gig. My brother treated me for my birthday. Hardly a treat hey, hanging around with motorbike heads pissed and reeking of engine oil. But I had bugger all else to do, so I went along.

Wayne, a bit of a short arse, blonde mullet cut, skinny, with a slightly lopsided mouth. Looked like he was almost smiling when he wasn't. He was with a group of razzers in the ute alongside ours. My brother had just met him, new bloke in town; they all seemed to get together, bike-heads. Anyway, we started going out together, and became you know, a bloke and his sheila.

At first, he was good to me, took me out to Chinese every now and again and didn't let me pay all the time. Unlike the others, he did not drink much.

Then he changed, things changed. It took me a while to cotton on. He got real nervy, jerky and irritable, then I found out he was doing speed. That's when he got stuck into the piss, like real heavy stuff, bourbon and whisky.

One day, out of nowhere, he bashed me. I could not believe it! I can't remember exactly what caused the burst of anger, but I bet it was petty. Probably something like not getting up from the kitchen table and getting him another bourbon and Coke. Whacked me right in the eye and I fell backwards off the chair. I was too scared to say anything, I just looked at him shaking until my eye closed up.

He frowned and handed me a plastic bag with a frozen cane toad in it to put over my eye; he laughed, and then went for me. He dragged me into the bedroom, I was shit scared. He raped me.

Next morning, he apologised in his own way, but said it was me who made him angry sometimes. I couldn't really blame him. I knew what he was like, and he was right. If I loved him, I should jump to it when he wanted something.

This went on for a while, him slapping and punching me and convincing me I was the cause of it all. At first, I almost looked forward to it like it was my destiny. As time went on, he got more professional at it because I bruised in obvious places. He knuckled and slapped me on the head; no one could see bruises through my hair.

One day he broke my little finger, snapped it back, and then punched me in the guts for crying. Wayne told me he'd kill me if I told anyone. My life was chockers with fear. This went on for six months; I couldn't really see a way out.

∞

I met her by chance. A new girl started at the battery farm where I worked sorting eggs.

'G'day,' she said.

Big sheila, I liked the smile, chubby cheeks, and a dimple in her chin. Dark hair, crew on top, long mullet to her neck.

'Name's Violet.'

'Mine's Brenda.'

We had a few fags down by the river after work, talking. Then a couple more times, just smoking, talking, and pumping more dumpers. I was guarded, hoping Wayne would not see me. He didn't like me having friends. Just him and me.

About a month later, we got off early. I offered to drop her home, we were on late shift, and I had the work ute that week.

She said, 'Come in.' A statement as much as a question.

We went in. She had posters of butch chicks everywhere. I'd never been with a woman before. Our lovemaking was too beautiful to be called rooting. We shared a fag afterwards, laughing and stroking each other.

I loved her big arms. She had tats on both meaty biceps. She saw me looking.

'Had to have them, initiation for being a warder.'

I remember being amazed, shocked and surprised. 'Warder?'

'Yeah, I was a jail warder, honey.' She winked and lit up another smoke. 'Bastards dismissed me for … er an indiscretion.'

'What sort of indiscretion?'

'Do you really want to know?' Her gaze hardened; it frightened me a bit. 'Violet the Violent, Vee the Vi, that's what they called me. Well, babe, I fucking-well nearly killed a sheila for spitting at me. Silly me lost a good job. They had good conditions for the staff there, benefits, you know, like free tucker, uniforms, use of a bloody shit-hot gym. Got the pick of some of the sweet little babes, too. Oh, those little honeys. Just for a favour, you know. Ha ha,' she mocked, 'There were only four blokes there, didn't like them, it was a women's prison.'

I could feel a steel-string simmering anger about her, I didn't say anything. She grabbed my hand in her catcher's mitt. Her look softened, 'I really like you, babe,' she whispered.

I felt safe then, but I had to go home.

∞

'Where have ya been, ya fucking bitch?'

He was a bit strung out and had just run out of white powder. I knew the mood he was in. Speedy amps.

'Had to work late …'

He grabbed me by the hair. 'You stink like you got bloke all over ya, eh? Don't ya?'

I protested, not too much though, because whenever I did, he got worse. I tried to pacify, pulled out my roster. 'Sssorry.' I pointed, 'Late shift, sorry Wayne, I thought we could do with the extra money.'

He was on to the next thing. 'Get me a fucking drink before I get really shitty, eh?'

I did as quickly as I could. I poured him several strong bourbons and Coke and hoped he would pass out. Eventually he did. Seeing him slouched on the couch snoring like a pig, drip of spittle hanging from the corner of his mouth, there and then I made a decision.

I'd tell Violet, I knew she would know what to do.

∞

'He fucking-well what?' she growled. 'He's cloutin' you about the place? Honey, what the ...?'

'I don't know what to do.'

'Well, I do, babe, I'll go and put a crowbar through his head.'

I felt a cold quiver at the outburst. I explained Wayne said he would not only snap my neck if I told anyone, but he would take it out on my family.

'The bastard! Look, honey, let me scheme up.'

She walked away to the end of the conveyor belt. At the end of the shift, she sauntered up. My insides shook at the way her eyes boiled. She ran a meaty paw through her crewie.

She had a plan, our plan. It was the only thing to do. She moved her bulk in a blokey way, legs apart, rocking backwards and forwards. 'Don't worry babe, Vee the Vi will sort the mongrel out. We're mates, and ...'

'And wwwhat?' I managed to say.

'Lovers,' she almost pouted as the tightness left her face. Her large hand reached out and stroked my hair. I'm sure she felt me quiver.

∞

That week, Wayne was in a better mood, he'd scored some more speed. Our plan had to wait. He was not too bad when he was buzzing and okay towards me except the third day when he lost his job.

He wanted a root. I played the dutiful bitch, but he was rough and hurt me. He slapped me a couple of times but not too hard. I didn't mind any more than I ever did, I knew it was just a matter of time.

A few days later, he ran out of powder, so I bought him two bottles of bourbon and two family size Cokes. The blows rained; he really belted the shit out of me, but I steeled it out. He fell asleep on top of me.

After a while I rolled over and manoeuvred him onto his back. He mumbled and snored, completely bombed from five days without decent sleep. Violet sleeked into the room; the moonlight highlighted her bulk. It surprised me she could pad so silently and quickly.

She wound a small piece of rag around his wrists, and I helped her tape them to the head of the bed with duct tape. 'Careful babe, gentle as she goes, no marks, no evidence, okay? Grab his ankle.'

My stomach twisted and gurgled, and my hands shook as we wrapped his ankles and secured them to the base board. We looped a four-inch-wide furniture strap around him and the bed.

She grabbed the ratchet. Click … click … several tight grunts followed. 'Hey honey, I heard him bashing you, I wanted to open him up.' A butcher's knife glinted in the moonlight. An owl hooted way off.

I think I wet myself. 'Vee …?' My heart pounded. The smell coming off her was animal, excited.

'Do not worry, babe I won't. We have a plan, right? Can't leave any marks on him at all.'

She stepped out of the room, came back with a black plastic bag, and then turned the lights on. The bag was a heavy-duty bin liner with *suitable for wet waste* written on it.

'Got it from the skip at the back of the shopping centre,' she said. 'Perfect fit, honey.'

I tried to be ready.

He woke and floundered for a moment. Then some level of reality dawned. 'Hey fuck, what the …? Fuck, you … hey … who the fuck are you?'

'Shut up!' the big girl barked.

My body trembled. He looked at her, not really understanding and then looked at me. Then he looked back at her. At that point he noticed he was tied up.

'Hey, what the fuck? Hey!' he screeched, 'and who the hell are you? Hey, Brenda … bitch, I'm going to kill you … untie me …'

'I said shut up!' Violet gave him a rabbit punch in the stomach, knocking the wind out of him. I'll cut that off if you don't shut up,' she added, pointing at his dick. She threw a blanket over his body and ripped a tea towel in two. She poked half into his cavernous mouth and clicked the ratchet two more notches. Grunts and strains muffled out the sides of his dribbling mouth as he tried to spit it out. His eyes looked like shiny paint tin lids.

She turned to me. 'Righto babe, give us a hand.'

We tried to ease the plastic bag over his head, but he wriggled and writhed and babbled.

'That does it,' she said and grabbed the duct tape. She gave a quick couple of karate punches to his mid-section and then taped his mouth up. Bits of wet towel stuck out. She punched him again, a couple of quick jabs, in the stomach to leave him in no doubt about what would happen if he continued. His eyes boiled with confusion and anger.

We managed to get the black bag over his head, and she jammed some blankets around the bottom to seal it. Muffled whimpering and freaking out noises emitted from inside. She half lifted him and poked a rubbish bag under his bum. I was about to ask why when she held her nose for a second.

Violet sat heavily on his stomach. 'I said, shut up, mongrel.' She formed a big fist and slowly turned to me. 'Let's get the hose babe, like we talked about, we have to do this, it's the only way.'

I must have nodded, because I could not speak. We went out to Wayne's ute and she opened the tailgate. I grabbed the flexi swimming pool hose as she started the car and backed it towards the window. She told me to throw the hose through the open bedroom window as she fitted the other end to the exhaust pipe. The V8 kept up an evil low-down thunder in the crisp cool night. We went back inside.

The room was already smoky with exhaust fumes and Wayne squeaked and grunted in his struggle to stay alive.

'See this?' said Violet, slashing a hole in the heavy liner. She gave me the other end of the hose. 'Poke it in there.' Her cheekbones seemed higher; a bull terrier excited.

The hose jiggled in my hands; it was hard to do anything.

'Come on, honey, let's do this!' She guided my hand and nudged me gently with her bulk. 'Wack some tape around it, need a good seal, eh?'

Then she went and turned the overhead fan on. Wayne's gurgled shrieks bubbled and pleaded from behind the duct tape. She punched him again in the stomach and grabbed the tension-arm on the strap.

Click. He grunted. Click.

The bed creaked tight and almost twanged. He struggled and violently jerked for parts of a minute, and then the bed and him quivered. My heart banged against my ribs; my mouth was a salt mine. I watched owl eyed as he jellied to a stop, took a minute, more, less, didn't know. The room stank of human waste … and evil. He jerked again, a final protest. I could hear the V8 ticking away outside. Burble, burble, distant thunder, faint, but there and not letting up.

'Okay babe, let's leave him a few minutes, just to make sure.'

We went outside for a cigarette, just like at the factory. It did not feel like the old days. The low drum of the V8 rumbled at an idle, parked around the side of the house. She kept glancing around to make sure it didn't stall, calm as. My hands shook so much I had trouble drawing on the fag.

We just looked at each other; she stroked my hair, gentle finger for such a big, strong girl. She took a big drag, glanced at me hard and fired smoke out of her nostrils. So calm. Calm enough to relax with a fag. Oh God.

'It's all going to work out great, honey. You done pretty good. Wait here.' Violet went over to the window, stood for a while, and looked around. A minute or two passed, her size was silhouetted against a half-moon light that seemed years away as she ambled out and disconnected the hose. The V8 clanked from park into drive and the revs increased in volume as she drove the ute into the garage and turned it off.

The stillness crept back with speed, like crisp, hard, sharp ice sharding down on me. It wasn't a very cold night.

In a couple of minutes, I returned to the world. 'Let's go back inside and sort all this out, eh? Babe. It's gunna be alright. Right?' I could see a hard smile in the reflection from the window.

I followed her in. She pulled the pipe out of the bag and threw it through the window. Then she wrestled the bag off his head. The sight of him, I just stood there and tremored, glued to the floor. His body was a rag doll in Vee's hands.

'Right babe, give me his clothes, wrench those stinking sheets off the bed and do a full wash, pillow slips and blanket while I set him up. Concentrate now, you've got to do a good job, okay?' She grabbed a handful of clothes as well as the furniture strap and disappeared.

I automatically thrust a pile of things in her direction. I stood there for some time, drifting, trying to anchor my whole being. Then the thunder of the V8 cranking up made me so close to shitting myself I wasn't sure. The place stank. For a moment or two I thought it could have been me. My head swam.

She came back into the laundry. 'That took some doing. He's slumped over the steering wheel with a hose coming in through the window from the exhaust pipe. Took a bit to clean the bastard up. Anyrate, Babe? Understand, eh? Terrible death, but he was so depressed, wasn't he? Arsehole, that's what he was, honey. By the way, I just put the fan on full in the bedroom just to get rid of the stink of that bastard and the exhaust fumes.'

She could tell I was fragile; she was good at that, she understood me. 'It's going to be okay, Babe, you'll see.' She put her big arms around me and played with my bum. Strangely, I did not feel that safe.

She lit up two cigarettes and gave me one. 'Now here's to us, babe. Right? What we have to do is make sure that you are spot on with what you've got to do, okay? In about half an hour it will be light, and you should ring the pigs. Remember?' She grabbed my shoulders gently and made me look her in the eyes. 'We've rehearsed plenty of times, okay? You woke up wondering where your dear partner was because he hadn't come to bed, right? Then you heard the car running ... that is when you discovered ... this terrible thing, honey. Just be natural, I know it's upsetting.'

We went back into the bedroom and made the bed with fresh sheets. My brain struggled to manoeuvre my hands but I got it done.

'Now honey, jump back in bed, and make it look slept in, just on your side, while I go and make a cup of tea.'

I know I didn't fall asleep; I just lay there scrolling the ceiling, unable to move. My eyes played some sort of rapid eye movement. I knew it was no dream. My mouth clicked and struggled for wetness. My eyes blinked in the darkness. At least the V8 had stopped. A low squawk filtered from down by the creek.

She came back. 'Right honey, drink this up, we'll fold up the stuff out of the drier. Then, I'll fuck off.' The big sheila stood; confidence boiled out of her. She stepped forward and grabbed my face, angled it up towards her lips and thrust her tongue into my mouth. A purposeful pash, full of power and aggression. She was on top of her game.

∞

Two months later, I moved out of the house and went to Darwin. The cops swallowed my story, I could not believe it; we really did our homework well. No one suspected anything. Story was, poor Wayne, drug addict, depressed, hopeless down and outer, one less dropkick moron around the place as far as the pigs were concerned.

At first Violet was real good to me. We went out a lot, got drunk, played with each other, had a great time. Then it changed. I knew it was me, my fault. She did not need to tell me. I provoked her. She only knocked me about the place for my own good. Then it came home to me. I knew I deserved it.

The End

Take note -

Sometimes a snap

Can jog our memory

Pocket Dial

Dell said, 'I've booked a table at Fleurs for seven o'clock Saturday night.'

'Pretty upmarket ... what's the occasion?'

'It's our eighteenth wedding anniversary you ninny.' Her brow furrowed.

Greg put his hand up. 'Ha ha, I knew.'

She glared at him, not unkindly.

He tried to make light of it. 'Well, I would have known as soon as I looked at my diary on the day. Anyway, yeah sounds good to me.'

'Okay, forgiven but you better get me a present. My sweet ever-thoughtful husband, nothing is too good for us, now, is it? We haven't been out for yonks except to the Thai restaurant up the road ... er hang on, we've only ever had takeaway from there ... um never mind. The kids are doing their own thing at the weekend.'

Greg thought it was a bit extravagant to be splashing out on dining out when the house repayments were going up with the interest rates. Also, his affair was costing a bit. Paula had expensive tastes. He wanted to end it but she made it difficult because her wild sexual needs were hard to ignore. *Also,* she wanted to leave her husband, him to leave Dell and marry her. It had started out as a quicky at the Christmas party. That was three months ago.

Dreamy Dell continued, 'We've had eighteen wonderful years, two great children and we are so compatible, not like most other couples I know. The lousy two-timing blokes all seem to be having affairs and their poor dumb wives don't even know it.' She gave him a smooch on the lips.

Greg quickly hugged her so he was looking over her shoulder and she would not notice his expression. *Maybe she knows something?*

He recovered. 'Right, next Saturday night it is.'

∞

On Saturday Greg busied himself with shed projects and some gardening. There was a lot on his mind. Paula had told him, *I'm late with my period* and was again pestering him to leave Dell. He decided to not do anything for the moment, hoping that some way out would leap up at him. He pushed it to the back of his mind and felt a little better for a while until they were in the car on the way to Fleurs.

Dell said, 'I'm really glad we are going out tonight just the two of us. We haven't done this for ages.'

Greg kept his eyes on the road. 'Yep, so am I,' and tried a smile.

'You know what I love about you? You're so considerate and loving towards me, even though you did forget our wedding anniversary I do love the flowers. The wedding present was a bit blokey but it brings out your sense of humour.'

He bought her a set of knives in a block for the kitchen.

She continued, '... And you know what else I love about you? You haven't run off with a floosy like most of my friends' husbands have.'

Dell turned to look at him. He managed to check the rear vision mirrors just in time to give him that extra second to recover. *How could she know? Nah. No way.*

She smiled. That made him feel worse.

∞

Fleurs was a very upmarket restaurant, carpeted, light music padded the air.

A young man at the reception area gave him a slightly confused look for a second and took their coats. He ushered them over to a waitress who took them to their table.

'You seem to be preoccupied, dear.'

'Um yeah, sorry, thought I recognised the bloke who took our coats, can't place him, probably looks like someone I met lately. Anyway, never mind let's get into it.'

The waitress returned and they ordered drinks.

After a couple of gin and tonics they decided to have a bottle of wine. They could get a taxi home. It was a night out.

The dinner wore on and Greg was able to push his worries to the back of his mind, the more he drank. The food was really nice and he figured he would be able to resolve his money worries in time.

The taxi home was a treat. She rested her head on his shoulder and snuggled into him. The look she gave him was suggestive.

∞

They strolled arm in arm up the path and to the house.

'That was a lovely dinner, maybe we should do it again sometime,' said Dell as the security light flicked on.

She fumbled in her pocket for the keys and pulled out a note. 'What's this?'

'Come on,' said Greg, 'it's cold or hadn't you noticed?'

The paper was neatly folded. She opened it and leant into the light.

'What does it say?' he said.

'I don't ... understand ...' she squinted in concentration.

He opened the door with his key. 'Let's go in, probably one of your shopping notes or something, anyway, I'm having a nightcap, what would you ...?'

Her look cut right through him.

He could only manage to say, 'Whaaat?'

'Is this true?'

She read out the note - *"Your husband, Greg, has been fucking my wife."*

A blob of sweat trickled down his back.

'There is a phone number here, do you want me to ring it?' Her acid gaze never wavered.

At that moment he realised with a shock, the man who took their coats at the restaurant was the same face in a frame on the bedside table at Paula's place.

The End

Nature can surprise -
Think things through
That is the best policy

Detail

'Oh, it'll rain sometime alright,' remarked the bobcat driver as he took a bite out of his white bread sandwich.

'You're pretty safe saying that, mate,' replied Johnno. 'I mean, of course it will rain sometime.'

It was June on the Sunshine Coast. The heavy dew had dried up in the Tea Tree not long after sun-up and the air had taken on a dusty gossamer.

The bobcat driver gave a gap-tooth smile and wrenched another half-moon from the remains of the sandwich. 'We missed the wet this year but even money says it'll rain.' He poked the crusts into his mouth with sausage-like fingers.

Johnno was on the verge of speaking when the man with the tree-trunk neck continued, with spit and food. 'And ya know what? Eh? I reckon it's gunna rain soon.'

'Why's that?' enquired Johnno who had only moved to Mudjimba from Sydney about a year earlier.

'Well, mate, see them ants there? Eh? Right? Them bastards know there's rain about.'

He pointed to a stream of black ants. 'And mate, them black cockatoos 'ave been squawkin' for the last few days.'

Johnno was not superstitious, but his interest was piqued. 'Do you really believe that, I mean, those things?'

The bobcat driver's brow furrowed. 'No two ways about that, there are indications everywhere. If you spend enough time in the bush, you just get good at reading signs. Take another example. Right?' He poured from a worn dented Thermos flask and gulped a slug of black tea, burped politically incorrectly, and continued.

'Yep, f'rinstance, see them parrots over there? Eh? Right? Yep, they reckon there's rain on the way.' Johnno followed the direction of his finger. 'Black fellers say that them bastards go troppo before rain, yep, gunna rain soon.'

Johnno was just about to say something when the big bloke interrupted, 'and I tell ya mate, she'll be decent rain.' He scratched his ear. 'Hope you've got insurance, might need it one day.'

'Yeah, no worries although I hate paying the bastards for nothing, year after year.'

Johnno smiled at the thought, he usually made sure that he made a claim for something every year though to cover the cost of the premium. Johnno was not too worried about what he was hearing. After all, the weather forecast was for dry weather, slight westerly wind, no rain in sight. Typical Sunshine Coast in winter. Also, he recalled that the long-range forecast was dry to November. Nothing but dry weather.

Johnno was keen to get the bobcat man back to work clearing alongside his house. He was not too keen to pay for someone having smoko. He was saved.

The big fellow got up. 'Righto mate, let's get into it, eh?'

The job was finished, and Johnno could not help being impressed that such a big bloke could get such a lot of work done with such a small machine. When the bill was presented, he could not believe how cheap it was; in fact, he thought that the big fellow had made a mistake. Johnno was not the sort of bloke who would mention such a thing anyway. He believed a few bucks in his pocket were better than in someone else's.

The bobcat driver stuck out a hand that looked like a big piece of meat and they shook. He pushed his crumpled hat up. 'Hey mate, you're a bit low here, eh? You should get a bit more fill, build it up a bit, this Tea Tree used to be all swamp ya know. Any rate, see ya later mate.' He gave a casual salute and took off in a cloud of dust and diesel fumes.

Johnno could not help but like the bloke - his price was right, his table manners were not the best and he was a bit of a know all, but what would he know about the weather?

∞

Two days later a low-pressure system formed rapidly up the north-east of Cape York. It was unheard of for that time of the year, a low of such intensity. Within a couple of days, a cyclone formed. In June. The cyclone hammered areas up north and instead of crossing the coastline, it hugged the coast just out to sea, down as far as Fraser Island before moving inland. It quickly became a rain depression, but the cyclonic winds wrought severe damage to the coast. The winds continued with decreasing intensity, but the rain continued steadily as it headed south.

From the office window of accountancy firm Matthew Ledger and Associates, Johnno looked out at the rain. The weather bureau advised that they expected the rain depression to weaken but minor flooding was expected. He could see Bangalow palms whipping almost double in the park over the road. The rain came at all angles and collided with the wind.

Staff was advised to go home and secure their properties, but it was expected that the winds, although savage, would die down with the rain, which had moved from light rain to showers. Heavy rain was forecast but it would ease up in the afternoon.

Water lapped the edges of Nicklin Way, but he arrived home in reasonable time without any real problems other than being redirected a couple of times because of minor flooding. He made a cup of tea and sat at the kitchen table to watch the rain. In a very short space of time, before he had drained the cup, it increased, and the wind picked up in gusty bursts. The rain sounded like gravel on the iron roof. For the next hour the rain increased even further and cascaded in solid sheets over the gutters. Johnno had never experienced weather like this and his confidence faded rapidly.

Like a man possessed, he darted from window to window, not knowing what he was trying to see because visibility was very poor anyway. Bolts of lightning thwatted nearby and rolls of thunder mixed with the wind. The dense grey rain made it seem like 5.30pm, not 2pm, so he turned the light on. He received a slight shock from the switch which jolted him to the reality that he needed to be careful as the air was close and damp. Ten minutes later the power went off and with it a *bing* emanated from the phone.

With trembling fingers, he turned on the tranny only to hear that the whole coast was out of power. He could just make out the back edge of his property where it joined the Tea Tree. Johnno thought that his boundary line was further back and then realized with a start that the line of water was well into his property, almost up to the Hills Hoist.

Anxiety increased when he noticed a fertilizer bag, a gardening glove and his green Esky floating out the door of the garden shed. It was only four metres from the edge of the verandah but the swirling water convinced him not to go out there. He had the back door open only a crack because spray whipped everywhere, and it was only the acute pain in his fingers that made him close it.

It seemed impossible for the rain to get heavier, but it did. It became so intense that it was almost impossible to see out. He quizzed himself, 'Surely the council wouldn't let the developers build in flood prone areas?' Surely not. Sweat stung his eyes. How could he sweat with all this rain?

After an hour or so the rain eased up for a few moments. He gave a mini sigh of hopeful relief, grabbing the phone. Instantly he wondered who he would ring, it didn't matter anyway because the line was dead. He opened the door again. The back deck was slippery as he quickly shone the torch around with an unsteady hand. The gloominess surrounding the beam was almost overwhelming. Every now and then lightning highlighted an unreal horror stage set. He quickly trained the light on the neighbour's house.

Fortunately, his house was a little higher than theirs, but water appeared to be up to the back door. Johnno glanced in panic at his car in the carport; water was halfway up the wheels. Leaning up against the wall was an extension ladder. His heart jumped as it dawned on him that he should drag it over and tie it to the post in case ... in case he had to climb on to the roof. Surely not.

The radio had just advised that all roads on the coast were closed; the weather watch had been upgraded because the low-pressure system hovered over the coast and residents in low lying areas were instructed to take emergency action and get out if possible. He shook his head, was he in a low-lying area? There were supposed to be regulations to cover all this. The water rose.

His hands shook. It wasn't really that cold. He'd gone from hot to cold. The rain commenced again with the wind and it all got wilder so he zipped back inside again. After fumbling around in drawers, he found a candle which took some lighting because the matches were as damp as the air. His fingers felt like he had wicket-keeper's gloves on. For a moment he forced himself to stop darting around aimlessly.

The house felt strange and his senses picked up the strange smell of damp filth. He put both hands over his ears as if that would make it all go away but he almost leapt in fright. Childhood memories flooded back of a young boy standing on a trembling platform hanging on to his grandmother's hand as a goods train thundered past. He shook his head, jolting him to the realisation that he had to regain control of himself.

Back to the door again. He edged it open a smidgen and waved the torch beam around. Visibility was poor as the lightning had ceased. Rain whipped in his face and the wind created a sheet of water that just threw the light straight back at him. Johnno felt the water rising. It was difficult holding the door open with the pressure of the wind, so he closed it again. He glanced quickly in all directions, as he paced around from room to room, looking but not really seeing what he was doing. He had an idea and started to grab what he thought were valuables and threw them on the bed.

He tried to be rational, to decide on what to take. *Take? Why?* He did his best to convince himself that it was just a precaution and the weather probably would not get much worse. Thoughts buzzed through his head. The rain will stop soon. This is a housing estate, people live here. We would not be able to live here if it was not safe. Surely.

By midnight the water licked his back door and then trickled in. The thought of using blankets as sandbags occurred to him so he packed them under the door to keep the brown stinking water away from the back step.

Then, above the din of the wind and rain, he just picked up a frightening announcement on the radio ... king-tide. The Weather Bureau warned that the water from the rivers would not be able to flow away if the rain did not stop soon. A king tide was expected at 7.32 in the morning. He knew a bit about fishing. No-one, not even God, could do anything about the tides.

Johnno found himself zipping from room to room, unable to focus on anything and he yelped in fright when he noticed water trickling over the rolled-up towels at the front door.

The rain and wind picked up again as he stared out with the torch beam over the rising sea that seemed to want to envelop his house. He was shivering, cold balanced with fear. Whether he liked it or not, there was only one option and that was to get on the roof and hope the flood didn't wash the house away. He was just thinking clearly enough to put on his raincoat and stuff the radio and all the things he deemed valuable into a rubbish bag. He also grabbed a plastic bottle of water and two tins of sardines.

He glanced wildly in all directions, trying to decide what might be useful, what he might need. He knew he had to move. *Quickly*. Out the back door he squelched as water gurgled in. It rose with every step. With the torch strap clenched between his teeth, he waded to the edge of the patio towards the ladder. Lightning flashed a few times which, although it helped to show the way, frightened him even further.

Every step was a major achievement; for a moment he stopped dead, his stomach was knotted, and he had the taste of bile in his mouth. He did not think he could do it. It was dark, the rain thundered around him and the wind whipped up spray. As he stood there, he could feel the water rising, it was up to his thighs.

He told himself, 'One more step, and then another, you'll be alright.' He reached the ladder and maneuvered himself on to the steps. His fingers were numb, and his feet kept slipping and missing the soapy steps. As he climbed, the weight of the rain struck him, and the wind nearly ripped him off the ladder several times. Rain stung his eyes and poured inside his collar. Johnno looked down on his car, water was almost up to the windows.

He finally managed to clamber on to the slippery roof by desperate grasps of the TV aerial. He could sense the swelling water below. It was almost pitch black and he used his torch to find the top spot of the roof. Clenched toes in his sandshoes hung on as his eyes darted in every direction and his whole body shook.

The wind howled, and the rain pelted and he tried to think that things were easing. Thunder rumbled in the distance. Thoughts crowded his head, what was he going to do if. If what? If the house washed away? With the aid of the torch and the odd flash of lightning way off, he estimated that the water was halfway up the windows. Over the next hour the rain eased marginally, and the wind became less gusty. The next few hours were uncertain as he periodically shone the torch on the rising tide. The rain became lighter and stopped a couple of times.

At least he was not lonely, a snake and two cane toads eased onto the island of hope along with him, just along the ridge beam near the end. He wondered where the birds and other animals were and he realized that he was not frightened of the snake even though it was black. It did not seem to matter. Every so often he thought he could see stars through the drizzle as the wind cut through him. Although it seemed like an eternity, hours passed.

Thoughts of building regulations buzzed around in his head as he could have sworn the house moved a couple of times. That did it. He started crying, there was no-one to embarrass, his face was wet anyway. Tears poured out. He did not know if he would or could make it. The water was now just below the roof.

Just on daybreak the rain ceased, the grey mass above eased slowly into oily, nasty, grey clouds that chased small scraps of blue. In a matter of hours, the wind became a breeze and a sunny sky wrenched shaky confidence from him as he gazed, horrified, at the destruction around him. He could see other people in the distance, two in a boat and one group of people on the roof of some flats in the distance.

The smell from flooded septic tanks and the evidence of the weight of human existence was almost overpowering. Rotting debris, logs, boxes, a dead dog and all sorts of flotsam and jetsam could be seen in amongst the flooded ruined houses and remains. The snake looked at him or that is how he interpreted it. Fear pricked his heart like a cold needle for a moment and then the reptile slithered away into the smelly water that he realised had subsided somewhat. He did not want to think about where the cane toads had gone. That pang of fear made him realize that he was still in the land of the living.

The flood rapidly retreated and around the middle of the day, Johnno felt game enough to make his way down to inspect the damage. The water level had dropped to floor height. He had heard on the radio that the Sunshine Coast was lucky because the rain had stopped in the catchment zone. Also, the king tide was at a minimum and the water had been able to get away. There was a big swell, the beaches had taken a pounding and the Sunshine Coast had been declared a disaster zone.

∞

He squelched through the house shaking his head, observing the mess. Wet and damaged possessions strewn at all angles reminded him of the area around a Lifeline bin after a wet long weekend. Almost everything was covered in mud and was completely useless. The premier, obviously pleased to get publicity, mouthed off about making sure the Insurance Companies honoured their obligations. Johnno tried a wry smile; he hoped it was nothing like the government's other promises.

Suddenly, he brightened. 'Bloody hell! Thank God, I'm insured.' He spoke to the smelly sewerage that swirled at his back step. The smile increased, he yelped and punched the air, 'Yeah!'

An idea shot across his brain. 'They won't have any idea what I lost, even if I didn't lose it. No worries.'

Johnno spent a very uncomfortable night shared with mosquitoes and the increasingly overpowering stench of death and rot. Some SES officers had called in during the afternoon in a boat. They gave him some water and a food parcel and told him to wait until tomorrow and report in at the emergency station a couple of blocks away when it was safe to venture out.

∞

The next day he struggled through mud and debris in the direction of the emergency station. He was thankful that his house was the only one left standing reasonably intact in the general vicinity. He had to take a detour because of the stench of a decaying horse that some blokes were trying to remove with a backhoe.

A woman from the SES in orange overalls told him that over a hundred people had died and she added, 'We're still finding 'em.'

She directed him to a caravan marked 'Insurance Claims and Information' where a man took some details.

'Just grab a seat at one of them booths there,' the bloke indicated with a lazy wave. 'There's a list of insurance company hot lines on the desk.'

He nodded and inwardly cringed at the dour public servant with half-moons of sweat under his arms. Johnno eased into the wooden chair; his hand trembled with anticipation as he dialed.

'Hello, AG Insurance, how may I help you?' gushed a female voice.

He recited his particulars and was asked to hold for a few moments.

'Right, now, Mr. John Edwin Pearson ...'

'Yes,' he blurted, perhaps too eagerly.

'Well, we have you insured with us, sir ... but, let me see, yes here it is, in the fine print. You opted for our No-Frills Policy, sir, the one with no flood damage cover.'

The phone hit the desk with a thump. The public servant glanced over, 'You orright, mate?'

Johnno did not hear him. He just stared at the wall. It came back to him. In his haste to take out the cheapest policy; he had omitted to read the fine print.

The End

What we deserve

Could be there for the taking -

But there is still right and wrong

Entitlement

I looked around the room, picking up a few things here and there. Poor old Mum, spent all her life working and putting up with hardship – for what? To be rewarded with a stroke. And leave behind this rented house in Wallaroo; alright, a heritage building and yes, she kept it nice but what else? The only pieces of furniture or family treasures worth having, Dad smashed, sold or lost.

Dad was a bastard. I called him a Mongrel but not to his face, of course. He was known around town as Mongrel to his mates. Pretty good mates, eh? He belted the shit out of Mum whenever he felt like it and he belted me when he had the chance, or to be truthful, when he was drunk – which was most of the time – whenever he had money – stolen from Mum or from selling dope. It was very rarely from working. When I heard him come in, I used to hide but poor old Mum, well she copped it instead. That's when I was younger.

Mum had a stroke a few weeks ago, at work, and was admitted to hospital by ambulance, lasted a couple of hours, had another stroke, and died. I was sad because I never had the chance to see her then. Maybe I could have prevented her from ... nah, I can't think that, you go when you go. I did see her on the previous weekend and we had a good time, so that is nice to remember. We had her funeral day before yesterday. A lot of people turned up, too.

Not much of value to keep, just a few mementos, a bit of cutlery, a few plates, and cups, that is about it. Heaven knows I could do with something of value. With Jeff down to two days a week and the kids ever demanding video games.

∞

Back to Mongrel. I stayed at home longer than I wanted to and by then I was big enough and more able to stand up to him. When he got stuck into Mum that last time, I belted him across the shoulders with a lump of wood from the wood box. I was shitting myself because I thought he would turn on me then. Mum was cowering on the ground, dizzy from a punch in the head. Right at that moment our neighbour, Mr Phelps, who must have heard the screaming, was standing at the front door, mobile phone against his ear. Fortunately, Mongrel was dazed enough to sit where he was. He glanced around, shocked that I had hit him, and it was with all my might so he must have been sore.

Sergeant Blackland took Mongrel to jail and I heard later that Blackland, who played footy for Wallaroo and was a big bloke as well, told Mongrel that he would beat the shit out of him if he was seen around town ever again. Wallaroo is a small country town and Mongrel was known to the authorities for all sorts of antisocial behaviour including not paying fines and things. I guess the police gave him the option, piss off or we'll book you.

That did it for Mum and me and a few of the blokes from the footy club came around and fitted security screens on the house as a gesture, just to make sure.

Mongrel made himself scarce and then about a year ago I heard he robbed the Port Broughton bank agency with a no-hoper mate of his called Don Jergens. They must have been out of it because they used a car with no numberplates. Jergens disappeared as did the money and Mongrel was left carrying the can. Silly bugger came back here, and they noticed the car out the front. I was a bit alarmed about that for a sec when I heard but I realised Mum wasn't there, she had gone to Adelaide to get new glasses.

Mongrel got six years. Jergens was found some time later floating face down in Streaky Bay. No money was ever recovered.

∞

Earlier this morning, a neighbour had taken one of the beds because I didn't need it, but I wanted the rug, from underneath, for the kids' room. With some grunting I managed to roll it up but then I noticed a square of Masonite tacked down near the edge of the floor. Strange, that. I prised it up with a knife and there was a hole in the floor. Under the floor was a toolbox.

I lifted the lid. On top was a pile of cheques stapled to a letterhead, Bank of Port Broughton. Underneath was crammed with used bank notes.

For a long moment, my insides froze. Then contemplation took over.

The End

Our station in life

Is a challenge -

Some people cannot see beyond

Dave Cobb

'What do you want?'

'Um … morning Mister Cobb, I've come here to speak …'

'Well, mate I don't want to speak to no one.'

'Sir, Mister Cobb, I've been asked to …'

'Piss off! I know what you're here for.'

'Mister Cobb, er can I call you Dave?'

'What?'

'Can I call you Dave?'

'You're not takin' me boys.'

'Er … Dave, we have to think of … umm … everyone's safety.'

'Safety? What the hell is this?'

'Dave, please, I'm here to talk, just talk, you and me. Please mate, put down that axe handle, hey? Talk, that's all … man to man, right?'

'Ya not takin' me kids.'

'Mate … Dave, they have to go to school, they haven't been for two weeks.'

'Who the root da ya think you are, eh? Big deal welfare public servant, eh? You bloody-well come here and tell me I'm not being a good dad, eh?'

'No, Dave, no. Look mate, I know it's hard for you, wife not around anymore, must be very hard, eh? Thanks, yeah, just leave it there on the ground, I'm here to talk, right?'

'Ya not takin' me kids, right? I'd do anything for me boys; you bloody-well know that.'

'Dave, they need to be fed, need clothes for school. Mate, it's the drinking, it's … it's getting out of hand again. Yeah? Isn't it?'

'I … I only have a few, not all the time …'

'You haven't been meeting with your group for a while; they asked when you were coming back. You can't go on like this.'

'It's alright for you, eh, earnin' big money, flash car, things runnin' easy for ya. You don't know what it's like, missus pissed off on me, left me with two boys, bitch, pissed off with that Barker arsehole. Left me on me own, eh.'

'Mate, no one's going to take your kids away, they'll be nearby, you can see them when you want …'

'I tell ya straight up, ya not takin' 'em, unnerstand?'

'Dave, you need to go back to the group. Your drinking is causing a few problems. There's trouble with the police, you know, firing that rifle of yours at night, frightens people. If you go to jail, you'll be no good to your boys, will you? Mate, please put that bottle down, we need to talk.'

'You've got no idea what it's like, tryin' to make it on ya own, look after two growin' boys. You probly think its funny watchin' a bloke with the arse out of his strides cryin', eh?'

'Dave, no, I don't, course not. Oh, my friend. Most blokes have been there, mate, one way or the other, you're not alone. You need help.'

'I tol' ya, I'd do anything for me kids, right?'

'Dave, the best thing you can do is let us get them off to school and give them a few square meals …'

'I'd do anything for me kids. If they aren't gunna be here with me, life ain't worth livin'.'

'Dave! Dave … mate, please put down that rifle … if you really love your …'

'I'd do anything for me kids, love me kids.'

'Dave … Dave … no Dave … put it down … please Dave … listen to me …oh God …'

The End

Sneaking around

Behind the scenes -

Can become complicated

Hollow Victory

Anne's smile was translucent, 'We'll work something out.'

Larry was not convinced. He was edgy and distracted as he lay back with his hands clasped behind his head. They were nude. She lit two cigarettes and handed him one as they stared at the ceiling in silence. Both knew something had to be done. It had been six months and they could not go on like this.

A chance encounter, he left work late on a Friday night, needed to tidy up paperwork. The workload had been heavy, and on a whim, he decided to go and see a movie. Larry needed to separate his mind from work. She had seen the film with a friend; her husband was away on business for three or four nights. After the show the two women walked out and had just parted company.

He saw her. 'Hi Anne.'

'Oh? Hi Larry.'

That is how it started. They had known each other socially, for a couple of years prior to this, but not very well. Then, they became lost in the passion and as time rolled on, they had hoped things would resolve themselves. But really nothing had, in fact it was worse now for a whole range of reasons.

Larry did not feel very good at that moment, nor did Anne. They both knew they were going to be found out, sooner rather than later.

∞

At a hospital near the city, a man lay on a bed, confused, and tired. The blackness began to ease as the trickle of a concerned voice slowly solidified in his consciousness. The lights became brighter, even though his eyes were closed.

'Ah, Mr. Morrow, Tom, that's better, isn't it? You're among friends; you've had a nasty knock on the head.'

His eyes opened into slits but the light injected shards into his head. He tried again; this time he was just able to make out a shadow near his face. Light from the window and the fluoro tubes made it hard to focus.

'It's good that you are back with us. My name's Steve, I'm a nurse, I know I look like the janitor.' He chuckled and dabbed Tom's forehead with a cool sponge.

'Ooooooh … what's …?'

'It's all right, mate, how's the head?'

The light still reflected off the tiles and ceiling, but he forced his eyes open a little more.

'What am I doing here?'

Hospital noises bounced down the corridor.

'You were admitted yesterday afternoon; a pair of pliers fell from some scaffolding and hit you on the side of your scone. You were lucky mate, because it just glanced off, also the pliers had rubber grips. If it had hit you on the top, right there, you might very well not be here now.'

He tried to pull himself up a little bit higher in the bed.

'Just relax Tom. Here let me help you.' The nurse grabbed a pillow from the side table. 'There we go. Would you like a sip of water?'

'Yeah, thanks, that would be good.'

'You might have a sore head for a while and you are slightly concussed, but you will be right in a few days. We need to keep you in hospital for a day or so just to keep an eye on the concussion. They dug out a business card from your wallet and rang your home but no one was there. Is there anyone we can contact?'

'No, not really. My wife is away at the moment, difficult to contact, won't be back until tomorrow night.'

'Fair enough, you'll be out of here by then anyway, I think. Right, I'll leave you with it, just take it easy and I'll drop in on you later.'

Tom gently ran his hand over the bandage. 'Ouch!'

He lay back trying to rein in his thoughts. What had happened? He remembered getting out of the lift, and walking past a building site. Yes, he remembered that. Things went hazy and sleep overtook him. Over the next few hours, he drifted between sleep, unconsciousness, and an unusual reality.

The next day he felt a lot better, although drowsy and vague. There was something else too, something to do with his mind, or his head, or his, what? He thought he knew what other people were thinking. He knew people who claimed they could read people's minds but he was doubtful that anyone could actually do it. However, he had that same feeling now.

About an hour earlier, the doctor had been talking to the person in the bed by the corner. The old man, Arthur, had said, 'Did you get it all, Doctor?' The doctor had replied, 'Yes, no problem, you'll be free to go home soon.'

It was evident to Tom, that the old man knew something was not right. Also, he sensed the doctor was thinking, *I'm not sure, I don't think we did get it all. Best not to alarm him, he is very old and will die soon anyway because his heart is weak.* The old man then said, 'Is there anything else I need to know, doctor?' The doctor was having trouble trying to balance truth, reality and compassion. 'You'll be right, Arthur. Just relax.'

The inner thoughts of these people were all crystal clear to Tom; he knew what the doctor and patient were thinking. During the day these extra powers seemed to come and go. He knew that the janitor could not wait to knock off. He knew the ward sister was very irritable about a problem she had with her son who smashed up her car. He knew what the other doctor was thinking too, when he came to examine the footballer. The doctor was musing over another operation that seemingly went wrong and he was wondering how he could wriggle out of it.

Tom was relieved when the female doctor came to see him. He knew she was honest when she said he would be able to go home tomorrow and that there was no serious damage, but he also had a feeling that she was having trouble with her boyfriend.

Steve, the male nurse called in and dealt with the other two patients in a friendly and efficient manner. He brought a jug of orange juice over. 'How are you feeling, Tom?'

'Pretty good thanks, mate. My head is a bit sore though,' he mumbled bravely.

'Yeah, that's to be expected but you will be right in a day or two. The doctor says the bruising will go down and aside from the headache you should make a full recovery within a week. Right, let's just get your bed organised, eh?'

Tom knew the nurse was genuine, but he also knew that Steve said similar things to everybody.

Tom Morrow was a happy man. He had a beautiful wife, lived in a green and stable suburb, and had a business that was steaming along. He worked very hard for this. His university days were spent wasting money he did not have and enjoying himself like most young people. Since then, after stumbling on an idea about computers, most of his time was spent with business activities. The life he shared in a fashionable home with his wife Marie was comfortable and predictable.

∞

'He's bound to find out about us,' said Larry. 'I don't like it.'

He paced, naked, taking measured drags on his cigarette.

'Larry, I've got something to tell you,' said Anne.

He stopped pacing, turned, 'Yeah?'

'I'm ... I'm pregnant.'

'What?' he snapped, eyebrows in a bold line.

'I'm ...'

'You are bloody-well what? You're not serious, surely.'

He took an angry hit on the cigarette.

'Yyyes, I'm sorry, I forgot to take the pill; I thought it would be alright but ...'

'We agreed, remember? Don't you remember? We talked about this subject many times. You said you were on the pill, remember?'

He butted out his cigarette furiously.

'Yes, I know, but ... I only forgot ... um only once.'

Larry turned and looked hard at her.

'Well, I only missed taking it a couple of times, I didn't think ...'

'Didn't think! I can't believe it!' He sat on the edge of the bed.

She touched his shoulder; he shrugged her off.

'What in the fuck are we going to do now?'

She touched him again; he let her hand remain. 'Larry?'

He looked up.

'Larry ... there's ... there's more.'

'What? Oh, Christ Almighty, how could there be more? You ... you're not thinking of keeping it, are you?'

'I have to, I'm you know ... er I sort of have to, I'm .... I have to, Larry.'

'What? That does not make any sense in our situation!' he said sharply.

'And there is something else I have just found out recently - my husband, umm can't father children.'

'Shit. So, you are pregnant, it's my kid, we're having an affair, your husband doesn't know about us and he can't father children. Right? Bloody great.'

She just looked at him.

'You'll have to consider an abortion; there's no other way. I mean to say, your husband is no idiot, he knows he can't father children. He'll know that you've been having an affair. Christ Almighty, Anne what a bloody mess. I don't know. You sort it out!'

He threw his hands up, shook his head and then looked down at the floor. He felt lower than a dachshund's guts. There was nowhere lower he could look.

Larry was dressed, pacing. 'Look, Anne, you're going to have to have an abortion, it's the only way. I mean, if he finds out we've been carrying on behind his back ...'

His words hung in the air like powder. He was too agitated and troubled to react to her in the bed, nude with a sheet just covering her knees.

'Larry, I can't. I just can't. I didn't think I would feel this way, it's your baby too Larry, not my husband's. I can't just ... get rid of our child, just like that. Let's run away. We've talked about it a lot, let's do it.' Her voice sounded like a ten-year-old in a school play.

'Run away? Where? How do we live? Where is the money coming from?' He waved his arms helplessly.

'Your business, our business, there's plenty of money.'

'My business, our business? Your husband is my business partner, are you bonkers? Do you really think he is going to give us half of the business, in cash and wish us well? How thrilled do you think he's going to be when he finds out his mate and business partner has been banging his wife for the last six months, eh? And, get this, an added bonus, she's pregnant as well!'

She lay back on the pillows, crystals seemed to fill her eyes. 'Larry, we've got to find a way out of this.'

'Look Anne, you have to get rid of it. There's really no choice.' He ran both hands back through his dark hair, pressing it down. It stuck up again as soon as he took his hands away.

∞

By Sunday morning Tom was feeling much better and ready to go home. The doctor had called in earlier and given him the all clear. Tom's wife did not know he was in hospital as she was still away camping with a girlfriend. At a pinch he could get a message to her, but there seemed no point, she would be home Sunday night anyway.

Anne was always doing things; tennis, the gym, netball. She was physical and loved sport. He did not mind, he always had plenty to do at work. In fact, there was no limit to the number of things that needed to be done at the office, his second home, or his first home as she often called it. Hopefully, by the time she arrived home he would be almost fully recovered except for the lump and the bandage around it.

The extra powers, being able to read other people's thoughts, came and went, sometimes he knew what people were thinking and sometimes he did not. He lay back listening to the squelch of rubber shoes and wheels down the corridor, and the ever-present antiseptic whiff.

The previous week

'I'm going away camping with Savannah this weekend,' bubbled Marie.

Tom looked up from the morning paper. 'Right, great, where?'

'Out to Cripple Creek Campground, if we can get in. They've got firewood there and dunnies, hot water too.'

'We should go out there, just the two of us one weekend,' suggested Tom.

'Yeah, great idea, although you probably wouldn't like it much out there, no fluoros, no desks and no computer jacks.'

He laughed; she was always doing something, out here, out there, visiting friends, bushwalking, or playing sport. He knew she would probably get bored with him anyway because he would take paperwork and the laptop too. She spent a lot of time with Savannah, a friend of hers from school. They were inseparable.

Friday morning

'Tom, I won't be here when you arrive home tonight,' said Marie piling bedding near the door. 'Savannah and I are knocking off at lunchtime and we're off to Cripple Creek; we want to make the most of the weekend and the weather as well.'

'Yeah, fair enough. I have a late one tonight anyway, that Kangaroo contract, it's a biggie, got to make sure everything is okay with it. I'd better be off hun, I've got a lot to do today. Have a good time, and give my best to Savannah. Must go.'

He kissed her lightly on the cheek, grabbed his briefcase and headed out to the garage.

Friday afternoon

Tom thought he would go to the shop on the corner and get a couple of sandwiches. There was a lot on his mind and he was not concentrating on the job in hand. He stood in the lift for a second or two before realising that he had not pressed the button. Then he walked out of the building and turned the wrong way. He had the Kangaroo contract on his mind, and no one to discuss it with. He did notice that a cold westerly was blowing and the sky was blue; he had forgotten to put his jacket on.

He did not notice a sign that said, *hard hat area* as he walked along the footpath underneath some scaffolding and he should also have noticed the arrows that were painted on the ground and along the safety fence line. It was poorly laid out by the safety officer and should have been marked more clearly because Tom was just following another pedestrian who had made a similar mistake.

About 20 metres away, a Bobcat was working and accidentally nudged the scaffolding. A pair of pliers someone had left innocently sitting on a plank high up was dislodged and fell, hitting him a glancing blow on the head. It knocked him out instantly and would have killed him if the pliers had not had soft insulated rubber grips. Workers gathered around and an ambulance was called and Tom was rushed to hospital unconscious.

The present

Tom was well enough to take a taxi home. It was another pleasant but cool spring day. He tried to recall what day it was, eventually deciding it was Sunday.

After the taxi dropped him off, he picked up several rolled newspapers that had seemingly landed with precision on the front verandah. He unlocked the door, walked in, and dropped the papers on the table. Marie was not home yet; still away camping. When he thought the word camping, the strange feeling returned. His mind was confused but he realised she would be home soon. He also realised that she would be concerned, and that made him feel good.

He thought about the Kangaroo contract as he put the kettle on. Not a problem with that, he could sense it was going to make his company a lot of money. He made a pot of coffee and took it outside to the verandah. The cushions on the cane chair felt comfortable as he put his feet on the stool. Tom fell asleep. Not long after, the coffee went cold.

He awoke to the sound of the automatic roller door whirring. Marie was home.

'Tom, you there?'

'Out here.'

'Hi darl, how're you go …? What happened to your head?'

'Had an accident, walking past a construction site, pliers fell on my scone.'

'Are you alright?' Her brow tightened.

'Yeah, no problem, had to go to hospital though, since Friday, just precautionary.'

'You'd better rest up and take it easy.'

'How did it go?' he asked, not wanting to talk about himself.

'Me, go?'

'Yes, camping.'

'Oh yes, sure, great, did plenty of walking. I'm really tired, need a shower.' She kissed his other ear lightly and went in the direction of the ensuite.

That strange feeling came over him again. He certainly knew she did not need a shower and he knew she was not that tired. Then the Kangaroo contract came into his mind again, and many other things; it was very confusing. His head hurt so he went and got some Panadol and a glass of water. As he lay down on the lounge, things crisscrossed in his mind, Larry Quinn, his business partner, the Kangaroo contract, camping, Marie, hospital, Savannah.

It must be a confused dream, concussion, that is it. Then Larry and Marie surfaced; why were they together? Nothing made any sense.

∞

Larry paced like a caged panther. 'That stupid fucking bitch.' He lit a cigarette. 'Bloody idiot!'

He could not understand it. They had discussed the topic on several occasions earlier on in the relationship and she had agreed to continue taking the pill. He knew it was a mess; after all, his business partner was her husband. If only he had acted earlier and ended the relationship with Anne because the spark of the first few months had already died. He had become tired of her in recent times because she had become increasingly demanding. It was clear his business partnership would come to a halt, and it was also clear that he did not want to spend the rest of his life with Anne. No way in the world did he want children, especially with her. He ground out his cigarette and grumbled.

∞

Tom did not want to admit anything to himself, but in his mind, he had strong thoughts and feelings that his business partner, Larry Quinn, and his beautiful wife Anne-Marie, were having an affair. He tried to shake it, but it kept coming back.

He knew his head had been damaged, possibly his brain as well, but what about his mind? It disturbed him, even to think that any of this could be true. This last week Larry Quinn had been away on business, their business, down the coast. Marie had been away camping with Savannah. He could not shake these thoughts from his mind.

The next day, Tom made some discrete enquiries from a couple of friends in the industry, and they confirmed that Larry was at that meeting on Friday. Also, he had a reservation at the Oxford Hotel, and it was confirmed that he had stayed there.

Tom did not feel good about checking up on people, particularly his friend, and his wife, people he knew or he thought he knew. He rang the National Parks and Wildlife. 'Yep mate, got their names down here.' The Ranger confirmed that a permit had been issued in Anne-Marie's name for two people at Cripple Creek.

The feeling left him and he started thinking that everything was all right and it was just his paranoia. After all they had been vindicated and he felt lousy about doubting them.

∞

Late Monday afternoon, Larry came around to see how he was feeling, and to talk about business. Anne-Marie made him a cup of coffee. Tom picked up an intimate communication between them, although Larry was much harder to read. Larry Quinn seemed pre-occupied, deeply troubled about something. Tom became uneasy about everything again as doubts crept back.

He went to his local doctor and tried to explain what was going on with him. It was very difficult trying to make clear to a medical person that you had extra powers that allowed you to know what other people were thinking. He was informed that everything was all right, and it was just his imagination, possibly due to his recent accident but it would resolve in time. He was advised to rest. Tom knew the doctor was not very interested in the case; it seemed he was more interested in thinking about sex with his secretary. The doctor also suggested a psychiatrist, but Tom knew that he was not sincere; all he wanted was a referral fee. Tom Morrow was now at a very low ebb.

∞

Anne-Marie felt ill; she could not eat, could not sleep. Her life was torture. It was not all to do with the pregnancy. She knew she could not tell her husband about her and Larry, much less tell him about the baby. When Tom looked at her, she felt strange. There seemed to be something unusual about him and the way he looked at her. She knew their marriage would be finished if Tom knew about the affair. She recalled a conversation they had just after getting married. He said if she ever had an affair, he would not make a fuss, would not lose his temper. It would simply just be all over.

Further complications sifted through her mind. Tom's business was originally kick started with money borrowed from her father. Also in recent weeks, she felt that Larry was getting tired of her. Unfortunately, she became acutely aware of this after she discovered she was pregnant. The thought that Larry did not want a baby disturbed her; she thought he would be happy. His reaction when she told him had shocked her.

The news that Tom could not have children also came recently because of tests they had both been having. Initially she had thought she would tell Tom that it was his child, if Larry didn't want to marry her, then the news came back about the tests.

She had naively thought that things would sort themselves out. Thoughts, scenarios, and realities tumbled around in her head.

∞

Larry Quinn had made a decision. He was not proud of it, but after all, what else could he do? It was her stupidity that got him into this mess. He knew Tom would find out everything sooner or later. Yes, he had to take steps to save himself. The wheels were in motion.

∞

It had been three days since Tom had come out of hospital. Larry was managing the office and the business as he rested at home. Tom was not imagining anything that was happening, he knew with absolute clarity, and he also knew he had to confront them both soon. Being a cautious sort of person, he decided to investigate a little further just to be sure. He rang the ranger again and found out that no one had used the campsite.

It was a nice day so he took a drive down the coast and spoke with some of the staff at the Oxford Hotel. Tom had to wave a few $50 notes around but he found out that Larry had stayed there. But, one of the kitchen staff recalled delivering some food to the room and had commented that a woman was there as well. Tom showed him a photo of his wife and he confirmed that the woman looked very much like her. He further noted from inside his head that the people he spoke to were telling the truth.

As Tom drove back from the coast to the city, he thought about the whole situation. He was deeply hurt. His wife of eight years, was having an affair with a good friend, his business partner, behind his back. He was not angry or mad, just sad, and depressed. Tom knew that he could not father children, but he figured that should not really have had any bearing on anything, because that news was a recent thing. What about his mate and business partner? They had gone through university together and there had been football and women and surfing, and more. Telling things started to crowd his thoughts; money, business, marriage.

Tom made up his mind to talk to Anne-Marie first but she was not at home when he arrived. He wanted to hear it from her lips before taking any action.

He made a few business calls and did some work on the Kangaroo contract, but his mind was elsewhere. Larry Quinn could wait, that was going to be difficult because money was involved as well. He lay down on the couch and fell asleep.

∞

The phone rang, sharp and relentless. The feeling came back, he knew the call was important.

'Tom Morrow speaking.'

'Mr. Morrow? This is Sergeant Don Winston speaking, sir. I understand you and Mr Larry Quinn are business partners?'

'Er … yes?'

'Well, sir, we have arrested Mr Quinn on charges of falsifying documents and forgery, in relation to a trust account in your name sir. Would it be convenient if …?'

'Falsifying documents?'

'Yes sir, apparently, this afternoon Mr Quinn attempted to withdraw a large sum of money. The bank security people suspected something and contacted us straight away. There were some other irregularities as well which included your safety deposit box and some other assets, that's why we would like to talk to you, in person of course. Do you know anything about this sir?'

'No, of course not. This is quite a shock.'

'Would it be convenient if we came around and talked to you now?'

Tom rubbed his eyes with his free hand. 'Yes, of course.'

∞

He hung up and sat boring holes in the lounge wall with his gaze. The bright rag rolled suede effect on the wall should have cheered him up, but there was no vision of it. Not only having an affair with his wife, but cheating him as well.

He barked, 'What a fucking bastard!'

Then he wondered if the two of them were planning to run away together. His head was in a bigger jumble now. Reality returned with purposeful knocking on the door.

'That was quick,' he mumbled.

He opened the door to two uniformed police officers.

'Mr Tom Morrow?' enquired the female police officer.

'Yes.'

'Mr Morrow, could we come in please?'

'Yes of course.' He opened the door wider, stood back and ushered them in.

'Would you like to grab a seat?'

The male officer remained standing, shuffling his feet. 'Sir, I am Sergeant Max Freeman and this is Constable Jasmine Hill. I'm afraid we have some bad news for you.'

Max Freeman? What happened to Sergeant Don Winston? At this point, he had no idea and could only assume they were about to tell him about Larry Quinn raiding his bank account.

'Would you please sit down. I'm sorry to have to tell you this, sir, but your wife is … um … dead.'

'What? Dead?'

Constable Hill replied, 'Yes, we found her about an hour ago down near the tennis courts.'

'What! Are you sure it is my wife? How did she … er die?'

'We believe it is your wife, but of course we will need you to formally identify her. At this time, we believe she committed suicide, sir. There will be a full investigation but that is the way it looks. And at this stage there appear to be no suspicious circumstances. Again, the investigation will later confirm the facts surrounding her death. I am very sorry for your loss.'

'Suicide?'

The police officer stared, 'Sorry to have to tell you this, sir, but it appears that she … er fixed a pipe to the exhaust and died of carbon monoxide poisoning.' He added, 'She had also taken a large number of sleeping tablets as well.'

Tom put his hands on his ears and leant back in his chair.

Constable Jasmine Hill spoke gently, 'Is there someone we can call, someone who could be with you?'

Tom just sat there unable to process what they were saying to him.

'Sir?'

'What?'

'Is there someone we can call to be with you?'

'No, I'll be alright, thank you … thanks.'

The two police officers saw themselves out. As they drove out of the street, they acknowledged another police vehicle.

'Aah,' said Constable Hill, 'That looks like Don Winston from the fraud squad. 'Wonder what the hell he's doing out this way?'

'Probably just driving around to kill time. They get it easy, those blokes,' laughed Sergeant Max Freeman.

∞

Tom Morrow should have felt relieved because he did not have to confront the two closest people in his life, but there was no relief, just an indescribable emptiness and sense of betrayal.

Although distraught, he was a practical man and with the advice of his lawyer, figured that he would gain full control of the business if he downgraded the severity of the fraud charges levelled at Larry Quinn. The death of his wife would never give him joy, despite the knowledge that she had an affair behind his back.

One thing had become apparent, and much to his relief, he no longer had those feelings of being able to read thoughts inside other people's heads.

A few days later, on a cold, bleak spring day after enduring the funeral of his wife, a letter from the coroner's office awaited him. It stated that his wife had been pregnant at the time of her death. Knowing that the child would have been Larry's because he could not father children, made his depression weigh him down even further. He did not bother to read on, dropping the letter on the kitchen bench.

He made a pot of tea, picked up the letter again and wandered out to the back verandah to his favourite cane chair. Tom re-read the letter with great sadness and then he sat bolt upright. The DNA and blood type of the baby matched his.

Four months later

Tom sat at his desk, surrounded by paperwork and folders, each one a new business opportunity. In recent months he had been working obsessively to keep his mind busy and away from dark thoughts.

His phone rang. 'Tom Morrow speaking.'

"Good morning, Mr Morrow, I am Detective Inspector Patrick Symonds from the Murder Investigation team. I am just calling about the investigation into the death of your wife. I have to inform you that we are ruling her death as suspicious as we have discovered significant complexities surrounding her life in the months leading to up to her death. I would like to come to the house to discuss this with you more fully. I should add that we have a suspect in custody. May I come to see you now?'

The End

Looking young
And beautiful -
Can be dangerous

Jail Bait

Kelly ran her hands along the products wondering how many choices people really needed for breakfast cereals. Blonde, blue-eyed, flat chested, in school uniform and wearing a dress higher than her mother would ever have approved of. She wanted to show off her tanned legs, shapelier than most schoolgirls'.

'Excuse me, dear, could you please read that out for me?' The stout middle-aged woman with a generous bottom held up a packet of cereal.

Kelly clicked out of her pseudo dream world. 'Er pardon?'

'Sorry, dear, I don't have my glasses.'

'Yeah, like sure,' she replied, with the *like sure* said softly. She gave a coy, friendly look and then read out the details.

'It's really hard to work out exactly what is in the products these days and of course where they come from.'

Kelly replied, 'Sure,' thinking that saying, *like duh?* would really be pushing it.

The stout woman pulled out a pen from the nest of brunette rinse retreating from greying roots. 'Thank you,' she said, made a mark on the list and placed the product in her trolley. She had kind eyes. 'And what is your name, dear.'

'Kelly.'

'That's a nice modern name; I like modern names.'

Kelly nodded.

The stout woman with kind eyes said, 'Well, I better be moving on now, I'll only get what I want today because without my glasses, you know, I really can't see.'

'I've got, like, all the things I need,' offered Kelly, 'I can like, help you with your shopping, and stuff, if you want.' She pointed at the stout woman's shopping list, hoping she did not sound too eager.

'That's very kind of you, love.'

They shopped and chatted, distant but parallel and as they neared the checkout, Kelly's heart rate accelerated when she saw the headlines and quickly stood between the stout woman and the newspaper stand. The older woman insisted on paying for Kelly's groceries.

They stood outside the supermarket and Kelly was about to offer to help the stout woman with her trolley.

'Kelly, would you be ever so kind as to the wheel my trolley over to my car - see the white Hi-Ace van, over there?' She pointed. 'I have a bad leg, you know, arthritis, plays up in winter.'

Kelly looked around as it started to drizzle. 'Yeah, sure, like, that one over there?'

They passed a stooped old man, a down-and-outer, pushing a shopping trolley full of plastic bags - pushing his whole life in a wire basket with wheels. He stopped to talk to a middle-aged couple, loading their boot with groceries.

'Best to put things in the side door, dear. Here, I'll open it for you.' The stout woman with the kind eyes leant across in front of Kelly and slid the door wide open. 'We'd better hurry with this rain; I'll hand the bags to you.'

Kelly quickly loaded three plastic bags of groceries and when she turned to grab the last one, she noticed that the kind eyes of the stout woman had changed.

The older woman made a purring sound that turned into a growl. *'Kurt will love a cute little blossom like you.'* She grappled Kelly in a headlock and tried to ram a chemical smelling rag in her face. Kelly's training kicked in; she jagged her elbow as hard as she could into the other woman's stomach and was about to deliver a hard right to her face when the old man, who was now without his trolley, arrived.

'You're under arrest' he yelled at the stout woman with the generous bottom. The middle-aged, boot loading couple appeared out of nowhere and grabbed the woman and threw her hard up against the side of the van.

The old man without the trolley turned to Constable Kelly Rathdowney. 'Doesn't look like you needed us, Constable.'

The stout woman with nasty eyes had turned even more into a mean machine. She screeched, '*What the fuck ... you can't prove a ...*' and tried to struggle with the middle-aged couple, who now looked younger as they forcefully pulled rank and handcuffed the stout woman.

'Took your time, Sarge,' said Constable Kelly, and she started coughing. 'Couldn't believe it, I thought I was ready for the old bag, but she was so bloody quick and, mate, she was as strong as, too.' She wiped her eyes.

The other two officers dragged the vicious, violently protesting old woman over to a police van that just pulled up.

∞

'You okay?' Sergeant Porter looked over from the driver's seat.

'Yeah, I'll live.' Kelly picked up one of the papers from the seat between them. 'The press don't help us very much, do they?' she said as she looked down at the headlines.

'Second body found. Police closing in on serial killers. Police believe the abductors to be a middled age husband and wife team ...'

'I was really packing it when we got near the newspaper and magazine section, I did everything I could to steer her away to another checkout. I thought there was a big chance she was onto me, too because she took her time asking me to help wheel her trolley over to the car.'

Sergeant Porter lifted a hand off the wheel and gestured. 'You did well on your first real assignment, and ... er you look pretty hot stuff in that schoolgirl get-up, too.'

'Ha ha. You really looked the part of that old down-and-outer too, Sarge.'

'Bugger. You sure know how to hurt a bloke, Kell.' The smile left his face. 'Thank Christ, we finally caught those mongrels.'

She hit the siren twice. They looked at each other.

'Two for the dead girls, Sarge.'

Kelly shivered, thinking how easily she could have been number three.

The End

Being pushed to the limit

Has consequences -

For everyone

House

The house was award-winning, no doubt about that. Stella had designed it all - from sketches of bush aspect to curved roof with landscaped gardens. Her passion for every conceivable glossy magazine on buildings, houses, and gardens had stirred her desire. She was one of those gifted people who already had the ideas in her soul.

Early in their marriage, he should have taken heed of the signs. Retorts like, 'This place is too small, I want a big house, something grand, not like this dump,' were commonplace.

Lance was a mild, easy-going sort of fellow. He worked hard at his job - delivering kitchens for a large manufacturer and in the early years he had worked in many building areas. His skills had helped amass a moderate amount of money as he had fixed, renovated, re-furbished, and tidied up properties they had procured. She kept him hard at it. Her job as a hairdresser did not bring in much, but after their first child she did not have the time for paid work anyway.

Stella was ambitious. She wanted more and bigger. She wanted. Not long after they had sold property number four for a handsome gain, they moved into property five, which was the worst house in the best street. A handyman's dream or nightmare.

Stella cranked up the pressure. 'Lance, we need to make more money so we can buy more land to build our dream home.'

He looked up from steaming off old mouldy wallpaper. Sweat trickled down his face. 'Where is the money going to come from? I mean, we could probably just buy the land but we'd have to borrow big money to build.'

'Yes, I know that. I've been sketching some designs; we could save heaps by using our skills to do the things we *can* do.'

He wiped his face with the rag, conscious that she had virtually ignored his caution. 'But, still, with the rest of our lives to upgrade, we're doing all right.'

'It'll take us forever to get the house we want; I'm going to take another job. Joslyn has offered me after hours work doing hair dressing visits.'

He looked on. 'Fair enough, I guess, but we can't neglect our daughter.'

'I know.' She ambled off to her office to sketch more designs. Stella had a way of saying *we* which Lance knew meant *him*.

He thought he should mention again that the magazines she insisted on buying were costing a fortune. He had suggested some time back for her to borrow from the library, rather than buy them. She had responded in a casual fashion that it was important to have them on hand. Also, she could refer to them, even if years old.

Six months later, they purchased a nice piece of land on Ninderry with a north-east aspect and a tiny blue vee of sea in the distance. Stella had pushed the deal with added pressure from the agent. Her husband had reluctantly gone along with it but had cautioned that they needed to consolidate because money was tight. Stella had another plan. Not long after, she secured another rundown property and convinced Lance they should sell their existing property and move into the one needing renovation.

He protested as best he could about it all but being of gentle nature he was no match for her. The word *we* had been used many times. She ignored his caution and waved a design in front of him - she was already thinking other things.

Life went on for both, she full of optimism and dreams, he concerned with finding time to be with his wife and daughter - and meeting the repayments.

However, *they* - it was really she - secured a loan and the process of building the magnificent house began. His concerns were ignored.

Every available moment, she was on site liaising with, and sometimes annoying the tradespeople. She let her part-time job go. Whenever Lance had a moment, he was harassed into building retaining walls, laying turf, digging holes, and planting gardens. Many people commented on the beautiful house. North-east facing verandahs, classy timber stairs, sheltered areas designed for those times of wild weather, polished blackbutt floors, spacious decks, and well-designed breeze ways. The mix of skillion roofs gave the place excellent, clean lines and an elegant feel.

One afternoon she came home from shopping. 'Lance, I've got some wonderful news.'

He was on edge in an instant; their relationship had markedly deteriorated, punctuated with arguments about money every day.

'Well, aren't you going to ask me what the wonderful news is?' Her eyebrows formed a bold line.

'Well, what is the wonderful news?'

'I'm going to have another baby.'

He was too shocked to notice there was no *we*. 'But ... what about our financial situation?'

Her forehead took on a bull terrier look. 'You should be happy, Lance. It's what you wanted, isn't it?'

He knew he wanted more children, but still, where was the money going to come from? He shook his head slowly and looked at the floor. There was a blackness about him.

'You'll just have to take on another job, Lance. You know, you could contribute more.'

He knew no such thing. He was worn out; the doctor had prescribed medication for his depressed state. But still, over the next week or so, he soldiered on and managed to secure a job stacking shelves after hours at a local supermarket. All against the advice of his doctor, who had been concerned enough to refer him to a psychiatrist.

The local building authority had nominated the house for an award. It looked magnificent on Ninderry, facing north-east with that tiny blue vee of sea in the distance.

Lance knelt on the cold garage floor. He would not mess this one up.

The triggers were taped together; both barrels were in his mouth.

The End

A fortunate life –

Job done

Friends are still there

Come In Spinner

Adam Peake rubbed his right eye with the back of a well-worn hand. The last truck's headlights had dazzled him, one blazing light more intrusive than the other. He wondered how that could be, probably the same type of light, identical model, wattage, and style, bought from the same spare parts shop but still, brighter than the other. One of the mysteries of the world, nothing to do with God, just the way things were.

It was late enough, 8.37pm on the clock. The wind-up travel clock on the dash, given to him by his wife, kept perfect time. The only thing was that the time was wrong, four minutes fast. Every time he looked at it was a reminder that it should be adjusted by the jeweller although the guarantee had well and truly run out. So, for years it had kept regular time, but the wrong time. He smiled because secretly it kept him honest, always a fraction early and that always paid off, kept him ahead of things. It also reminded him of her. He grabbed a tape, Joe Cocker, it was the top one in the box, and pushed it in.

Adam knew he needed a rest but was hanging on until the Green Spot Roadhouse, commonly known as the Grease Spot Roadhouse, which was the halfway mark. The CB provided a comforting *sound of the sea* fizz, turned down low, a lifeline for truckies, not used much these days but good to know it was there. He turned Joe up a bit and opened the window to get some fresh air.

'Six miles to go, Adam, my old son.'

He winked at the mirror, the dim light from the gauges reflected neat slicked-back hair with plenty of grey in it now, hair that used to be black. Now there were a few wrinkles strategically placed on his face. He gave the customary glance at the load through the rear-view mirrors. Then the old one-two-three-four. One, rotate head in one direction, two, same but in opposite direction, three and four, each shoulder up and down.

Ten minutes later the Green Spot Roadhouse lights became visible through the desert night. He knew the lights well as they had been a beacon for travellers for as long as he could remember. Down through the gears, easy these days as the truck, not a semi, just a large van, a Pantech, had synchro on all gears. Not like the old days, no synchro on any gears. Not in his truck anyway. Perhaps they were better times, all the old truckies reckon it was, having to double de-clutch through the whole gear changing process. Much harder work, the old crash box, and no power steering either, more of a challenge, maybe that is what it was, more of a life skill. However, he was secretly grateful for the ease with which he could drive the truck, very little effort, no stress. He knew that was not necessarily an advantage as on some occasions in the modern trucks it was difficult to detect a lazy wheel or a slow flat. Sometimes even a blow out for a distance. Adam knew that modern technology made it easier in many ways but not all. This was a lonely outpost, not mathematically half way but strategically so. It made the last stretch a bit easier.

The country closer to the destination became more barren - sand, clay, salt-bush and stunted gums. It was flat in most directions and uninteresting to the city people although wheat and sheep seemed to survive in patches hundreds of miles apart. Good years provided a harsh living for farmers, bad years, and there were plenty of them, gave nothing but heartbreak and sometimes suicide. As he pulled off the bitumen, Noghead Coombes gave him a blast on the air horns and thumbs up as they dribbled past each other. The high canvas covered load headed in the direction he had just come from, locking an updraft of dust in suspension as the retreating Christmas tree of trailer lights slowly diminished in the desert night. There were two other semis parked nearby, lined up with an old wreck of an army Blitz tow truck, lined up as if they were motor bikes at a military tattoo. He smiled; truckies took pride in order. Adam pulled up at the diesel pumps, turned the engine off and jumped down. He stretched and yawned.

Donkey Richards' blue heeler, Wheel Bearing Richards, who crouched under one of the trucks, gave the first of many paranoid high-pitched yelps. It had to be acknowledged that it was a dog's job; heelers tend to be that way.

'Hey, Bearing old dog, hey, it's only me,' Adam soothed. He had to try to calm the dog down, otherwise it would have yelped nonstop until Donkey turned up. Funny thing was, his owner never seemed to notice. Wheel Bearing was getting on a bit in years too, he realized, yeah, not so long ago it seemed he was just a pup.

Adam was not sure who the other semi belonged to as he did not do this run regularly anymore and there were always new blokes having a go from time to time. He reached into the cab for his denim jacket; the night had a slightly crisp edge to it. There was a gentle breeze, he could feel and taste the dust. Noggie's truck could be heard slowly fading into the distant desert night.

'G'day Adam, how's it goin', haven't seen ya for a spell, old mate.' Mitch Kelly, who was known as Singalong, smiled and scratched his ear. He was owner, mechanic, driveway attendant, part time cashier, sometimes cook and cleaner. The other half in the roadhouse was his wife.

Adam smiled, 'G'day mate. Naaaaah, only do this run when our usual blokes have a break. Anyway fill 'er up thanks Sing.'

His usual drivers both had the flu. It was really a two-man drive, not only to keep each other awake but to assist with the loading and unloading at the other end. Adam had organised the overnight transport people to take care of the latter when he arrived at the destination.

Singalong cranked up the bowser and began filling the tank. He also tried to hitch up his dirty work trousers with the other hand.

'When are you going to get a belt, mate?' queried Adam good naturedly.

The other man had a piece of three-eight rope wrapped around his middle and it had been that way for as long as they had known each other, some twenty or, thirty years … and the rest.

'Now why would I do that?' he mumbled through an unlit soggy cigarette.

They both laughed.

'Might go and order some tucker,' offered Adam, stretching, and feeling that twinge of arthritis in his lower back.

'Leave it with me mate, if anyone else arrives they can use the other pumps, don't expect it to be like Rowley Park here tonight, or ever again for that matter. Anyways, you'll hear 'em.'

Adam pocketed the keys and strolled over to the roadhouse. Dust hung in air finer than lace, not visible, just there. Millions of miles above, stars kept an overview with the occasional wink. He pulled open the flywire screen door, noting that a big blow fly buzzed against the inside of the screen, and he ambled into the relative warmth of the Grease Spot Roadhouse dining room in the direction of the only occupied table. Slim Dusty twanged away quietly in the background from a regional radio station. Donkey Richards and Garth Tracey sat chatting.

'How's it going fellers?' ventured Adam Peake.

Both looked up. 'Orright, mate.'

'New truck, eh Spence, never thought you'd get the moths out of your skyrocket and get a newie,' Adam teased.

Garth Spencer Tracey just scratched his unshaven face and smiled. 'Well, the Kenworth had done five and a half million miles mate, so the time had come as they say. I can tell yas, it was rooted!'

'Well, if I remember rightly, it was rooted when you got it,' piped in Donkey winking at Adam.

'Enough of your insults Donk,' smiled Spence with a characteristic sideways nod of the head, 'I'm on me way anyway fellers, some of us have to work ya know. See ya next time, eh?' He stood up, wiped his mouth with a serviette just as Toni Kelly, *the missus of everything*, flittered over. She had the knack of being there when needed.

She looked at Adam and nodded coyly. 'Good to see you, what'll it be, Peakie old mate?' They fell into comfortable familiarity with her disarming smile.

'Usual thanks Toni, only the two eggs this time.' He smiled back.

She was petite and birdlike in her movements. Her voice had a gentle but high-pitched warble quality about it too. Years of smoking cigarettes had not made any difference to her voice but had given her spider's web wrinkles around the mouth and eyes. In another life she would have been a ground cover bird. Now in her sixties at least, her hair had not greyed off, it still remained the colour of straw. One day, overnight, it would go white. Her job as *the Missus of Everything* seemed in contrast to her gentleness. She could hold her own against big tough men in blue singlets with big trucks and was known to sort out trouble makers, drunks, and idiots out for a drag race and a fight. Either way it seemed; she did the best mixed grill around the area. However there really was not anything to compare it to.

She grabbed the two finished plates and two cups, balanced them with ease on one arm, and quickly wiped the Laminex table with a dish cloth. Adam noticed with a smile; the latter action was just moving the grease around. She moved off at the same time as Spence in the direction of the cash register. He turned and nodded to the other two blokes as he fumbled with his wallet and moved from foot to foot inside sloppy elastic sided RM work boots.

Adam looked at Donkey. 'How are things with you mate?'

'Pretty good, mate.' He opened a packet of rollies and worked the tobacco into a tube, picking off the ends.

'You've been doing this run for a while, haven't you?'

'Yep. Nearly forty years,' he laughed. 'Gunna give it away at the end of this year.' He cupped his hands although there was no need to and lit the cigarette with a match.

Adam surprised himself by saying, 'Yeah, 'I guess we all will, sooner or later.'

They chatted for a while about running the country and then Toni appeared with Adam's meal.

'Thanks Toni.'

'Gotta build yourself up Adam, you've got a long drive.' She winked and zipped away.

Donkey ground the butt in the astray and drained the remnants of his lukewarm coffee which disturbed a buzzing blow fly that had been sizing up his cup for some time looking for something to die in.

He stood up. 'That's my signal to go mate, you've got to eat, and I've got a fair drive ahead of me.'

'Yeah, I understand, see you on one of the next trips, eh?' His smile was passive.

They shook hands.

Adam started eating. Donkey Richards hauled his big frame, with an oversize stomach hanging over his belt, towards the cash register.

'Make sure you drive that new truck of yours carefully,' said Adam with a wave. It was difficult to smile and talk with a mouthful.

The screen door slammed, Toni disappeared into the bowels of the kitchen and Adam ate alone, except for another blowie and a couple of moths. He carelessly leafed through dog eared Pix and Post magazines, all from another era.

Adam noted an EH Holden pulling up at the petrol pumps, two blokes swapped the driver's seat, both having a good chat which included hand waving and laughs with Singalong. He loved to chat with people, it was all there was out there, apart from rolling cigarettes, putting them in his mouth, waiting for them to get soggy and then replacing them with a freshly rolled fag. Having given up smoking some years before he continued with the ritual but never lit up. Some of the truckies joked that the acre or so of the roadhouse grounds was to the discerning eye, all but knee deep in unsmoked roll your owns. The two blokes in the Holden must have had the correct money because it changed hands and Singalong headed back to the workshop.

Just as Adam eased white bread around his plate, the screen door creaked, and a man walked in. He looked around, smiled, and ambled over.

'G'day mate, er mind if I...?'

Adam nodded, 'Yeah, no worries, mate, pull up a thumb and rotate.' As a truckie you had to grab it when it presented itself, otherwise a bloke could go for a day or two without talking to anyone, particularly on the long hauls.

'Bit soldier's bold out tonight,' the visitor mumbled rubbing his hands.

He was clean shaven with boyish good looks and dark hair slicked back. He had *the wild one* look, an ageless face. His clothes, although work drill, were clean and tidy. 'Nothing like a spring night in the desert, eh?' He had his sleeves rolled up above the elbows showing muscular arms.

'Yeah. Come 'ere often?' Adam ventured, still tidying up his plate with another piece of bread.

The bloke leant forward; on his right forearm was a tattoo, a bird of some kind. 'Well, I used to; I mean yeah, a lot when I was younger. I know the area pretty well.' The latter part was stated with a conspiratorial nod.

Adam drained his coffee and was about to look towards the kitchen when Toni appeared. She reached across, topped up his cup and looked in the direction of the other bloke. He smiled a negative nod and lifted a hand in a stop sign. She darted off.

Adam was wondering what this bloke was after, perhaps a lift, maybe just being friendly. In the old days hitch-hikers would try to steal a ride by chatting to the truckies inside the roadhouse. He remembered that the management tended to move them outside, especially the sheilas, particularly if Toni was on duty. There used to be more staff then. Funny thing was, sheilas, no matter what they looked like, never had any problem getting a ride. Women can do that; they are all beautiful in their own way he thought. Some poor blokes could wait days for a lift. Something that would never change.

Adam warmed to the newcomer; there was a friendly way about him. He was just about to say something when the bloke put out his hand.

'Oh, by the way, my name's Steve Hawke ... er as in the tattoo on my arm. Hawk will do, with or without an e.'

He indicated the elaborate artwork on his forearm. A hawk in flight, very neat, not too big, it fitted his arm well.

'So, you're from around here, eh?'

'Yeah, grew up 27 miles from here, just down the road in local speak, farm boy. Knocked about the area, worked on most of the farms around here, roustabout, diesel fitter, mechanic, welder, you name it, like most young fellers in the bush; you need to be able to do most things. How about you, mate? Truck driving all your life?'

'That's about it, yeah, started young, the old man taught me on the Isa run and up in the territory, you know, everything measured in cartons of beer and bottles of rum. Bastards used to like a few quiet ones in those days. There were a few pile ups but probably no more than today, less vehicles on the road too.'

There was a short comfortable silence.

The newcomer nodded and said, 'I haven't seen you here before.'

'No, I only do it on and off these days, did this run for the first time about thirty or more years ago. Did it about once a month for the first year but I got put on the other shorter routes doing relief, suited me, you know, wife and kids, more time at home.'

'Yeah, right' Hawke inclined his head to one side, interested.

'But, like I say, these days rarely, just to keep my eye in so to speak, being the owner, or part-owner with my brother. Kids grown up, you know, no real responsibility, missus, er, wife died a couple of years back.'

Why was he telling this stranger these things? He never spoke about his wife any more, it hurt too much. Adam was just thinking of another coffee for the road when Toni re-appeared.

'Good timing Toni, thanks, tah.'

The visitor nodded in the negative again and she disappeared.

'Well mate, I might just finish this and give the track a nudge. Er, need a lift?'

Hawke smiled. 'Lift?' He seemed slightly surprised 'No thanks. I just dropped in for a chat, got my own transport thanks. Gets a bit lonely out here mate, don't get an opportunity to chin wag with people much at all. Been good talking to you anyway, mate.'

Adam drained his cup and stood up.

The other man stood as well. 'See you outside, mate, something I'm sure you'd like to see.'

It all seemed natural enough. 'Yeah, righto, I need to splatter the boots first, and the bill.'

Adam used the 'gents' and then ambled over to the counter a couple of minutes later. He pulled out his wallet just as Toni turned up. She knew where everybody and thing was in her domain. A fluoro light nearby buzzed in direct competition to a blowfly, maybe the same fly that did the rounds. Several moths attempted suicide missions into the light.

'Now, your diesel tab's here,' she said rifling through some loose papers.

He paid up and she handed him some change.

'Good to see you again Adam. Your usual blokes, are they sick?' Her look probed. A friendly concerned look.

Adam smiled, 'Yeah, both got the flu, pretty bad too, lucky me, so far anyway.'

'You shouldn't be doing this run on your own. Long way. I guess we're all getting a bit old for this, eh old friend?' She smiled, exhaling a slight sigh.

'Yeah, suppose you're right, Toni, but ...'

Their eyes locked and they spoke at the same time, 'But what else could we do.'

That brought gentle laughter from them both.

'Righto, must go Toni, see ya.'

'Take care on the road, mate,' she replied, looked at him for a long moment and then busied herself playing with receipts at the cash register.

She was getting on in years but he noticed with a smile that she could glance and pout as powerfully as ever.

The door opened with a creak from the spring and he stepped out into the lights from the Green Spot sign on top of the roadhouse. The door clicked behind. For a moment or two, he thought Hawke must have gone. Singalong was changing a tyre in the light of the doorway to the workshop some distance away. Then he saw the other man, arms folded, leaning against his truck.

Adam walked over. There was another vehicle parked on the other side.

He stopped in his tracks. 'Sheeeeeeeez.'

Hawke looked on. There sat a light cream coloured Ford Customline, in absolute showroom condition.

'See, I told you you'd like it.'

'Like it, root a boot, it's, it's ...' Adam slowly circled the gleaming vehicle. In the filtered roadhouse light, it appeared to have red leather seats and a cream steering wheel. 'Hell, mate I haven't seen anything as beautiful as this for a long time.'

The only sounds in the clear desert night were Adam's footsteps in the gravel, and a punctuated hoot from an owl somewhere off in the scrub.

'Hell mate, did ... did you restore all this yourself?'

The other bloke leaned on the bonnet and laughed, fingering the chrome delta-wing aeroplane emblem that gave the car that distinctive rocket look. 'Nah, they all say that, but no, it's original, all but brand spanking new. She's a 1954 side valve Ford Customline, a limited edition, Canadian model.'

Adam thought he may have misunderstood the question. Either way, it was an elegant piece of machinery. Truckies understand and appreciate beautiful pieces of workmanship, especially anything to do with the internal combustion engine. Both men looked on, a comfortable space and time, lost in their own dreams and thoughts.

Hawke interjected. 'Well, sorry to say, mate, I have to go. I bet you do as well.'

He stuck out his hand. They shook warmly. Hawke opened the driver's door, the interior light came on, and he slid in behind the steering wheel which sported a chrome horn ring. The keys were in the ignition. The six-volt system kicked and the starter motor cranked over the engine. Eight cylinders bubbled into life. The V8 was not loud at all, it just rumbled like a storm approaching in that uncoordinated perfect rhythm.

'Righto Adam, must go, I'll keep an eye out for you, maybe next time eh.'

They shook again. A nod and smile from ... *the wild one.*

'Yeah, right, mate, see ya.' The wink was friendly.

Hawke closed the door; the light went off and he gentled the column shift into first gear. The clutch release was smooth, and the vehicle eased away. He draped a loose arm out the window and gave a placid wave. The low revving side valve V8 burbled off, slowly gathering speed in the gravel and then on to the bitumen, into another gear ... the dust hung.

Adam stood there, the two round bright red, currawong taillights slowly diminishing in the settling haze. The gear change from second to top was there somewhere, somewhere around 50 miles per hour. After about five minutes he thought he could still detect the distant burble but eventually, all sound blended into the desert night. Cold, clear.

Adam centred himself and realised that he had been standing there in a sort of contented trance, staring into nothingness.

'Finger out Adam, let's get cracking!' he exclaimed to the dark night and that brought him back, he was with it again, time to go. He climbed into the truck, kicked it over and fiddled with the CB radio.

Singalong looked up from a flashing blue welder and waved as the truck edged out towards the highway. He gave a blast on the horns as it moved on to the bitumen and then the speed increased through the gears. On the approach to the service station was a high semi full of sheep that he quickly recognised as belonging to the Aldenhoven boys. As they passed each other, one speeding up, one slowing down; Adam had to laugh as Rover Aldenhoven's brown kelpie, Ruckman, had his head out the window barking like billy-o.

Rover was laughing too, undoubtedly drunk and yelling something, definitely a barrage of swearwords but it was all lost in the noise and the speed of passing. Adam observed the fading Green Spot Roadhouse and the other semi's tail and side lights in his mirrors.

He watched it fade in the rearview mirror as the truck slowly picked up to its comfortable operating speed. There was just the road ahead and Adam settled in for the long haul, six, seven hours to the transport company depot. There was always a need to stay alert all the way to the destination. The road and surrounds hid many dangers in a long haul but falling asleep was the big one. There were other things to consider like kangaroos, emus and other animals, sheep, cattle and horses, and there was always the chance of a blowout too. He knew staying awake was paramount. It was all chance.

Adam fiddled with the CB radio again, turned it down and selected a tape, Tom Jones. He smiled, his daughter used to laugh at him and his taste in music. She could talk! She had given him the Angels, to 'bring him into this century' as she put it but he had only listened to the first track to be polite. It was a terrible noise to him. He was an *old fifty sixer*, Elvis was his era, Jerry Lee, Johnny O'Keefe,

John Mayall and others. His only compromise on the present-day singers was Joe Cocker. He liked Joe, a soul singer.

A shooting star to his left grabbed his vision. The sky took on a light show for a splintered second.

His thoughts could not let go of the beautiful Ford Customline. What a great piece of motor car. They did not make them like that anymore. He wondered why a bloke like Hawke would live out here, in the middle of what many would call nowhere. Still, he figured, you had to live somewhere, and the bush, or desert had its own special charm, if born out here, family, friends, attachment, yeah, enough reason. But still, what a beaut car.

He stopped every hour and a half for a brisk inspection walk around the truck. Always checking, had to. There was a need to be vigilant. A lazy tyre, a hot drum, a loose nut, dangling rope or wire, light not working, always checking. The intense cold was the necessary stimulant to keep him alert. By the time there was any indication of light in the vista, he had all but exhausted the tape supply. Funny thing was, he never really got sick of the music in the cab. There was always the radio for back up for something different too, regional radio.

Adam felt lucky when a new day arrived. The stars, still visible, slowly making way for the day, the sun below the horizon pushing up. The desert was the place to see a proper sunrise, night into day. He believed he had beaten God at his own game, cheated the old rascal of yet another day. Even if it happened to be his last, at least he'd had the privilege of seeing the start. He knew many people would not see today.

Many of his friends had died on the road, that was the way it might be for him too, although he was much more careful now than he used to be. Maybe that *was* the way it was going to be for him. Age did strange things to people; it wasn't a conscious decision they made. He did not wake up one morning and say, "I'm going be careful from now on." No, it was more subtle than that. When he was young, he could not picture old age, almost impossible to visualise. It is just something that happens; you slow down, different priorities.

When he was younger, he did this run at least an hour less each way, terrible roads, and quite often as drunk as a wharfie. In those days everyone was either pissed, on biddy beans or powder, could not do it without. Now, in the early eighties, some of the drivers drank but most did not on the job, or did not much. The cops kept a keener eye on things these days. The good old days were over, which he had to admit, was not altogether bad. No, things were just different, that is all.

Back on the never-ending tarmac he noted wallabies and the occasional old grey roo by the side of the road, sometimes alerting him to be wary. It was never certain whether one would jump out into the path of the truck. Every so often a huge eagle or bird of prey would majestically lift into the thermals of the road.

He always drove slower at this time of day, same as dusk. He had hit many roos in his time, also buffaloes in the Territory. Bloody big bull bars, not too much of a worry, had enough weight to shunt the animal out of the way. Being careful, there it was again.

Adam did not want to smash up the front of his truck. But that was not really it. These days he had a greater respect for the wildlife, not that he did not in times gone by, but when he was young, he did not give a root. Yes, he had more respect now, every creature had a place in the scheme of things, a more significant place than he could have imagined as a youth. He cruised on steadily, magpies, eagles, crows, and flocks of galahs scattered as the day picked up. The wildlife seemed to disappear into hideaways, only to come out again at dusk.

Once again, he thought of Hawke and that wonderful Ford Customline.

∞

Yawning, he pulled into the overnight transport yard just as another semi was leaving. Adam did not recognise the driver, but they waved and tooted anyway, it was a club. Big Maddie gave him the thumbs up and some semaphore signals. He backed in, smiling to himself, keeping her in his mirrors. Actually, it was hard to get her out of his mirrors as she was quite a big woman.

Big Maddie, Madeline, thus called because someone felt it necessary to not confuse her with her husband Mathew, who was known as Little Maddie. However, he was bigger than her. Either way, she was the boss of the overall show which was their marriage and the transport business, and that was it. There was nothing a bloke could do that she could not do. In her younger days she got up to all sorts of things but overall retained respect from everyone. But still, he mused, people always have a past and sometimes that past has the potential to be colourful and he felt good people should see it that way. The big figure waved him in, expert use of hand signals, to within one inch of the loading dock. Maddie had driven trucks before too, better than most blokes. He folded himself out and stretched just as she ambled up.

'Nice work Peakie, haven't lost your touch, eh.'

The big woman with dark frizzy hair like a bunch of springs, smiled as she juggled a clipboard, a pen, a tape measure, and a manifest.

'Hard to lose silky skills like backin' a truck in, Big Maddie,' he laughed. 'Anyway, how're things in the transport industry, or shouldn't I ask?'

The first part of his reply raised a laugh, but the second part was greeted with a roll of the eyes. Adam was reminded that she was still a beautiful woman, and upper middle age, whatever that meant, had only made her more attractive. It was hard to tell if she dyed her hair, probably not. It had always looked the same to Adam. She was one of the lucky ones who never greyed off, or if she did, there is no way she had let on.

'Well, best not whinge about that, always been hard going but, aaaaah, well, we're still making a fist of it nowadays, that's when that bloody husband of mine, doesn't piss the profits against the wall at the pub. We'd be better off buyin' the pub. But, when you do something for a long time and you just fall into being good at it, well ya stick to it because it's comfortable. And we don't know anything else.'

His turn to laugh.

None of it was said with any heat, then she turned very businesslike.

'Right, full load?'

'Yep. Here's the paperwork.'

'Thanks, Peakie, gunna stay tonight?'

'Yeah, I reckon I will, been a long trip, always is.'

'Fair enough, I'll get that husband of mine to organise the boys to unload ya. Your stuff is there, see?' She pointed to a neatly stacked mountain of boxes. 'We've got two truck-loads in later, so they may as well get you fixed more or less straight away.'

Another truck started up nearby, she waved at the driver, he hit the air horns.

Adam could see that she had things to do. 'Shall we go to the office?'

'Yeah, the crew is on smoko. Little Maddie has been goin' nearly all night, he'll be happy to use you as an excuse to go down the pub and sink a few marines.'

They walked side by side to the office which was one of two prefab buildings 20 foot by 15.

She stuck her head in the door. 'Hey, you drop kicks, guess who just blew in?'

Little Maddie, on seeing Adam, pulled himself out of a groaning chair. 'How're ya goin' you old bastard? Haven't seen you out this way for a bit.'

'Hey,' interrupted the big woman, 'Dearest, could you organise those two useless pin heads to unload and reload Adam's stuff.'

Adam smiled at her efficiency.

'Yep, no worries, love, leave it to me, although I'm just about knocking off, seen that Peakie is here, time for the pub I reckon, how does that sound to ya, love?'

She looked at Adam. The smile was held in control, but her eyes went north. 'Told you so, there goes this week's profit. Peakie, don't let him go 'till Spot gets here, right?'

Adam nodded and tossed her the keys. He did not trust anyone else. She took a good catch, gave the thumbs up and took off. The men shook hands.

'Feel like a few quiet beers, mate?' inquired the big bloke as he lit up a rollie.

'I'd probably have one with ya, but I won't have too many, going to leave about sunup, so can't be nursing a hangover, now, can I?'

'Right, I'll just organise the boys, they're in the smoko room.'

Just as the two older men stepped out of the office, another bloke strolled in the gate.

'Here comes Spotty now, he takes over from me. We can piss off to the pub, the first one won't touch the sides,' explained the big fellow. 'How ya goin' Spot?'

'Aaaaah, not too bad thanks fatso,' he said, nudging Maddie with a tattooed lower arm, a gentle fore-arm jolt as he shaped up like a boxer. 'Hey who's ya mate? G'day Peakie, long time no see.'

Sixty-nine years had not faded Brian Lain's freckles. Sunspots had just added to them.

'Alright Spot. Thought you'd retired hurt, you're old enough anyway,' replied Adam getting into the spirit of stirring up an old mate.

'Cheeky bastard, eh Little Maddie?' chipped in Spot. They were all of the same era. He scratched his grey hair and bounced around like a Cockney.

'No doubt about that, Spot. We're off to the pub.'

'Half ya luck, s'pose, wish I could join yas but I'd better check with the big sheila.' He winked at Adam, 'We're all shit scared of her round 'ere. Maybe see ya directly mate, eh.'

Adam remembered that Spot had given up drinking a couple of years ago because the doctor told him that if he did not, he would die. That was the truth about most blokes. He figured there would not be too many true-blue Aussie blokes who would give up drinking unless they had to. Truckies were top of that chain and he reckoned that the decision for Spot would have been hard.

Adam and the big bloke walked out the gate, both waving to Big Maddie. She gave them a dismissive wave followed by a stern school teacher index finger meant for her husband, and yelled, 'Remember you have to organise the late shipment, orright?'

It was clear that this was no request. She jangled Adam's keys and indicated the office, normal procedure to lock the truck and deposit keys in the office. She supervised and kept a very sharp eye on the whole operation.

After a couple of hours and a few beers they returned, Big Maddie had gone home for a bit of watching the eyelids from the inside as her husband called it, leaving Spot in charge until Little Maddie returned. Adam grabbed his keys and the big fellow took on some paperwork, or pretended to, with bleary eyes. There was not too much going on for a couple of hours and he was already falling asleep. Spot offered to give him a call later.

Feeling tired, Adam grabbed his kit bag from the truck, the few quiet beers had done the job. Twenty, thirty years ago he would have kept drinking all night and then driven twice the distance he was going to drive after eight hours sleep. Just as well, the way he was feeling.

They had already crimped off the lead seal on the lock, so Adam headed for the Great East West Motel only thirty or so yards around the corner. Just the place where a truckie could sleep lulled by the constant sound of vehicles coming and going, air brakes, and a railway shunting yard nearby, twenty-four hours a day, dull, thudding, noisy action with the occasional egotistical blast of air horns. The life blood of a truckie.

Polly, widow of many years and proprietor of the Great East West, looked up from a pile of paper work as the bell on the door clinked. The web of wrinkles around her eyes became more prominent with the smile. 'Oh, Mister Peake, haven't seen you around here for a spell.'

'No Poll, other blokes are on sick leave, thought I'd hone up my driving skills. How're things with you?'

'Managing to make a living, not old enough yet for the Onkaparinga rug over my knees and the soft food,' she laughed.

They chatted, two people who had known each other for a long time, they could not be anything other than friends.

'How long you staying?'

'Just tonight, be leaving at about four.'

'I'll give you a reminder, breakfast?'

No need to look at the menu. 'Yeah, the usual,' replied Adam. The usual was eggs and bacon, toast, and coffee. He figured that it would be hard to get anything else around the area. She gave him the keys to a room at the back, probably marginally less noisy than the front.

He showered, lay down for a while, then strolled back to the pub for a counter meal. There were few familiar faces, just the odd g'day, so he ate, sunk a few beers and went back to the motel. Tiredness crept up on him and he fell asleep with the TV ticking away on the regional channel. Half way through the night the snowing screen woke him, so he turned it off only to hear a goods train shunting backwards and forwards in the yards.

'Morning Adam, 20 to four, time to get up, did you sleep well?' crackled Polly on the blower, she always seemed to be on duty since her husband died.

Adam shook the furry no man's land from the end of slumber. 'Aaaaa, mmmm ... morning Boll.' He could not manage the P. 'Yeah, out like a light ...'

'Have a shower love; brekky will be at your door in eight minutes. I've already put the kettle on, remember, I'm Polly?'

'Thanks Poll.' He smiled at the fact that he was alert enough to catch her wit.

After breakfast he walked swiftly to the office to hand the keys in and pay. Polly seemed as if she had not moved.

'On your way then?' Only slightly more a question than a statement. She presented the bill.

'Yeah, got a fair way to go.'

She looked at him, one eyebrow higher than the other. 'Take it easy on the road, Adam.' She brightened, 'See you next time, eh?'

'Yep, although it won't be till the lads have their holidays.'

'Until next time then.' The spider's web increased.

Adam returned the smile. 'See ya,' and turned.

He pushed through the doorway into the greyness that was promising day. Stars persisted. He reflected on Poll's words; he would have bet ten bob to a pinch she had said those words to her husband before he went out that last time.

A team of kookaburras began a noisy squabble, getting it in before the light.

The early morning was very cold; he pulled his jacket collar up and hunched his shoulders. Although early, there was plenty of action in the overnight transport yard. Big Maddie was directing traffic, waving manifests, and giving orders in the bright floodlit area.

'Mornin' Adam, fighting fit?' She scratched her springs with the blunt end of a pencil.

'Fighting fit isn't the exact terminology I'd use, but pretty good thanks. I'll be out of your hair as soon as the diesel warms up.'

'The wife's best friend is having a sleep, the lazy so and so. When will you be back this way, Adam?' She peered at him tilting her head gently on an angle. Her smile was not all business, it was soft and warm. He knew he was privileged.

'Oh, probably a few months,' he replied, throwing his kit bag into the truck.

'You've got the life of Riley, Peakie.' Her look moved on a little. 'Nothing changes much here, although that husband of mine and I are considering having a holiday soon.'

Adam laughed. 'Do you realise that you have said that to me every time for the last ten years.'

Her brow furrowed. He thought he had said something he should not have. There was a pensive look for a second or two, then she laughed, deep down mirth, her bosoms heaved inside her drill shirt behind the pens in the pockets.

'Maybe you're right, I hadn't thought about it in that way. I'll just have to do something about it then; maybe I won't be here next time you visit.'

'I doubt that Big Maddie, time to make some dust, say see ya to the big bloke.' He started the truck.

'Certainly will, drive safe Adam, God with ya. Some of us have a job to do.' She winked and headed off to the loading dock.

Adam noticed for the first time that she was looking a bit older or maybe just more tired.

'You're not on your own dear,' he mumbled to the cassette deck as he slipped in Elvis' Greatest Hits as the motor warmed up. Then he jumped out and did a 360-degree visual check of the truck. He clicked the heater on and glanced back at the loading dock as the truck eased out the gate. He turned up the CB, and then turned it down, so it was just decipherable. In the rear vision mirror he noted the action in the yard as another truck pulled out and went the other way. Within a few seconds it was all gone and there was, as ever, the road ahead. The road ahead was really the road behind when he thought about the trip, quick glimpses in the mirrors confirmed that.

The cab warmed up and he turned off the heater. For a short while, day teased with night, slowly stealing darkness, a given absolute, then very quickly it became what could only be deemed as light. Black smudges turned into grey shapes that turned into salt bush and the occasional tree. Some of the things that moved turned into kangaroos and the blurs that lifted off the ground became crows or wedge-tailed eagles. The stars eventually gave up and allowed the day its rightful place – only until the next dark. Every so often when a tree presented itself, flocks of galahs blotted out the intense first sun, and his ears inside the cab with the noise of the diesel and the tape deck, still did not escape their screeching. The occasional remains on the road of a slow creature unaware of the road rules provided tucker for the unstoppable crows.

He left the side-lights on for some time and settled in for the long haul across the desert, en route to home, via the Green Spot Roadhouse. The next few hours were occupied by repeats of his favourite tapes, counting various creatures and regular stops to check aspects of the truck. The day had warmed up considerably and he was always keen to get back in, so he could drive along with the windows down.

Not far from the Green Spot he was jerked into reality. An old grey kangaroo sat on the white line in the middle of the concrete causeway; at least that is what he thought he saw. In fright he grabbed the wheel, smashing his knuckles on the door jam, and tried to wrestle with the lurching tonnage. Old skills kicked in as he frantically steered the wheels in the direction of the skid. The power of the careering load was too much for him until, by a smidgen of luck, one rear wheel caught on the edge of the bitumen which corrected the lurch and he was able to bring the missile to a shuddering halt. Dust billowed around him for what seemed like ages. The engine had stalled so he started the truck again and pulled further off the road. He sat there for a few minutes, sweat clouding his vision.

'Shit, that was close,' he challenged the shimmering roadway and airborne bull dust as he jumped down out of the cab. The diesel idled. His eyes darted. The smell of burnt rubber assaulted his nose.

It had been a long time since he had done that. He must have nodded off, *just* nodded off but that is all that was needed. Nod off? Surely, no. He leant against the hot truck; a deep-down low-level shake took over his being. In the early morning, he stood motionless in the desert, except for his shaking and shimmering hands.

His CB burbled and crackled in the cab. *Come in Spinner.* That's what he thought he heard. He looked at his hands; they still shimmered from a deep-down body tremor. After what could have been five minutes, he willed himself to a greater level of control. What was that? Someone looking for Spinner? He did not know any Spinner.

Adam walked back, shaking his head, trying to think clearly, noting the gruesome thick rubber strips snaking along the road. It was several hundred yards back to the concrete causeway. He could not find the kangaroo, or any blood. Had to be something, some evidence, some explanation. He had trouble working out the skid marks and recreating the event.

He was thankful though and spoke to the flat desert. 'Thank Christ for that. The bugger got away.' There was no desire to think any further in case the animal was dragging itself around in the bush, badly injured. He scratched his head, not seeing any animal tracks.

Back at the truck it took a few minutes to compose himself before driving off again. Fortunately, it was not long before he reached the Green Spot Roadhouse. His recent experience had a profound effect. Adam had always prided himself, particularly in latter years, on his safety record and powers of staying awake, being responsible.

He pulled up at the pumps, fortunately there were no other trucks around, other than the old Blitz tow truck parked in line with a couple of forty fours. The place was always reasonably quiet but it seemed to be more so now. Singalong was over at the workshop with the welding mask pushed up on his forehead, Toni was handing him a cup of something, probably tea. Adam needed to talk to someone, he could not let on about the near miss, there was just a need for the comfort of other humans. He tried to think of something good and the vision of the beautiful Ford Customline calmed him. He walked over to them.

Toni looked up. 'G'day Adam.'

She drew heavily on her cigarette, pinching her mouth and then smoke seemed to leak out of her nose. She did not smoke in the restaurant but certainly made the most of the breaks.

'Yeah, how's it goin', mate?' retorted Singalong taking off the mask and hitching up his pants. The three-eight rope around his middle was old and frayed.

'Er, fine ...'

'I'll get you a cuppa and a meal in a ... you alright love?'

'Er ... yeah, no worries ... just tired. No hurry Toni, with the cuppa, I just need a decent break.'

Adam felt the urge to carry on talking, there was a need to fill what he thought was a void. 'Hey Toni, remember that bloke, the fella, that was in here a couple of days ago, the ... he sat with me, tattoo ... er tattoo of a hawk on his arm ...'

'Mmm, no love,' she said and stole another suck on the cigarette.

'He sat with me when I was here two days ago, Hawke, that's right, Steve Hawke.'

Cocking his head to one side, suddenly interested, Singo dropped the butt of the soggy cigarette, ground it out even though it was out, and replaced it with freshly rolled grubby new one from behind his right ear. 'Steve Hawke?' he exclaimed.

'Yeah, remember? He had that showroom condition Ford Customline, parked next to my truck.' Adam felt the need to point to where his truck was.

'Gee mate that's a long time back, poor bastard got lunched in a terrible pile up just out of town at the last causeway. Hey, you're havin' a go at us, aren't ya? That was in the fifties.' Singalong looked at his wife with intense eyebrows, he continued, musing, 'Yeah, I remember the car, balltearer, there was a bit of controversy at the time, he claimed it was a Tri-Spinner, you know, three spinners in the front grill, but ...'

Adam stared.

Toni continued to fill the space with cigarette smoke.

Singalong dropped the newish unlit grubby cigarette on the ground and stepped on it. 'Yeah, brand new, it was the Canadian model, some argued that the front parking lights were spinners but that was subjective because me old man said that Ford never put out a Tri in that model, and if you look closely, you'll see that them things on the side are actually side lights, parkers, not spinners.'

Adam felt strange, he looked at the ground not seeing the hundreds of cigarette butts, washers, O-rings, springs, and workshop debris.

Singalong groped behind each ear looking for a cigarette.

'Yeah, really bad, bloody awful smash, they reckon he tried to avoid hitting a roo at the concrete causeway, you went through it, about three miles out. Died on impact so they reckon. Hell, it was a while ago though mate; let's see, nineteen, yeah, the same year as the Ford, 1954. You're pulling my leg, aren't ya?'

Adam continued to look down; a calmness slowly enveloped him in a warm embrace. Come in Spinner, he now knew exactly what it all meant.

The End

Life may be hard

History is there to be repeated -

Ah, the perception of youth

Dangerous Days

'They lived in dangerous days orright,' mused Nugget with a gulp from the bottle. 'My grandad and his offsider would chop a few notches up each side of a tree, and I'm talking about a real tree, eight/ten foot across the base, then they'd stick a plank in each notch and move up to where they were going to start work, say about ten foot up. Dangerous as hell! They'd chop a vee out of one side and then the blighters would start sawing with a huge crosscut saw.'

Nugget threw a handful of sticks into the middle of the fire. 'Aside from the fact that they could fall from them planks or a branch would snap off high up and fall on 'em, there was always a chance to cut themselves with their tools, but the real danger was when they wuz near the end of the cut. If the tree fell how and where they wanted it to, all well and good, but you can imagine that half the time it would go this way or that!'

Nugget remonstrated with his arms. 'I tell ya, a big tree like that, used to kill at least one bloke a month in his gang of ten and when they used wedges, well, I tell ya. That was in addition to all them normal things like cuts, abrasions, broken bones and snake bite! And crook guts from eating rotten tucker! Yep, they wuz dangerous days orright fellers.' He took another swig and handed it on.

'That's nothin'!' piped in Bluey Sampson, 'my grampa was one of the first blokes to get a bulldozer, in fact he had two, out western Queensland in them early days. Him and Dogger Doherty would string a big chain between 'em, I mean a chain as long as half a mile and with links five-foot-high, and they'd put them dozers in low gear and crawl through the bush. Trees crashed down all around them, sometimes a tree would land on the machine and the blokes used to get bad injuries, and snakes! Man, I tell yoo, king browns mainly, would land in their laps. The old bloke lost eight drivers one year, couldn't get the fellers to hospital, weren't none nearby, no anti venom stuff neither in them days. Yep, no doubt about it, they were dangerous days those blokes had to deal with.' Bluey tossed another stump on the fire.

'Hey, stop hoggin' the bottle, eh?'

'Child's play!' Dropper O'Brien paused to light up a fag. 'My uncle was a miner at Broken Hill in them early days of the mines. Strike a light! It wasn't uncommon to lose twenty or thirty blokes in one cave-in. Admittedly cave-ins weren't that common but when it happened, whewwwww!' Dropper nodded up and down, eyes big, begging belief from all and sundry. 'And old Uncle Bert reckoned that most of the blokes, that's the ones who didn't get crushed or weren't injured with machinery that reached the age of forty, would die of some sort of lung complication 'cos of the dust! Or broken backs, end up crippled with bone problems. The ones that got to that age, which was an old codger for a miner, usually died anyway of getting some sort of alcoholism poisoning. Liked a drink in them olden days, no worries, I tell ya. Yeah, you'd have to say things couldn't be much more dangerous than in them days, that's for sure.'

He looked in the direction of Sterlo who seemed to have taken ownership of the bottle.

'I'm not so sure about that, Dropper,' commented Swayer Lynch in a dry tone. 'Sounds almost like running into an open goal to me, almost easy! What about the Anzacs? Eh? What could be more dangerous than living in those times, eh? Blood and guts everywhere, broken bodies, limbs gone west, the stench of death, bullets and shells flying all over the shop. Blokes screaming, men crying! Grown men actually crying! Crikey, if that aint dangerous days, then what the heck is, eh? I ask you *that!*

Swayer kicked the end of a burning stick into the fire. 'Hey, where's that bottle?'

'Well ... these days ... er ...'

The only sounds that followed were the crackling of the fire and a far-off night bird. They all looked at John Woods, the youngest in the camp.

'Well, Jarrah, come on,' stirred Spider McPharlan, 'what dangerous days can you report on, eh?'

There was a rumble of toned-down mirth.

'Er ... well, we live in dangerous times now,' stammered the young man, eyes bright in the flicker.

'What do ya mean? Nothin' dangerous about these days, is there?' Spider tried again to stir up the youngster.

'Yeah, well! What about ... about leaks from nuclear reactors ... and ... AIDS, and malaria ... overpopulation ... and pollution ... the rise of fanatical religions. Eh? And what about ... about the oil companies, and the banks, and the Middle East ... *and* those mental cases ... Bush and Bin Laden ... eh? What do you say to *that*?'

The little bloke did not need to stick his chest out.

The impact of realisation gathered them all. No doubt about it, these days were *far* more dangerous than ever before.

The End

The depth of mateship

Is forever -

Who are we to judge?

Hellfire Pass

September 1972

Edward Johnson and David Gilmore had returned to Kanchanaburi in Thailand for a reunion with some of their mates who had all been imprisoned by the Japanese in World War Two.

They had taken the train to Hellfire Pass, the place where a memorial had been built in memory of the lives lost and the almost overwhelming hardships endured on the Burma Railway. Most of their friends had died, along with many they never knew, soldiers from the allied armies, and many local Thais, as well as other Asians. The almost impenetrable jungle, disease, cruelty, and accidents in the construction of the railway took its toll.

The men spent half an hour standing, hands in pockets, staring at the old rusty railway line still visible. Most of the rails and bridges of the original line had faded into the jungle or been salvaged for local building. The pass, carved through solid rock with no mechanical means, was a feat in itself. Only the solitary word and audible sobs punctuated the hot humid jungle as those brave enough looked around, hoping not to catch a glance from a comrade.

On the way back the two friends stepped off the train, which never went any faster than a slow amble, and then sat down on a patch of grass.

'Glad I didn't bring the wife,' said Ted.

They watched as the diesel tourist train rumbled on and slowly clickety-clacked over the River Kwai.

'Same here,' replied Dave.

'Mate?' said Ted, inclining his head, 'there's something I'd like to …'

'Yeah?'

'Bluee begged me to kill him,' continued Ted.

John *Blue* Foster was a soldier just like them but senior because of his length of service. Doc, who was called that only because he knew a little first aid, had to remove Bluee's leg, with no anaesthetic, after a truss crushed it. For two weeks he lay deteriorating in the sick bay.

'Yeah, he was in a bad way, poor bugger was going to die, nuthin' surer, he had further infections in the upper leg, he had malaria, jaundice, dysentery, and the rest.'

Ted turned. 'When I was there, he asked Hidako to shoot him, but the mongrel just gave his yellow toothed grin, whacked Bluee with his cane and walked out laughing, bastard. So, Bluee asked me to smother him with a pillow. The wag managed to smile when he said it because no one had any bloody pillows – he had a heap of old rags rolled up in his shirt. I told him I couldn't do it and walked out. Anyrate, about an hour later I goes back and Bluee's dead.'

'Yeah?'

'I noticed he had slight pink marks on his wrists as if he'd been held down.'

Dave turned, eyes pooling with tears. 'He ordered me to do it.'

Ted put a gentle hand on his friend's shoulder. 'I'm not judging you, mate, I didn't have the courage to do it. You did.'

They both looked out at a fishing raft drifting down the River Kwai.

The End

Doing our best –

Might be the best we can do

Others may also carry some of the burden

Collateral Damage

A collection of five short stories based on characters from my novel

Crucial Step

A Party to Remember

'Happy Birthday! Hey, how's my little man?' Vince clapped his hands, pivoted like a drunken sailor, and then stumbled into the birthday party. Theo's hyperventilating puffs had just blown out six candles much to the delight of the other children.

'Aaaaah!' Vince caught the edge of the rug and stumbled head-first into the kitchen-tidy. Some children shrieked with laughter. Most then realised something was up. Theo's brow tightened. The room went eggshell quiet.

Gail stood shock still for a second, framed by the kitchen door. Then she rushed over and used all her strength to hustle her husband to his feet. He flustered and shoved and tried to push her away but was too bombed to have any effect. She glanced at her friend Carol, whose eyes were like saucers and her hand covered her mouth. Gail steered her swaying husband out the door and down the passage, his feeble blubbering protests muffled further when the bedroom door closed.

Theo's mouth reduced to a shivering prune and his face grew rosy. Tears threatened. Silence was his enemy and his saviour.

Carol waved her hands into a semblance of order and clapped a couple of times. 'Um, hey, how about some birthday cake? Who wants cake, eh?'

The silence broke and the children yelled, 'Yeahhhh!'

Gail walked back into the kitchen. She mouthed a word in Carol's direction, 'Vietnam …' As if that would explain everything.

Theo's pinched forehead somehow managed to bridle the tears. He shoved his chair back and whipped out the back door in the direction of the chook house.

The End

Chook House

'Theo, love, come out.'

'Don't want to.'

'Your friends have gone, sweetie, it's alright. Come on. Hey? Let's go and look at your presents.'

Theo's head eased around the corner of the henhouse. Pinched mouth, eyes red and moving fast.

'Daddy didn't mean it, dear. He's ... he's sick. Come on, over here.'

Gail put her arms around him. He buried his head in her apron and started to sob softly. She looked up into the clouds. A tear glistened on her cheek.

'It's alright, dear, Daddy fought in that terrible war. Since he got home, he ... he's had trouble ... adjusting. He didn't mean to spoil your party.'

She had been up most of the previous night mopping Vince's brow with a flannel. He had been re-living the screams, and the explosions, and the bullets; and the horror. And then he had been mixing the pills with whisky, beer, and wine chasers.

'There, there,' she coo-ed to her son. It was hard to explain depression and shell-shock to a small boy. 'Come on, let's go up to the house and have some cake. Your mates took a piece home with them, but Auntie Carol made sure there was plenty left for you. Alright?'

She ruffled his hair and turned to go. 'Oh! quick Theo, close the gate, Margaret will get out.'

Margaret the hen, always on the hunt, spied a gap into freedom but Theo managed to zip over and latched the gate just in time.

He looked up. She smiled at him. He did not completely surrender his demeanour, but his brow lifted, and his mouth softened into a semi-smile.

The End

More than Sorry

'Jesus, Vince, that was one hell of a party trick. Of all days, you had to pick your son's sixth birthday to OD on uppers and booze.' Gail, hands on hips, glared down at him sprawled on the settee.

'Fuck, I ... I just had a bad day, that's all.' He took another swig from a West End tallie. His hand shook.

'Look Vince, I know things aren't easy for you at the moment, but you really need help. You need to go back to rehab, not the local Doc. Mixing prescription drugs and alcohol, it's no good.' She sighed, slowly moving her head from side to side.

'Get off me back will ya, I'm going in tomorrow to see those dick-head doctors. I'm just a bit shell-shocked. Not just from the war, alright? We risked our lives over there. For what, eh? For fucking-well what! Right, then we get back here and bamo! Everyone treats us like fucking criminals.'

She leant over, not fazed by his outburst, and patted his hand several times before gently grasping it with both hands. 'It's alright, Vince, it's alright. What you are saying is true.'

He pulled his hand away, not violently and it seemed he was ashamed he was treating her that way. Vince could not, however, leave it at that. 'You know what I fucking-well think, eh?' Not waiting for a reply. 'Well, I agree we shouldn't have gone in the first place, but we bloody-well did, right? We didn't have any choice; we just got conscripted, lied to and then sent overseas, just like that. Yes sir, no sir, Uncle fucking Sam and all the way up the Khyber with LBJ. Yep, we did bloody-well go and now here I am.' He started to roll a cigarette; some of the tobacco fell on the ground. 'Fuck it all,' he growled.

Gail shook her head, no point in talking to him. She opened the fridge. 'Hey Vince, did you drink all the wine?'

He looked down at the empty wine bottle at his feet and then lit a badly rolled cigarette.

'Vince, Vince, Vince,' she breathed softly, 'you'll have to sharpen up. Can't have your boy seeing you like this all the time. He thinks the world of you. Poor little bugger, he looks up to you and you keep disappointing him. You'll have to talk to him, he doesn't understand much, but ...'

'Bloody hell, Gail give us a bloody break, will ya?' He looked out the window, seemingly at nothing. It somehow had a calming effect. The light picked up his wet eyes. 'Yeah, I know everything you are saying, yeah, all right? I know.' He took a big breath and blew out his cheeks. 'I'm going to say sorry.'

'It might take more than sorry, Vince.'

'Yeah, don't ya think I know that, eh?' He shook his head and then upended the remains in the West End bottle down his throat.

The End

Smoke Signals

'She was pretty embarrassed.' Carol flopped down and dropped her cigarettes on the kitchen table.

'Poor old Vince, poor old Gail, poor little Theo. Poor anyone who has to put up with a Vietnam Vet.' Charlene clicked her lighter, took a big draw and blew a funnel of smoke at the cracked ceiling.

'Yeah maybe, but it must have been a terrible time out in that place, fighting … and all that? I'm glad Dean's marble didn't come up.' Carol tapped out a cigarette from her packet of Kool. 'It must have been hard for both Gail and you. I guess it's one thing to marry a man, knowing he's in the army. You'd expect them to go to war. Another thing to get conscripted, the government change the rules, and then they have to go.'

'Yeah, although they did actually have a choice, not much but still …'

'Umm, how's Jack?'

'That bastard? Oh, you know him. He's bitter about how some people treat him, but he brings it on himself. Baits people and when they find out he only has one leg they back off. His behaviour is a pain in the arse. Drunk all the time, same old bloody thing.'

'Does he know about … er …?'

'Yeah. He knows. When he came back on leave from Pucka last year he suspected. He accused me anyway. I mean, silly prick must have known I'd be lookin' around a bit. When he was away at Pucka he was putting it about, betcha. And away, R and R in Saigon, rooting those Asian sheilas and expecting me to wear a chastity belt. Ha! Fuck that. He wants a divorce. Beat me to it, arsehole, I was gunna say the same thing.' She screwed the cigarette into the astray where it continued to smoulder around the smear of red lipstick on the filter.

'I'm … I'm sorry …' Carol's words fell away. Not much to say about a marriage that was over before it started.

'He's a selfish bastard, always was. We should never have got hitched in the first place. Anyway, I don't want to be saddled with a one-legged bloke with a lump of wood on his shoulder, *and* shit on the liver with everyone around the place as well. Bastard aint sharing his pension with me now, either. Stopped my access to his wages. I would have been better off as a war widow.'

'Umm ... yeah.'

'Jack reckons he's going back to Thailand, mate of his has a bar over in Bangkok. Good riddance, he can root all the slopes he can get his hands on, much as he wants. Yeah, he wants Vince to go over with him, ya know, mates, high adventure, all that shit.' She fingered out another cigarette, lit up and exhaled through her nose.

Carol shook her head. 'Naaah. No way, Vince has his boy, idolises him. If he didn't have Theo, he might consider it I guess but there's Gail. They are going through a rough patch alright but she's clawing on to the rim with her fingernails. For the present anyway. Must be hard for her. Vince is out of his head most of the time, taking biddy beans, uppers and downers and in betweeners, as well as hitting the bottle of whatever he can get his hands on. Gail's got a lot to put up with. Poor Vince is really in no condition to go anywhere now, anyway.'

'Yeah, poor everyone.' Charlene continued to fill the space between them with smoke.

The End

Dead Right.

The front bar of the Enfield buzzed with post six o'clock swill. The smoky air played with the balance of noise.

'Hey, Jack, over here!' Vince did a top of the head salute. He lit up a rollie with difficulty and moved aside as Jack slid from crutches to a stool. Vince sculled the remains of his glass and waved at the barman for two more schooners.

'How're they hangin' Vince? Hell, you don't look too good, mate.' Jack's eyebrows pinched. 'Jesus, your eyes don't look too flash.'

'Aaaarh, you know. My head isn't liking much of anything right now. Keep hearing all sorts of noises and … everything else. Not s'posed to be drinkin' but, er … who cares?'

'Yeah, spot on mate.' Jack pulled out a Marlboro Red from the crushproof pack and snapped his lighter. 'Hey, here's cheers,' and they clinked glasses, Vince nearly spilled some before finding his mouth. 'Hey mate, maybe you *really* shouldn't be drinking as in not really having a drink.'

'I'll be right. Anyrate, how is the new leg?'

'Lot better, much, much better than the old one. Er … not me real one, mind you.'

They both laughed.

'Yeah, the Rehab docs were really good. It will take a week or two to feel like almost a real one. Some of them at least, know what we are going through. There are a few bastards that didn't see any action are putting in claims too, pretending injuries. Anyway, you should go and talk to the medicos, mate, no good going on like you are.'

'Not fucking–well you too?' Vince shook his head.

'What?'

'Gail's on me back all the time. Do this, do that …' He dropped his soggy cigarette butt onto the floor.

'Yeah, I know, Vince, I know. We've got every reason to be pissed off. Everyone I bump into hates our guts. We risked our lives for everyone here in Australia and what thanks do we get? Eh? Fuck-all!'

'Yeah.' Vince pulled out a paper and tried to roll another cigarette.

'Anyway, mate I'm going to piss off to Thailand. We could both go, eh? Buckets has started up a bar in Bangers, doing very bloody well. He wants to crank up another one in Phuket. Got access to some good *artificials* too, pretty good stuff, could be just like Saigon all over again. He's knee deep in horizontal female you know what, too. Sounds like a good proposition to me, he needs a bit of a hand. I've got some dough from my pension, so I might get the hell away from here for a while. I feel like a leper, me, in my own country. Fucked. Wanna come?'

'What does Charlene think?' Vince fiddled with his rollie.

'Here, stop fucking about, have one of mine.' Jack tapped out a Marlboro and handed it over. 'Charlene? The bitch has been getting a bit of in-out from every Tom, Dick and Harry around the place, but mainly Spoggy. He always was a backdoor man, arsehole. We're getting a divorce. Fucking bitch has been cleaning out my bank account all the time I've been away. She aint getting any of my pension though. I've switched banks. Teach her a lesson. Maybe she will have to charge for it from now on. Ha! No one would pay to root her, so she'd have to get a real job, probably kill her.' He took a gulp. 'Look, mate it's been over for ages. Last time I was here, first leave from Pucka, I found out she was getting a bit from Spoggy.'

Vince shook his head, tired matador. 'I can't go, mate. Got me boy. Gail and I aren't getting on that well, but we have to stick together 'cos of Theo.'

'Yeah, yeah, yeah, I know … *Hey!* Watch it cock-head,' barked Jack as a person carrying drinks accidently bumped into him. The man was about to make something of it but noticed the crutch. He shook his head and walked on. 'Cock-brain!'

'Another beer?' Vince signalled the barman.

'Hey, mate,' said Jack, 'You shouldn't be drinking like this, eh?'

'Who gives a flying fuck, mate?'

'Yeah, yeah. I know exactly what you mean. Fair enough then, let's have a rum chaser, eh? And the whole world can go and get fucked, right?'

'Yeah, dead right.'

The End

Fulfilling desire

Can be good -

But reading the play is important

Briefcase

She was one of Michelle's acquaintances from netball. The three of them were supposed to be going out to dinner to celebrate being together for a year.

Michelle rolled her hand. 'Look, Max, you'll like her, come on ...'

'But why does she have to come out with us, I mean, it's our celebration, nothing to do with her, shouldn't it be just the two of us? I've never met her.'

'Come on hun,' she pouted, 'it'll be fun. She's pretty lonely at the moment; her boyfriend has gone to India for a month and things aren't working that well.'

Max was becoming increasingly annoyed with Michelle's overbearing behaviour. Also, he suspected she was seeing someone else behind his back.

∞

Laura's imagination floated. Her boyfriend, Charlie had gone to India. *Well, I'm not going to sit around and twiddle my thumbs waiting for him.*

She had seen this young man around the place. His vibe radiated disinterest, maybe it was because he was spoken for. She knew he was. At the shopping centre last week, she had parked near the loading bay. He was unloading some furniture. Initially, from a distance, she did not know it was him. As she neared, she recognized him. The strong brown arms lifting, shoulders squared, back ramrod straight. He was not aware of her presence. She stood still, just looking at him, pretending to be confused in case anyone was watching.

Somehow, he sensed her presence and turned his head. His eyebrows arched up. With the glare of the sun, she could not tell if his smile was genuine. She ran an index finger under the shoulder strap of her halter top, almost caught out. *Bugger Charlie, he can sort himself out in India.* 'Umm … hi.'

He turned further and wiped a casual hand over his black hair. Deep breath, big square chest. 'Er … g'day, nice day for shopping.'

'Yeah.' She did not know what to say. 'Don't lift things that are too heavy, you might hurt yourself.' It sounded rude; she had not intended it that way. 'Got to keep going … umm … see you.' That sounded worse.

He nodded, 'Yep, see ya.'

∞

They were already sitting down when Laura breezed in. Her auburn hair made a strong statement.

'Hi!' Eyes flickered in the lighting. 'Sorry I'm late.' She shook her mane, droplets of water flew off, some hung and glistened. Diamonds. Then she did her best to hide a double take when she saw the man from the shopping centre. Max's eyebrows shot up, recognising her too, at the same time. He nodded a greeting.

Michelle waved her hand to indicate it was not a problem. 'No need for apologies, we haven't been here that long.' She introduced Max.

Max waved towards the bar. 'You're just in time for a drink, what will it be?'

'Gin and tonic, thanks.' Laura hung her shoulder bag on the back of the chair.

The young, dark-haired waitress came over.

Max looked towards Michelle. 'Same again?' She nodded. He turned to the waitress. 'A G and T, a glass of McWilliams Chardonnay, and I'll have another draught beer, please.'

The girls settled quickly into verbal banter, things to do with netball. Max leant back. He was happy to be left on the outer. It gave him the opportunity to check Laura out. Occasionally a question was directed at him for a comment. He obliged and smiled his best. Laura was trying to be nice to him.

They ate several courses and with each round of drinks they grew less inhibited. Max could not help glancing at Laura occasionally. Low cut top, shapely mounds obvious. He averted his eyes just before she glanced. The wine kept coming and several bottles went the way of the first.

Dessert arrived. He got caught; she looked up at the same time. Their eyes held for a long second.

Michelle piped up, 'I'm off to the ladies.' She grabbed her bag.

They watched her depart, an unstable weave towards the foyer. Their glances returned to each other.

She touched her hair; the voice was soft and distant. 'It was nice seeing you at the shopping centre the other day. We should meet … again … some time.'

He held her gaze. 'Yes … soon.' Max could not believe what he had just said.

There was a long space in time. The waitress asked if they wanted more drinks. They nodded yes. They looked up quickly as Michelle appeared a short distance away. A mobile phone tune tinkled from her shoulder bag.

Michelle put the bag down and pulled out her phone. 'Hi … yeah? … mmm … yeah.' Her brow slightly knotted and her body language took on a slightly apologetic pose. 'Yesss … okay … okay … yep … right. See ya.' She looked up. 'Look, guys, you won't believe this. I've got go back to the office and sort out this travel business. Just when I'm starting to enjoy the night, too. It won't take long. You people know each other well enough to keep entertained, don't you? Look, guys, I won't be long, I promise.'

Max looked at her. 'Who was that on the phone?'

Michelle took a second to answer. 'Err … umm … Perry. He can't fathom my figures, can't blame him. Anyway, I won't be long. I'll buzz you and you can pick me up.' She grabbed her bag and walked out.

∞

143

Laura was more than sure Michelle was having an affair with Perry. Her thoughts drifted back to the shopping centre; the scene became vivid. Max lifting and stretching. Now, at the restaurant, Michelle disappearing, probably up to no good. She could not keep the lid on her feelings. Her gaze was hot, she could not control it. He looked away a couple of times.

She gushed, perhaps too quickly. 'Let's ... go ... outside.' She wanted him, she would deal with the guilt later. She would not consider caution; doing the right thing did not come into it.

He stammered, and mouthed the words, 'But Laura ... Michelle ... she's, my *girlfriend*.'

Laura tried to bring things back on track. 'Yes.' She looked into his big brown eyes and eased out a coy reply. 'I know ... she's ... my friend, too.'

Max shook his head as if to clear the cobwebs of guilt. He stood, pulled out a couple of notes and dropped them on the table. 'Come on ... umm ... let's ... walk.'

Michelle wandered back towards the shopping centre, enjoying the buzz of alcohol in her head and happy Max and Laura seemed to be getting on. Perry waved from the entrance. Good old reliable Perry, he had no need to tell her what he was when he applied for the job. She smiled, as if she could not pick that he was gay.

'Sorry to drag you back, Shell, but ...'

'No, that's okay Perry; we have to sort it out. Better now rather than later, in fact I've got an idea how we can actually make some money on this one. Now, where is that file?'

∞

They walked out of the restaurant, brushing against each other. Electric contact. He glanced towards the car. She quivered, could not stop herself. Light rain glistened on the roof. Max manoeuvred her, gently pushing her up against the car, then onto the edge of the bonnet, one hand around her bottom. His left hand, fingers extended, was embedded in her diamond studded auburn hair. Her response was instant, almost aggressive as she returned the pressure.

Frantic tongues explored, lips locked and kissed. He went for her panties, her hand dropped to help. Mutual urgent need. Laura raised her legs. Her clumsy hands tried to undo his jeans.

A crunch of gravel, crisp in the cold night.

They looked up.

'I ... I ... I forgot my briefcase,' stammered Michelle, eyes wide in the moonlight.

The End

Some stories are sad

But in fiction

Can be beautiful

Incomplete Picture

Liz picked up the photo. 'I suppose they asked someone from the Pokhara Lodge to take the photo, that seems to be the last time anyone could recall seeing them, alive that is. They disappeared without trace well over twenty years ago.'

'Pokhara? I have heard of it.' Connie dangled her wire-rimmed, reading glasses by a wing.

'Yeah, it's about a day by road from Kathmandu. People go trekking from there, one of the most popular spots in Nepal. I found this out from a friend of mine who regularly goes hiking in places of interest. Pokhara is the starting point for what is called the Annapurna Circuit and you can make it as hard or as friendly as you like. The whole circuit takes a week or two at least although tough campaigners probably do it in less. Beginners can just do the lower reaches. See, they both have walking boots on and trekking jackets.'

'Right. First up, why me?'

Liz took a sip of water. 'Well, I know you reasonably well from yoga and you are a bored, retired, investigative journalist ... and you did say you wanted to write something different, something possibly meaningful, anything, a novel ...'

Connie pursed her lips, almost Daffy Duck style. 'Yeah, I suppose I did.'

Liz quickly pressed on '... and there's probably a story in here somewhere - I mean you can be the judge of that, of course and ... I wanted someone who I could trust, I mean it's all very personal ...'

'Trust a journalist? You know what we are like.' They both laughed. 'Righto, what have we got?' A spiral notebook appeared in front of her. 'Don't worry too much about the delicate stuff, I'll go over what I intend to write with you, that's if indeed there is a story worth, you know …'

Down to business straight away, Liz was impressed by her friend's attitude. 'Thanks Connie. Well, there are two stories here. Firstly, I have an envelope which includes a personal letter to my mother from my grandmother as well as the photo.' She placed the photo back on the coffee table. 'We can go over the photo and the letter later, but I think it worthwhile to explain the sequence of things. The dates are intriguing.'

Liz explained that the letter, addressed to her mother, Elizabeth, at this address was dated 27th of May 1989, the envelope stamped a day later at Pokhara, then stamped Kathmandu, and *finally* stamped Connaught Place, New Delhi ten days later.

She continued, 'Right, now the original letter was placed in a larger envelope and addressed the same, why I have no idea, redirected by someone in the post office in India, probably. *Then* this larger envelope goes to Bombay, now called Mumbai, to the, see this, *Mail Exchange - Locked Bag 37 - Australia* dated three weeks ago, like I mean, 21st January 2017, the receipted date-stamp of Sydney GPO. *Then* it was delivered by our local post office to this address which is the original address it was supposed to go to way back in 1989.' Liz held up her hand to stop Connie asking anything.

She continued, 'And the beat goes on. This larger envelope has date stamps all over the place and who knows exactly the path it took. So, this postal item seemed to have disappeared for something like twenty-seven and a half years from May 1989 to January 2017 - that's your story if you want it.'

Connie looked up; forehead scrunched.

'Just kidding, although there is a story there somewhere. The second story is the real story of what did or didn't happen to the two women in the photo.' Liz pointed to the woman on the right. 'That's my grandmother on the right, Pearl Montgomery.'

Connie placed her glasses on the end of her nose. 'Who's the one on the left – she looks slightly … er … Asian?'

Liz opened a loose leafed folder. 'Yes, her name is Bhavisana, she was born in Nepal in, let me see, 1914. My great-grandfather worked for the British High Commission in New Delhi, well before partition and somehow or other she was adopted from an orphanage in India. Maybe my grandmother needed a playmate - and that plays out later, maybe - she was a year older than Sana, that's what they called her as Bhavisana was a bit of a tongue twister I guess.'

Liz continued to explain how the two girls were inseparable until Pearl was married, in 1937, to Bellamy Ashton, and Elizabeth, Liz's mother was born. Bellamy, Liz's grandfather, worked for the British Embassy in India and then in 1949, emigrated to Sydney. Sana went with them but took a job in Melbourne and seemed to sever contact with the family. Liz's mother said Pearl was devastated because there was no information as to where Sana had gone. In about nineteen sixty something, Sana turned up. Evidently, she had worked around the country in secretarial work. Liz's elderly mother, on a recent visit at the nursing home, was sketchy about it all, not only because her memory was coloured, but throughout her life she was not privy to the goings on of her parents. Then, Sana lived in the servant's quarters at the Sydney house with Bellamy and Pearl seemingly in harmony. Liz leaned back and exhaled a long breath.

Connie stopped writing and took a sip of water. 'Phew, big story there but I'm not sure what it is.'

'Wait there's plenty more. Just before Grandpa ... er Bellamy died in 1982 they sold the main house. It was a heritage dwelling and they didn't have the money for the upkeep, so they moved into the servant's quarters, right here where we are now. Pearl and Sana lived here until 1988 when they disappeared seemingly off the face of the earth. As I mentioned before there was an investigation and they were tracked to Pokhara. Nepalese and Australian authorities put it down to misadventure and no one knew any more than that until this letter arrived in May this year, 2017, addressed to mum.'

Connie looked over her reading glasses, willing the question.

'Yes, I opened the letter, I mean my name is the same as mother's but ... you know she's been in care for nearly a year now. I did go and try to tell her, armed with resolve, what was in the letter, to explain what I could but she couldn't focus on anything, let alone what I was trying to say. All she could say was, 'What a lovely photo. They look like they love each other. Who are they?" Liz turned away, hoping her friend did not see a crystal tear.

'And? What was in the letter?'

Liz composed herself. 'Sana had inoperable cancer and she wanted to go back to the roof of the world to spend her last days. She said the two of them had made a promise to each other that if one became ill, they would both face it together. Grandmother, in the letter - and I could actually *feel* her apprehension, um maybe shame ... no, depth of feeling - said she felt terrible about it all and asked her daughter, my mother, to forgive her for not confiding in her. My mother will die wondering, but maybe not.'

'Mmmm, seems a bit kind of sad for your mother, her daughter, and you for that matter. But, Liz, people do all sorts of things in life, some we're ashamed of or embarrassed. Many people can't bear to keep living without the other. How many times do we read about couples that take that path?' She did not look for an answer. 'Bear in mind they were both elderly ... well into their seventies. Maybe she was ill too? Personally, I think it takes great courage to make a promise like that, and to keep it. I guess Pearl just couldn't bring herself to tell everyone she was about to ... er ...' Connie obviously felt ill at ease to say the words.

'Commit suicide, you mean.' Liz sighed. 'There's more. Pearl said they were lovers and had loved each other since they met as children. She makes mention of the fact that Bellamy never suspected as far as she knew. It seems he may have because I do recall several times where there was trouble in the camp, even as a kid I picked up on it.'

Connie placed her glasses alongside the notebook. 'A human story, a beautiful story and a very sad story as well, Liz. I guess in their time, when the world frowned upon that sort of behaviour, you can sort of understand. And besides, if the letter had not been lost your mother would have been able to form her own views on the matter. And never know, maybe your mother *does* know all about this.'

'Pearl went on to beg her daughter's forgiveness for ... for being a lesbian.'

'You can make it up to her by telling her stories about how wonderful her mother was, and maybe Sana as well, your choice, my dear.' Connie touched her friend's hand and smiled.

Liz made a pot of tea. 'So, can you make a story out of any of this?' She asked.

Connie looked serious for a moment and then smiled. 'Well, my dear, it is a sad story but beautiful at the same time. Remember, we all have our own stories and maybe your mother can share yours? Right, must go.' She grabbed her things off the table, 'We'll get together again soon and formulate something. Every photo tells a story, doesn't it?'

'Yes ... but probably never the full story.'

The End

Life can be exciting

The best decisions

Are usually the most obvious

Man In Paris

Earlier in the day Hedley tried, on several occasions, to convince the women not to see the wonderful sights of Paris in a two-seater Fiat. Where was the driver going to sit?

'Why don't you accompany me tomorrow, in comfort, in the tourist bus, well it's not a bus, it's a minibus, but I can assure you it *is* a much better option.'

'Oh, come on Dad,' soothed Lisa-May, 'how about some of that adventurous spirit, get down and dirty *with* the people.'

'Tabby, can't you talk some sense into your daughter? No way am I going to travel in that sardine tin when I can sit in a proper seat. I mean, the bloody car is a wreck, and the way they drive, too – probably not insured and the three of us jammed in there – plus the driver.'

Anton had done his utmost to avoid showing them the mode of transport in question, but Hedley had persisted. A wide range of excuses were put forward but eventually the prized Fiat was made available for their observation. The women were wide eyed for a few moments, but the sense of adventure sent them into fits of laughter. Hedley shook his head.

'Well, I think it would be fun, plus it's half the price of the tour and the driver knows all the places worth seeing,' quipped Tabatha, clearly on her daughter's side.

3.40pm.

Hedley slung his arm over the back of the bentwood chair and took a sip of his coffee. They do not make coffee as well as they do at home, he thought. Why would that be? Like most of western Europe, coffee had been part of their cuisine for centuries.

He had already been on his tour and was due to meet them at the hotel café at four and figured a coffee would be just the thing to keep him upright until dinner.

It was wonderful to see Lisa-May again. She had been living and working in London and just come out of a messy divorce. Her ex was a pompous bloke, she would be better off without him, mused Hedley. Thankfully there were no children to squabble over. She had taken a coach across to meet them in Paris because they had a six-day break in their tour.

When his daughter wanted to do something, she was hard to shift. Anton, the snappy waiter in the dining room, had convinced her to see gay Parree in his brother's tiny Fiat. It did not escape Hedley's keen eye, the way young, dashing Anton and, his sometimes-pouty daughter, Lisa-May looked at each other. Anton went out of his way to make not only Lisa-May, but Tabatha as well, the centre of attention. He smiled; flattery will get you everywhere he figured.

Before they left, he gave his wife and daughter a hotel business card with their room numbers jotted on the back.

'What's this for?' said Lisa-May.

'Just in case the car breaks down and you have to walk; you can easily get lost in a city this size.'

'Ha! Do we get a whistle each, too? And a cup with our name on it?' added Tabatha.

They all laughed. He was known to be a catastrophist.

3.55pm.

He knew they would rib him, when they arrived back at the hotel, about wearing a suit and tie today. Tabby pestered him as to why he would even bring a tie on holidays, let alone a suit.

Hedley knew he was worried about retirement. Lines gathered on his forehead for a minute or two because he knew Tabatha was concerned as well. He tapped his lip with an index finger. That fateful gold-watch-day was looming 13 months from now – but he was not counting the days. Sure. The boss suggested he take some long service leave to get the feel of retirement.

They had visited their daughter in the UK twice since she moved there four years ago, and this was a good opportunity to see her again.

Stubborn Lisa-May took after her mother, that was for sure, not him. It was good Tabby went on the sightseeing sojourn, mother and daughter, bonding, and all that. He smiled again, mother and daughter used to fight like cat and dog during Lisa-May's teenage years. Now they were the best of friends. It warmed his heart to see them together, 23 years difference in their ages and they acted like gushy teenage girls, friends forever.

4.10pm.

'Coffee again, monsieur?' enquired the slim, blue-eyed waitress, slightly bowing in a polite, disarming fashion.

'Oh. Umm, no thanks ... er no merci.'

They should not be too much longer, he thought. The hotel café was slowly filling up. If they did not arrive soon, he figured he would head for the bar. Hedley looked down at his ankles and chuckled. Tabatha always chastised him for not rolling his socks into a ball, after washing them, before putting them away – not that he did any of that sort of thing anymore, anyway. Hedley argued, logically as far as he was concerned, doing what she wanted always overstretched the elastic and made them slip down. Tabatha did not trust him to hang the washing out these days but did allow him to bring it in off the line, but only when she was unable to do it, naturally. She would not let him put things away because as far as she was concerned, he did not do it properly. He would have to point out the over-stretched socks-elastic to her when she arrived back, just to illustrate his point.

4.22pm.

'Where are they?'

Just then there was a commotion near the service desk. Hedley looked up. The slim, blue-eyed waitress pointed excitedly in his direction. A flustered gendarme hurried towards him.

'*Pardon,* Monsieur, pardon,' he panted, holding up a hotel business card in a shaking hand. Sweat speckled his brow, '*Mon Dieu, Monsieur,* there has been … *an accident.*'

Hedley did not notice everyone in the café staring at him. The rumbling in his head became louder.

The End

Commitment –

Mates –

And Honour

One I Owe Ya

1969

'Let's get outa here!' screamed Howie from the steaming thicket. The incoming chopper hovered in the din and dust and eventually spread-eagled in the rice paddy near the edge of the dense humid jungle. Mortars exploded everywhere and bullets zipped and fizzed. Sergeant Peter *Howie* Howard waved his heavily tattooed arms like a mad-man. He screeched and yelled, pointing in the direction of the grounded chopper and another one preparing to land.

Norm Arnold lay as low as the earth would allow. Sweat clouded his eyes and he wiped a filthy sleeve across his face. Every so often he would bench press the machine gun above his head and whack out a clip in the direction of the jungle that camouflaged the Viet Cong. The tinkle and clink of shells added to the sharp gunfire. Fear kept him going. He saw himself as an average sort of bloke, doing an average sort of job. Everyone called him *Anchorman* because he was solid, dependable and … average. Everyone that is, except Howie Howard.

The choppers, bursts of increased firepower from the jungle and shrieks from everywhere, cranked up the tension. The stinking, buzzing jungle was not damp enough to stop the choking dust kicked up by the rotors.

'Let's go, you useless cock-heads!' screamed Howie again, dodging and weaving.

In contrast to most of the others, he was gutsy, brave as hell and afraid of nothing. Howie stood up again, as if defying the whizzing bullets to take him. He emptied a clip into the jungle again and yelled at his men to get to the choppers. The blokes all knew Howie had a chip on the shoulder. A big piece of wood. They did not know if he had the short-arse syndrome, because really, he was not that short and everyone said he had muscles in his shit. Or whether he failed at school or whether he was just born on the wrong side of the railway line. It was rumoured he was ushered into the army as a last measure to keep him out of jail. They all knew Howie was never happy with what life had dealt him. But he was brave, tough and with a street-smart meanness.

He was loyal to his men in the field to the point of death. Most other times they saw him as a plain bastard and a bully. Howie boasted about killing a bloke in Brisbane a couple of years before joining the Army. He constantly picked on others but never anyone who could handle him. He was a loner, no one socialised with him. They knew it was very important to Howie to be the top man. Many fights broke out over the ego games but they all realised how important their sergeant was in keeping them alive when on patrol. Howie always led the charge, often putting himself in danger to save the men he seemed to despise back in barracks.

Out in the jungle hell, where insect bites, sweat, injury or death awaited them, they had to kill or be killed. Simple rules of war. They all begrudgingly respected his intelligence and unquestioning bravery under enemy fire. Howie was a professional soldier. All the others in the unit, bar two, were conscripts like Norm Arnold; young men, less than twenty years old. They knew they had to stay alive. Howie gave them that. For some unfathomable reason he really had shit on the liver about Arnold. The sergeant never called him Anchorman.

Heavy machine gun fire tore pieces of earth and sludge into the air. Arnold ran in a practiced crouched position and turned his head looking for others. Howie was the only one left, directing traffic under extreme pressure, on the crouch, sprinting in Anchorman's direction. Suddenly a loud burst of fire hammered out of the thicket, Howie staggered, his legs jellied and his body jerked like a rag doll for a split second before collapsing into the dirt.

Anchorman glanced towards the Medics who were dragging casualties towards the choppers ahead, and his mate Don Martin waved him back. Howie then became obscured from everyone by of a patch of elephant grass.

Arnold did not think. He flung his machine-gun towards Martie, turned, and ran in the direction of Howie. He did not know why, he just did it. All he could remember when talking about it later was the hot sweat in his eyes. Others said he bellowed like a bull. Arnold ran the 30 metres in seconds, others said he ducked and weaved like a madman.

Howie, covered in blood and muck, lay twisted in a shallow ditch. Sparse foliage on the perimeter of the rice paddy and jungle gave no cover. Bullets fizzed all around and lumps of turf and pea soup water flew in the air.

Howie, the professional soldier, was just conscious, covered in blood from the waist down. 'Yyyyyou fucking dick-head, you disobeyed an order.' His mouth tried to form words, 'Get – the - fuck – outa here …' The last part faded.

Once again, Anchorman did not think. If he had he may not have done what he did. He grabbed the sergeant by the lapels and slung him over his shoulder. He was aware of the damp warmth that soaked his shirt, it had to be blood.

Fortunately, the first helicopter managed to struggle airborne and was hammering the Viet Cong positions with machine guns. Martie stood like a statue at the door of the other chopper emptying the firearms, at his disposal, into the jungle. Anchorman ran as quickly as he could, with the extra weight of another man, bullets whizzed past as he dodged and weaved in the direction the waiting helicopter. Just as he reached the machine, he felt a dull forceful thud in his right shoulder; the force threw him and Howie almost into the open carriage. Several hands grabbed at them, someone screamed, 'GO!' and Martie piled in on top of them. The chopper lifted off sideways in the dust and din as bullets ricocheted cow-bell noises off the cabin floor.

Arnold felt warm all over, he knew it was blood, whose it was did not matter. Someone rolled him over and there was Howie with bulbous eyes. For a moment Arnold thought the man was dead.

A weak smile crept over the sergeant's muddy lips. 'That's one I owe ya, Anchorman.' A trembling, bloody hand on the end of a heavily tattooed arm grasped Arnold's shoulder, the grasp was strong but then it faded fast.

Arnold realised that the bastard had called him Anchorman for the first time. He lost consciousness to the rattle of rivets, the ping of stray bullets hitting the underside of the vibrating floor and Hendrix's Purple Haze.

The Present Day, 1994.

'Hell mate, I couldn't believe it, he said we cheated him … us.'

Norm Arnold held the phone to his ear. His hand was moist, even though the day was quite cool. 'How in the hell could he say that?' he replied frowning. 'I mean to say, he was happy with our work, and hadn't he forgotten that he still owes us 400 bucks each?'

'Blowed if I know. You shoulda heard him go on. I'm bloody dizzy with it all,' rambled Warren *Burra* Smith, who was Norm's partner in a small carpentry business. 'The mongrel says he's gunna come round and smash ma place up with a cricket bat if I don't pay him back half the money he paid us. I mean… hell, I can't believe it.'

'Look, calm down Burra, there's got to be some explanation. Anyway, come 'round for a chat.'

They hung up. Both stood motionless in their environments for several minutes.

A Few Months Earlier.

'That sun's got some clout in it,' murmured Burra as he pulled his hat brim down further to cover his freckled features.

'If ya hadn't got stuck into the piss last night, ya probably wouldn't notice it,' laughed Anchorman.

They struggled and cajoled another heavy lump of wood six metres long into position. Even though he was older by about twenty years, and was favouring a weak right arm, he could still put in a pretty decent day's work.

'Hope the rain holds off until this evening. We need to get these bits of timber in position and tied down so we can put the floor on, soon. Any chance of that mate of yours, Pommy Granite turning up to give us a hand? He's a clown, it's within his interest, could save himself quite a bit of money.'

Burra rolled his eyes and jibed sarcastically. 'Can't ya see? He's already been here. Look he's moved all that floorin' to the side of the building and restacked those studs, just like he promised. Also, he was a great help mixing that concrete for the stump holes.' The timber had not been touched and they had mixed all the concrete themselves.

They laughed at the thought. Larry Taylor, who everyone called Granite because he was a Pommy, had employed them to build a small cottage. Initially he had repeatedly stated he would help, which would keep the costs down. They were familiar with statements like; *That's somefing I can do,* or *I'll get here early and clean da place up,* or *I'll go ta da village and get the 'ardware in da 'igh street, save youse goin', know what I mean?* or *I know a bloke oo can get it cheap, aw-wigth?* There were many similar statements and the two carpenters often referred to them and just as regularly, laughed. Granite had done absolutely nothing in contribution to the job. He was always too drunk and stoned, or not there, but mainly not there. Even if he had been there, he would not have been there at all. Burra pressed the fact that he was a reasonably good bloke and paid on time so they agreed to work for him.

'All the more money for us, mate,' interjected Anchorman. 'Why does he keep dribbling on to us about how he's going help all the time? He's done absolutely nothin' since we started.'

'Oh, he gets stuck into the piss something frightful,' laughed Burra. 'It takes him three days to get here from Brisbane. By the time he has a few beers and a smoke, argues with the missus and kids, and has a few more artificials, half the day's gone. Then he probably realises he's out of petrol. Then he has to dig up his money from the jar in the back yard. Then he must get some more beer for the drive, and so it goes on. How he doesn't get picked up for drink driving has got me beat. It certainly takes him a while to get here alright.'

They were used to the antics of Granite. He was an old acquaintance of Burras from years back, when existence was simple. Burra had a place out in the bush and all sorts of people stayed there.

Granite was always bombed and it was hard to believe he could get it together to grow dope out in the forest, but he did. Nothing had changed; he still grew dope and got drunk all the time. Granite had somehow saved enough money to build a place of his own and after mysteriously disappearing for a few years he had bobbed up at Burra's. Burra wanted to do the job, but his mate Anchorman was not too keen because the house was to be built without council approval. For obvious reasons Granite did not want the authorities involved, because the money was illegally obtained.

'What happens if the Building Inspector comes along and says, 'Who built this?' questioned Anchorman at the time.

'She'll be right, mate they'll never know, it's out past oodna woop woop, miles from anywhere. Granite says that he'll just tell them it was a working bee amongst a heap of mates, no worries.'

Burra won, even though Anchorman, true to his name, was not too happy about it at the time. The day wore on and in the early afternoon the humidity increased and the rain came. It belted down, as only tropical rain can, for well over an hour. All they could do was cover everything up and sit in the car and have a cigarette. When it stopped the ground steamed.

The wet season had created many problems for them from day one. When the timber had arrived, the delivery truck became bogged just inside the gate and the timber had to be offloaded there. The stacks had to be split so they could carry each stick individually. Anchorman and Burra were the individuals who had to do it. Unfortunately, when it was re-stacked, most of the timber warped. Had the Granite put a decent road in, none of this would have happened. They had asked him to do that before the job commenced and he said he would do it, but never did. At the time when the timber was dumped at the gate, Granite had said, *Yeah, no worries lads, I'll move it all over to the house, save youse, aw-wight? Know what I mean?*

The two tradesmen believed him then but they became wiser as the job progressed. Even though the weather was inclement and problems arose from time to time, they were happy with their effort. So was Granite, or so he said many times. *You blokes 'ave done a smashing job.*

Often, he was a week or so late but he usually turned up with their wages, one way or another. Also, he brought a carton of stubbies, or more correctly, he brought a carton, half full of stubbies, as he always managed to drink a few on the way. It all seemed like good natured stuff. He was a big fellow and constantly reminded them that as he was from a cold climate, it was important to keep his fluids up in.

The job progressed and the carpenters put in long hours to get the house to a stage, when Granite told them that he was running short of money and things would have to wait until the next crop came in. They pushed hard and managed to get the roof on, as a special effort to keep the floor and other stacked building material dry.

On the last day, Granite had pointed out, *You fellows 'ave done a job 'ere, a weal treat, know what I mean? Umm, by the way, I'm a little short of da folding, know what I mean? We can get it sorted next week? I'll drop it off next week, eh Burra, yeah, dats what I'll do. Aw-wight den?*

There was not much they could do, especially as he had not been fully cashed-up on several other occasions, and he had come good before, so they agreed.

The Present.

'Look I tell ya, he's right off his scone. He's got no brain cells left. He's got no memory! He reckons we talked him into *not* getting building approval from the council. Cock-head!'

'That's a pile of crap,' responded Anchorman. 'Remember? I made a big issue of doing it properly.'

'I know, I know, he's a mental moron, he's threatening to set fire to me house this time.'

'How come? After all this time and after leaving the job with him being really happy with our work? And him owing us money, too. How come he's off his rocker now? Doesn't make any sense.' Anchorman rubbed his jaw.

'Well, there's another idiot who did some work for him and apparently, he pointed out to Granite that a good amount of what we did was bloody wrong. Took me a bit to work it out but his bloke,

Gambo, has it in for me because I had to fix up a job he did a while ago. He made such a mess of it he got fired. I guess that's it.'

'Look Burra, this'll blow over, don't worry about it. If he rings up again, hang up. He's obviously mental.'

'That's all right for you to say, daddyo, but it's unnerving. You should hear him carry on! We used to be mates, but he's off his brain.' Burra rubbed his eyes and frowned.

They hung up.

∞

Anchorman picked up the phone.

'I got another call from hell last night, about midnight. That's on top of a call every weekend for the last couple of months. That Granite reckons he's gunna drag me behind a car this time. Every other phone call has been just straight out abuse and ridiculous accusations of things we did not do and things we did do, but now it's getting bloody serious, mate.'

'Calm down mate, did he smash ya place up? Did he burn ya house down? Look, people don't do things like that. Not unless they're bikies or the Mafia. He's too gutless to do anything, if he was going to, he would have done something by now.'

His mate and business partner was clearly unhinged.

'He said he's had a registered builder there who said we took advantage of him and did not do things properly. Bloody hell, you should hear him waffling on, it's sickening. Apparently, this Gambo character is filling his head to the brim with crap. He ... he ... he accused me of putting the weatherboards on wrongly. Well, when I said that we did not even *do* the fucking weatherboards, he said I was a liar. It just goes on and on and on.'

'Is there any scope for meeting him? I have copies of all the receipts, they don't call me Anchorman for nothing.' Anchorman tried some humour. It did not have any effect on Burra.

'Well, he wants to meet with me, so he can belt ma teeth out.' said Burra.

'Look mate, I've got to go and drop off a quote near your place, I might drop in for a quiet beer, eh?'

'Righto, see ya soon,' mumbled Burra into the phone.

'Have a beer, mate,' said Anchorman as he climbed the front steps with a six pack under his arm. Dudley, the dog thumped the timber deck a few times with his tail. He was getting on a bit in years but could still acknowledge visitors. Burra grabbed the stubbie and whipped the lid off. He was pale which was unusual as his complexion was normally ruddy, under a shock of fair hair.

'He wants all the receipts, everything.'

'How can that be right? We gave him all those at the time when we spent the money during the job.' Anchorman scratched his ear and frowned.

'I tell ya, he's out of his mind, he probably lost them all. I told him we gave them to him, all the paperwork. This is really cheesing me off, mate,' retorted Burra sharply.

'Well, as I said, I've got copies of everything. Maybe I should come too, I mean when you go and see him? We could go to the police. We can probably wriggle our way out of the building approval problem, it may not come up.'

'Look mate, there's something you should know.'

A prolonged silence.

Arnold tilted his head. 'Something I should know?'

'Umm … yeah. Some years back he bought a pound of dope off me, and well, he never did pay me. Anyway, not long after, he got busted, he was always as careless as buggery. The short of it is that he blames me for getting busted. Beat that! He blames me cos he got busted, *and* he did not pay me either. That's a real bottler, an absolute ball-tearer. Blaming fucking-well me. Shit a brick. He knows I won't go to the cops, for that reason alone. Why are you looking at me like that?'

'I see.' The older man said, deadpan. He walked to the fridge in the corner of the verandah and pulled out two more beers. Familiar territory among mates, whoever was up first, shouted. 'Where are ya gunna meet this lunatic?'

'Well, Granite suggested the Railway Hotel, middle ground so to speak.'

'How do ya know it isn't a trap of some kind?'

'Oh, I think it'd be all right, first up in the mornin', the stupid bastard shouldn't be too pissed at that hour and besides, I know the barman there,' replied Burra, as he took a swig on the beer. 'Also, Granite said, *Don't tell plod, know what I mean?* Dick-head.'

'Maybe I should go and hide behind the lounge door, just in case,' suggested Anchorman.

'No, she'll be right, I've godda do this, I mean, it was me who pushed you into the job. Don't worry, if there's any trouble my barman mate, Stem, er used to be a serious competition boxer, he'll sort him out quick smart.'

'Righto mate, but I'll be around the place.'

∞

'Yeah?' Anchorman picked up the receiver in a flash. He had been waiting eagerly for the last two hours.

'Only me,' replied Burra.

'Well, cobber, how did it go?'

'Ya won't believe it,' said Burra slowly. 'He reckons he's not happy with it all but he'll let it go. He says I won't hear from him again. Thank God for that.'

'Is that all?' the older man stood up, rubbed, and massaged his shoulder. The pain had eased somewhat.

'Yeah, he seemed pretty stoned but he wasn't pissed. He didn't ask for the copies of those receipts but I gave them to him anyway, tried to explain it all to him but he didn't seem interested. I expected him to threaten me but he wasn't too aggro. He did say somethin' like '*ya shoulda treated me betta, coz I did time fa you, know what I mean?*' I tried to tell him he did not do time for me coz he got done, not me, but he just babbled on about things that did not make a great deal of sense. His brain has gone west I reckon. Anyway, I'm pretty sure it got sorted out, in a way. Don't think I'll hear from him again. Hope not.'

Anchorman smiled into the phone pleased his apprentice had hosed down that festering sore. 'I guess we have to forget about the money he owes us, eh?'

'Pity, but yep. Win some, lose some. Righto mate, see you on the job, Monday.'

'Righto. See ya.'

Several months later

Burra looked black as he strapped on his nail bag, 'Bloody hell, mate, you won't believe it but the Granite rang me again last night. He just went on, and on, and on …'

'Not again, you should hang up on him before he carries on. I thought that it was all over?'

'Yeah, I know. He was blithering on about how he had to carry all that timber, and how him and his nephew dug all the holes, I mean he's cracked. Also, he said what lousy bastards we were getting that roofing dropped at the gate, and how he had to carry it all to the site. What the hell am I gunna do Anchorman?'

'Don't worry man, if he rings, hang up.'

'All right for you to say, he doesn't ring you.'

'True mate. Just try and relax. See ya at the job tomorrow, eh?'

'Rightoh.'

For the next couple of months Granite rang Burra intermittently during the week, and always on weekends and late at night. Burra could not seem to hang up on him quickly enough and he was always left with an ear full of threats. It obviously unnerved him and instead of being his usual witty self on the building site, he was subdued and depressed. Sometimes the quality of the job suffered. Anchorman had to constantly pull him up on safety issues and Burra occasionally belted his thumb with the hammer. Something he had not done for ages. Anchorman had been considering the problem and was trying to decide on a plan of action. He figured no one should be allowed to stalk people like that.

One Sunday night, when Anchorman was just about to go to bed, the phone rang. He picked it up casually, expecting it to be his daughter who said she was going to ring over the weekend. 'Yeah, g'day.'

There was silence for about ten seconds.

'Ya know who dis is? Well, I'm gunna pay you a visit, know what I mean.'

The line went dead. He slowly put the phone down in the cradle with a slightly shaking hand. He ran the other hand through his now greying hair. That night was spent without sleep, scrolling thoughts as he listened for sounds that were not there.

The next day at work Anchorman told Burra about the phone call. For the first time in ages the fair headed man laughed. He stopped abruptly.

'Sorry mate, I did not mean to laugh, it's just that I haven't seen you look like that since ya got ya foot caught in the string line.' He carried on seriously. 'My news is that I have a silent number, so that mongrel bastard can't call me when he's had a skin full.'

'That's not a bad idea, still I couldn't do that because I've got too many contacts and otherwise, it'd be a mammoth task to inform everyone of a new number.'

'I don't care; I never want to speak to that mongrel again. Er … I hope it's not going to be at the expense of you though Anchorman.' Burras' brow furrowed and a forced smile followed.

∞

Over the next six months Anchorman heard from Granite only twice, and on those occasions, he hung up quickly. Burra did not hear from him at all and things returned to normal, or as normal as could be. They concluded that the mental case only made threatening phone calls when the alcohol level pushed his mind into another realm, and they figured that he posed no real threat. So, they continued with their lives, living, and working.

One Saturday night, late, Anchorman's phone rang. It flashed through his head that it could be Granite, pissed out of his brain, so he allowed the answering machine to take the call. A panic-stricken Burra came on the line. 'Hey! Norm if you're there pick up, please …' He never called him Norm.

'Yeah mate; it's me, what's cookin'?'

'Crikey mate, I just got a real bad call from Granite. Hhhe was really spewin.' Reckons he's gunna shoot me dog! No fooling this time he reckons. I tell ya, mate he sounded the worst I've ever heard.

Trouble was he got the missus first and threatened her, said I thought I could hide my phone number but he had ways of getting it, he wasn't stupid. Told her he's been watching her. He must have been too 'coz he said he saw her walking to her car after tennis the other night. Said he liked her white dress with blue stripes … that's what she was wearin'. Bugger me mate, I dunno what to do.'

'Bloody hell. Listen, why don't you come round tomorrow, we'll have a beer and talk about it, eh?'

'Yeah, I'll probably be around about six a.m. coz I won't be sleepin' very much, that's dead set.'

'Don't worry mate. He's too gutless to do anything.' He spoke with more conviction than he felt. 'See ya in the mornin', whenever ya get here, eh?'

'All right mate see ya'

Anchorman put the phone down and stood in the dark for several minutes.

∞

Burra arrived in a cloud of dust and was almost out of the car before it stopped. He stumbled up to the front of the house and took the steps two at a time.

'How's it goin', mate?' Anchorman was as cheerful as he could be.

'Not real flash mate. This thing is drivin' me crazy. I don't know who gave the lousy mongrel my phone number, not that that matters anymore. Havin' a go at me is a pain in the arse, but havin' a go at the missus, well that's well and truly over the fence.'

'Yeah, I know what ya mean. What you need, mate is a smoke.'

'Like hell, if I had a smoke, I'd be too paranoid to do anything.' Burra was pale and he looked nervously everywhere.

Anchorman just looked at him. Things had to be bad for Burra to turn down a smoke. 'Look Burra, leave it to me, I'll ring the idiot dickhead and try to … to … sort something out. Don't know what though. Anyway, have a beer?'

'Bloody oath mate, got a tankard of the crinkly Beenleigh-bottle of rum to wash it down with?'

Anchorman smiled, appreciating Burra's attempt at humour. They had a few drinks and the morning wore on. Burra told him his wife was going down to the Gold Coast for a week to visit her mother and get away from the tension that Granite was creating. It was a bit of a relief for him to get rid of her. He felt she was a bit crook on him because she blamed him for being involved with Granite in the first place.

Eventually Burra went home and Anchorman was left pondering the situation.

That afternoon his daughter came out to visit because she was going to Sydney for a few weeks that evening. A dreamy girl, feeling at home as if she had never left, she threw herself down into a chair and smiled at her father, 'Hey Dad, something strange happened to me this morning.'

Anchorman was working on some plans at the kitchen table, only half listening to her.

'Well, do you want to hear, or not?' she questioned good naturedly.

'Mmm ... what? Oh, sorry Liz.'

'When I was at the shopping centre, this sort of out of it looking bloke came up to me and said, 'Hey beautiful, I've got my eyes on you. Frightened me a bit, out of the blue, someone comes up to you and, you know ... Fortunately Alex arrived and this creep took off.'

Anchorman clicked wide awake. 'What did this bloke look like?'

'Umm, he was pretty solid, had real red eyes. Er, he said something about doin' time for someone, sounded like a Pom. Said *'know what I mean'* a couple of times. Bloody mad man. Why? Why do you ask, do you know him?'

'No, can't say I do. Sounds like a down and outer, drunk, junky. You've got to be careful these days, promise me you'll be careful.'

They both laughed because he used to say that to her when she was younger and on her way out with some bloke or other.

'Of course, dad, you know I'm always careful,' she said, love laced with humour.

Later, when she prepared to leave, he insisted on going to town and driving her and her boyfriend, Alex, to the airport. She said it was not necessary but decided that her old man was just trying to be nice and she did not relate it to the earlier conversation.

When he arrived home that night the house was in darkness. Normally that did not bother him in the slightest but it did on this night. He had a piece of water pipe in his hand as he opened the door. He thought he knew that Granite would not have the guts to attack him. But there were doubts, deep down. He saw Granite as a gutless stalker who got thrills out of ringing people. But still ...

The coast was clear, and he grabbed a beer and sat on the verandah. He did not turn a light on, just sat in the dark wondering what the hell he was going to do. He was certainly not going to let some rotten low life mongrel bring him down, no way in the world. Very late, just as he was about to go to bed, the phone rang. It did not startle him. He knew it was Granite, he could feel it, sugar ants crawling up his spine.

'Good timin',' he whispered, as good a time as ever to talk to the stalker. He allowed it to ring a few times, a bead of sweat formed on his forehead.

'Hello?' he said into the mouthpiece.

There was silence for a few seconds.

'Know who this is?' said the familiar voice.

'I remember you. What's goin' on?'

'Oh, nothing's going on, aw-wight? Me an' your lovely daughter are going out to the forest ... and only one of us is coming back. Know what I mean?'

'Look, er Larry, what the hell is this all about, we need to talk...' The line went dead.

Anchorman put the phone down with a trembling hand. His right shoulder ached like mad. He now knew what had to be done.

∞

The next day he arrived at the job site early and was quietly working away setting up profiles when Burra arrived in a cloud of dust. This was unusual for him because he was always late, only a minute or two, but always late. It was almost as if he had to make a statement of that fact.

'Hey Anchorman, that bastard shot me dog! Dudley ... dead ... bastard shot him ... dead!'

'Oh no, crikey mate, that's the pits. I'm sorry. Old Dudley was a good little feller. I'm really sorry mate.'

'Not as sorry as that bloody Granite's gunna be!' Burra had tears of anger in his eyes. I'm gunna kill the bastard!'

'How do you know it was him?'

'Well, the half-wit rang me up real early this mornin', must have been about five thirty, and said 'I did time fa you, now it's time for you to pay me. Know what I mean? Hope you tied your dog up.' Then he hung up. Rotten bastard.'

'Listen mate, leave it to me, I'll see what I can do.'

It did not sound too convincing because Burra turned and said, in a shaky voice. 'That's what ya said yesterday and look what's happened now. What did ya do, antagonise him?'

'I spoke to him but he did not respond like I thought he would.' said Anchorman scratching his ear.

'That's because he's sick in the scone, I'm goin' to see the cops, right now! I don't care if he dobs me in for that dope, or the building approval. Right now, I don't give a rat's arse.'

'Take it easy, mate. Look why don't you head off down the Goldie and have a week with ya missus. I promise I'll sort it out.'

Burra sat down and covered his pale face with his hands. His fair hair was hanging everywhere and he looked a defeated man. Neither of them said anything for several minutes.

Burra glanced up and broke the silence. 'What can you do?'

Anchorman spoke more harshly than he had intended. 'Listen mate, do as I tell ya, go on holidays, *now*, grab ya stuff and go!'

This was the first time in a long time that he had used his rank of age. He realised he had pushed it pretty hard and his voice softened, 'Listen mate, leave it to me, alright? Look, I did not mean to yell at ya, alright? Trust me.'

'Yeah, maybe a few days off would be the go. What about my property? What about you?'

'I'll sort it out. Just go, mate, things'll work out alright ... you'll see.'

Burra moved towards his car. 'See ya next weekend, take precautions mate, that Granite is a mental case.'

'Yeah, no worries, have a good time and don't worry, all right?'

Four days later.

Burra hammered into the driveway in a cloud of dust and flying gravel. Had he not been in such a hurry he would have noticed a Toyota Landcruiser parked down the side of the house.

'Couldn't stop meself driving back today. Hey did ya see this?' he yelled and held up a newspaper to Anchorman who was sitting on the verandah. Burra leapt up the stairs two at a time.

Anchorman nodded; his expression cool. 'Yeah mate, I've seen it, there is a God after all. The miserable low life offed himself, saved the world a few problems, eh?'

Burra said, 'I have to read it aloud, yet again mate I'm so excited.'

FIREARM INCIDENT

Mr Larry Taylor was found dead after the firearm he was cleaning apparently discharged. Neighbours said that he was an alcoholic and often went on drinking binges. He was known to discharge firearms on his property. Although there were no suspicious circumstances, SGT. Jim Crocker said that this highlighted the need for tighter control of firearms. 'It is tragically obvious that this person should not have been allowed to own a firearm. He would be alive today if ...'

Burra's voice trailed off.

Anchorman's eyebrows showed concern. He spoke in a measured voice. 'Yeah ... I couldn't get him on the phone. Now we know why.' He stood up and strolled over to the fridge, negating having to look at his mate. 'Time to celebrate, what do ya reckon?'

'I never thought I would ever be happy about the death of anybody, but, mate, I tell ya what, this goes bloody close.'

Just then a door closed in another part of the house. Burra looked up. A moment later a squat, swarthy man with a pronounced limp came towards them.

Anchorman turned, 'Hey Burra, I'd like ya to meet an old mate of mine. Burra, this is Howie Howard, my old sergeant from 'Nam days.'

Peter Howard thrust out a heavily tattooed right arm and they shook hands firmly.

The End

Sometimes a down

Can turn into an up -

Grab the moment

Tea Towel

'**B**ugger.'

Road closed. The creek, now a river, was up after two days of rain. It took a while for the water to come down from the ranges. He had crossed the creek earlier that morning in heavy rain and only just made it. Now he had no show.

There was just enough room to creep the car around the warning sign on the crest and he stopped a couple of metres above the raging creek now turned river.

'Bugger,' he repeated as drifting tree trunks and islands of hyacinth jostled for position in the swirling torrent. He sat for a moment and lit a cigarette, allowing himself to be mesmerised by the wipers. The drizzle stopped and he stepped out of the car, leant on the bonnet, and stood listening. The water continued to swish and gently roar in its own league above the day creatures who seemed to be slowly conceding their noises over to the crickets, frogs, and night birds.

Campbell knew his life was a mess and there did not seem to be any *ups* anymore. Jackie left him, or more correctly, she had made *him* leave, said she did not love him anymore. He now lived in an old shed with no power on a pineapple and banana acreage nearby. The bloody bitch kept the car, a brand new 1974 Holden LH Torana that he was paying off. The car was in *his* name, because it was *his* car, wasn't it? She could not get work at the moment but needed the car to go to work when she got a job, so she said. Sure. Campbell knew he should have stood up to her.

He was now owner of an old rusty fish shop Falcon, that a mate had given him for a week's work, and a string of debts. At least he had a job, not much of a job but still a job. He had to. There she was, in an almost new house - he was paying that off too. And she had withdrawn all their savings saying she had bills to pay but would put the money back when they sorted out the assets. Sure. Campbell thought about the pay packet in his pocket knowing it would not last long. He lit another cigarette. Why did he smoke so much?

The worst thing was, he had gone guarantor for her beer-sodden, golden-haired brother to buy a car and he had smashed it up and then he pissed off. Campbell found out later that the bastard had not bothered to insure the car. *He* was paying that off, too.

He looked out into the middle of the torrent, wondering what it would be like if he just walked down the slippery bitumen, and just kept walking and let the water take him. Campbell shook his head and absentmindedly observed a huge log jam itself against the bank creating a neat little shoulder; a right hander. It reminded him of surfing at Double Island Point. An idea flashed. Things became urgent as quickly as the thought.

He moved back to the cab, grabbed a few clothes fresh from the laundromat and stuffed them into a crew bag. He then reversed the car up the rise near the sign. The engine idled and smoky exhaust hung in the damp air. The mossies and buzzing insects increased their tinnitus.

Campbell quickly strode up to the top and looked about. Almost dark, no one around.

Back at the car, he grabbed a tea towel from the washing basket and draped it around the steering wheel and the brake pedal. A very loose twirl, like how the cowboys in the Westerns tied up their horses to the hitching rail. He grabbed his hat, raincoat and bag and placed them on the ground nearby. He then removed the bulk of the money from his wallet, leaving only his license, and threw it onto the passenger's seat. Campbell broke off a thin green twiggy branch and jammed it delicately between the accelerator and the underside of the dash. The instant screaming of the engine frightened him for a second or two and he swallowed a couple of times to settle his nerves. It took several random pokes with a stick to depress the button on the drive lever but he eventually got it. He leapt clear as the wheels spun and the car propelled forward. It quickly gathered speed and skidded slightly to the left. His heart jumped, thinking the tea towel would not hold.

Everything happened so quickly and the rusty old vehicle launched itself with a massive whoosh into the boiling floodwaters. He did not have time to close the door and he watched the interior light fizz out as the vehicle performed a graceful slow motion body roll. He stood shaking as the vehicle was swallowed by the river.

Just then, lacy drizzle began again so he put on the raincoat and hat. He grabbed the bag and walked up the slope past the sign. It was almost dark, but he knew the way.

Campbell thought about a bloke called Nigel whose young gung-ho son he had rescued from the surf at Double Island Point about a year ago. Nigel wanted to give him money. Campbell was embarrassed and declined. Nigel had said, 'Any time mate, I owe ya, anything you need, anytime, alright? Just give me a ring.' Campbell had a phone number. He patted his back pocket, where his pay packet sat comfortably.

Nambour was only an hour or so away on foot and it was a dark, rainy night. Pulling down his hat he felt confident he would not be recognized as he boarded the last train to Brisbane. He was not missing yet, was he?

Campbell wondered what he would call himself from now on in Geraldton, Western Australia. He smiled for the first time in many months. Now he felt confident that he was on an upper.

The End

Our lives are not one way -

There are other directions

In a parallel universe

Parallel

'You can't keep moping around like this,' he said. 'Snap out of it!'

Bugger you, she thought. *You have no idea what it's like to lose a baby.*

'It's just as much a trauma for me, you know,' he growled. His body filled the doorway, right foot slightly forward, bald shiny head bowed like a bull ready to charge. He turned quickly and stormed out.

Crystal heard the screen door slam. She was glad Milo had gone out. *You bastard, stay out. I don't care if I never see you again.* She sat at the kitchen table, a small, frightened animal, looking and not seeing two magpies picking grubs off the lawn as they warbled to each other. Silent tears leaked down her face. She sniffed. A miscarriage. How could the prospect of new life end in such a hole? No way would she go through that again. *He blames me. My fault! How could it be my fault? Says I'm too small, should have put more weight on, should have eaten more, should have had more exercise, blah blah blah.*

Crystal dabbed her face and tied her blond hair back with the blue ribbon. 'I'm going out shopping,' she sniffed in the direction of the dog, grabbing a bag off the bench.

Fortunately, by seconds she avoided parking rage in the shopping centre car park. A sideways baseball-cap shape in a lowered Falcon tried to muscle her out of the spot she was half into. He gave her the finger. *Bastard!*

Prams, overtired and spoilt children fought for space with pensioners in the mall. Clatter and chatter bounced off the shiny surfaces. Whoomp whoomp pulsed from the CD and trendy fashion shops.

Why did I come here? Crystal felt she was floating on a cloud, a very dark cloud. Ever since ... the baby ... her world was another space. Nothing could be more real than almost being a mother, then not. Tears threatened again. She was jolted into reality by a toddler walking straight into her.

'Watch where ya going!' barked a battler of a breeding sow, pushing a shopping trolley loaded with white bread and fizzy drinks.

Crystal did not know if it was her or the child the woman was talking to. She wandered into a big department store to the lure of elevator music. It was not quite so crowded because the *home brand* people could not afford to shop there. She was not sure if the music was depressing or not. The jewellery section sparkled in front of her, diamonds, and glass: silver, gold, and shiny alloys. The watches caught her eye, there on the counter, right in front. She picked up a Seiko, delicate and intricate, beautiful. She palmed it ... dropped it into her bag and ambled away.

Then she stopped and heard herself saying, 'What am I doing!' *Did anyone hear me?*

A heavy hand gripped her shoulder. 'I think you'd better come with me.'

A young man in uniform with tattooed arms and a meaty nose, frowned at her. Other shoppers and staff stared, nudged each other whispering.

'I'll handle this, Brunella,' he said to an older female attendant plastered in makeup, who glared at her.

Crystal was crab-walked to the back of the store and pushed into a cramped, sweaty office.

'There, sit!' He towered above her and folded his weight-lifter's arms below a tag on his shirt pocket, *Roy – Security*. 'Right, hand it over.'

She did not say anything to him, just herself. *What the hell am I doing?* She pulled out the watch.

He snatched it. 'You're in serious trouble you stupid bitch. You'll cop a heavy fine or go to jail for this.'

'But … I … I didn't mean …' Tears erupted and poured down her cheeks.

'The waterworks aren't going to earn you any sympathy from anyone.' He looked thoughtful and stroked his chin. 'I can offer you a way out.'

'Way out?'

'Yep. You're not a bad looking sheila, bit skinny,' he sneered, confident of his position. 'Get your pants off, alright? We'll do it on the desk, and then I'll forget about your misdemeanour. I'll lock the door and no one will be the wiser. How does that grab ya, eh, gal?'

Five minutes later she walked out of the department store. Crystal heard her baby call from the bridge. She was on that cloud again, floating in a parallel universe as she made her way along the pedestrian path to the middle of the bridge. Cars whooshed past and dishevelled her dress and hair.

Crystal, free at last, jumped into the muddy Brisbane River.

Or in a parallel universe …

Story two

'You can't keep moping around like this, honey,' he said. 'You're going to have to snap out of it!'

Bugger you, she thought. *You have no idea what it's like to lose a baby.*

'I know it's a trauma for you. I'm not exactly over the moon about it, right? Stop blaming yourself, that's not doing you any good. It just happened, alright?' Milo stood still, large frame blocking the light, right foot slightly forward, bald shiny head bowed like a bull ready to charge. He threw his hands up in the air and shook his head. 'I just don't know how to help!' He sighed, slapped his thighs lightly and walked away. 'I've got to go to work.'

She was glad Milo had gone. The screen door clicked. She sat at the kitchen table, a small frightened animal, looking and not seeing two magpies picking grubs off the lawn as they warbled to each other. Silent tears leaked down her face. She sobbed and sniffed. A miscarriage. How could the prospect of new life end in such a hole? No way would she go through that again. *He's been good about it but I know he blames me; I know he does. My fault! He says it isn't my fault.*

I'm too small, should have put more weight on, should have eaten more and should have had more exercise. Should have done a lot.

Crystal dabbed her face and tied her blond hair back with the blue ribbon. 'I'm going out shopping,' she sniffed in the direction of the dog, as she grabbed a bag off the bench.

Fortunately, by seconds she avoided parking rage in the shopping centre car park. A sideways baseball cap in a lowered Falcon tried to muscle her out of the spot she was half into. He gave her the finger. *Bastard!*

Prams, overtired and spoilt children fought for space with pensioners in the mall. Clatter and chatter bounced off the shiny surfaces. Whoomp whoomp pulsed from the CD and trendy fashion shops.

Why did I come here? Crystal felt she was floating on a cloud, a very dark cloud. Ever since ... the baby ... her world was another space. Nothing could be more real than almost being a mother, then not. Tears threatened again. She was jolted into reality by a toddler walking straight into her.

'Watch where ya going!' barked a battler of a breeding sow pushing a shopping trolley loaded with white bread, fizzy drinks and a squealing, smelly, nappy clad babe in the front. For a second Crystal did not know if it was her or the child the woman was talking to.

'I didn't mean you, eh,' she said almost as aggressively. 'Little Duane's been a prick all day. Never should 'ave brought the bugger, runs everywhere, got ADHCC or sumpthink, eh.'

Crystal had to get away, so she headed into a big department store to the lure of elevator music. It was not quite so crowded because the *homebrand* people could not afford to shop there. She wasn't sure if the music was depressing or not, it was so clean with glossy polished tiles and lights, white tinkle everywhere. The jewellery section sparkled in front of her, diamonds and glass: silver, gold and shiny alloys. The watches caught her eye, there on the counter, right in front. She picked up a Seiko, delicate and intricate, beautiful. She palmed it ... and almost dropped it into her bag.

She heard herself saying, 'What am I doing!' *Did anyone see me?* Tears erupted.

A gentle hand touched her shoulder. 'Are you okay, love?' Through the veil of grief, she registered a badge, *Brunella* an older woman, head tilted to one side. 'There, there, everything's going to be alright. Come with me.' She turned to a security guard with a big nose and gently said, 'I'll handle this, Roy.'

Crystal could smell her make-up. Other shoppers and staff stared, nudged each other, frowned, and whispered. She was led out the back and into a space, tables and chairs, a deserted lunchroom.

'Sit down, dear. I'll make us a cup of tea.'

Crystal began sobbing and blurted out the sorry story of her darkness.

The older woman gave her a soft dry tea towel. 'You need support at a time like this, dear. Same thing happened to me. A long time ago. I lost a baby too, you know. You can never forget; you cannot allow yourself to forget but you have to move on. It's the way life is, whether there is a God or not.' She put her warm hands on either side of Crystal's face, 'We are given gifts but precious things are taken away as well. You'll be alright, love, you'll see.' Brunella kissed her forehead. 'Now, about that cuppa, milk and sugar?'

Half hour later she walked out of the mall on a different cloud into a brighter world, another parallel.

'Ah! Crystal!' he yelled. 'I hoped I'd catch you here, saw your car.' Milo spread his arms wide. 'Honey, I just couldn't leave things the way they were when I walked out this morning. We are in this together.'

She walked into his arms.

or ...

As she walked towards him, a car veered out of control and hit her. The driver, an old man, had a heart attack. Crystal was free at last.

or

They quickly walked towards each other. The lout with the sideways cap was fiddling with the car stereo, not paying attention, and accelerated into them.

or

As Milo hurried over, the sow was leaning into the backseat trying to discipline Duane and his sister, and accidently hit the accelerator. The rusty Datsun ploughed into Milo at speed …

Life goes on, or not, doesn't it?

The End

Picture Imperfect

Marlene and me. That's me, Sharon on the right, the one with the flowers crocheted on my top. The two of us, that's all it ever was from as early in my life as I can remember. The photo tells it all, doesn't it, two happy young sheilas at the most exciting stage of their lives?

I remember exactly the time and place that photograph was taken. The Kenilworth Rural Show, in the arvo of September the second, 1976. We'd just come back from having a few drinks at the pub tent with Jack and Dave. My boyfriend Jack had a mate of his from Darwin staying with him and I suggested he drag him along to the show, you know, to make a foursome.

Marlene for some reason didn't have many blokes in her life; I was always the one with boyfriends. It never seemed to worry her, not having a bloke to knock about with. I even had my first sexual thingo ages before she did. Brian King was his name. It was very clumsy, and both of us were embarrassed. I remember telling Marls about it all and she laughed saying she'd pick her bloke and pick her time.

That first time came, and afterwards she agreed with me that doing *it*, at least the first time anyway, wasn't all it was cracked up to be. In fact, she said she hadn't done it since.

Anyway, I keep the photo alongside my bed, a reminder of happy days and also as a reminder of how quickly things can change. A week later, Marlene disappeared.

Nothing was discovered for several months and one day someone found something. Some children playing at Charlie Moreland Park found a suspicious mound of dirt disturbed by dingoes.

The bodies were identified as Marlene and Jack. I cried and carried on for ages, everyone could see I was distraught.

The buzzer resonated through the bars and cold concrete.

The warder yelled, 'Lights out in five minutes.'

I now have plenty of time to reflect on what I did.

The End

Being a martyr

Has its drawbacks -

It pays to keep an eye on things

Multi-tasking

'Pardon?' said Wally.

Natalie continued as she picked up toys. 'Why don't you listen to me? Are the dishes in the dishwasher clean?'

Silence

'Well? *Hell-oh*, come in, over!' She opened the dishwasher and switched it on. 'It's alright, stop worrying, I figured it out for myself.'

Wally looked up; eyebrows pinched. 'Aaaaah, yeah, what? Sorry, I was just trying to decipher this computer, I mean the people who design these bloody things, I don't know …'

'That's the trouble with you blokes, you can only do one thing at a time … and that's not very well,' the added extra thrown in to crank up even more attention.

'Alright, alright,' offered Wally, forced to stop what he was doing. 'Might I be so brave as to suggest that you are wrong about that. But you may very well be correct about being able to do only one thing at a time, blokes I mean. And by that, I mean one thing properly.'

'Ever since I got up, I have tended to Bubs … and that takes a fair bit of doing, right? Then I sorted clothes, did the washing, watched the TV, made breakfast, read the paper, and did …'

Wally made waving actions with his hand. 'Sure, ya did, but how many of those things did you do properly, Eh? Do you want me to remind you of your record last week?'

'What?'

The baby started crying.

'For starters, I bet you put on Bub's nappy with the safety pin digging into her skin again. Do you want to look at the dyslexic effort you made with the crossword? And my drawer had some of your underwear in it, I had to go to your drawer to get mine.'

That must have created the tiniest element of doubt about the safety pin because Natalie zipped over and picked up the baby who had been rolling around on the carpet.

She said, 'I'm late, some of us have to go out.'

'And ten bob to a pinch of you know what, you probably forgot to put detergent in the ... still, I'll fix that up for you later when I go to unload the thing and find the dishes dirty, like last ...'

'Stop! Why do you have to be so, so critical of me?'

Wally put his hand up in a stop sign. 'You started it.'

Natalie picked up Bubs and placed her gently in the pram. 'See you later, Mister Bloody Perfect.'

Wally chuckled, noting how hot she looked in black, skin-tight leotards with her straw-coloured ponytail sticking out the back of her American, baseball cap.

Outside, Natalie sighed, fitted her earpieces, and jogged off, smiling at Bubs. By the time she arrived at New Farm Park, Bubs was asleep. She rang Katie and then stopped, gave the pram a gentle rock and began her stretches as she talked to her friend.

She heard someone yell.

Her first thought as she looked up, '*My baby!*'

Twenty metres away, the pram wobbled, slowly at first and quickly gaining speed, it tumbled over the edge into the murky Brisbane River.

The End

Some sins

Are worse than others -

Be careful

The One

That very first time his spine tingled. The way she held herself. His heart pounded and his insides went to junket. Her smooth curves; clothes could not hide how beautiful she was. People looked at her.

The club encouraged expensive clothes and displays of wealth. Very much the private school set, knowing someone and having big dollars ruled membership. Even applying for an anchor point one had to have recommendations from the big end of town. Most tables had ego displays - bunches of keys with tags. Jag, BMW, Merc.

Jason was with a friend, John, whose father was high up in Western Global. John's girlfriend Kirsty was with them.

Then, *she* walked in; he could not help notice other blokes track her across the room. Jason was drawn to the effect she had. Instantly alert females speared glares at their men.

The young woman walked across the long deck; half-moon shapes of lower bottom escaped her perfect undersize denim shorts. In the smooth, tanned, exposed mid-riff, a stud glinted. Bringing it all together a white shirt was knotted casually, showing just enough chest higher up. A light silver chain around a graceful neck caught diamonds of light shimmering off the water. High heels and legs! Hell, she had beautiful legs. He had never seen such a stunning combination. She walked up to them.

Kirsty looked up. 'Hi Jody, great to see you.'

John smiled, 'How's it going.' Then he nodded, 'By the way, this is a mate of mine, Jason.'

He stood, or more correctly, stumbled up, if that was possible.

She put out her hand. 'Hi Jason,' and smiled, turned to Kirsty, a dark ponytail swished. 'Sorry I'm late, road works.' She pouted and looked at him again. Can't believe how much road works are going on these days.'

He sat down in a measured way to make sure he did not miss the seat. Could not believe it, the most beautiful thing he had ever seen, at his table. Kirsty had said she was going to bring a mate, but ...

It was an awkward night for him. Every time she looked at him, he felt weak. Fortunately for him, the girls chatted, they were friends. At the end of the night, she stuck her hand out and they shook. Her hand was warm and her eyes willed him.

∞

A week later, he could stand it no longer, she was the one. He flipped open his phone and pressed.

'Hi, Jody speaking.'

'Jody? It's me er ... Jason. Jason.'

'I know who you are.' The voice was smooth and dreamy. 'What took you so long to ring me?'

He searched for an answer. 'I ... I've been quite busy; you know how things are.' More confidence.

'Yeah, it's been a bit that way for me too. What can I do for ...'

He blurted, hoping it was not too quick. 'Hey, wanna go out one night, Saturday night?'

The response was measured. 'Yeah, why not. Where to?'

∞

They went to a pub and the noise defused the tenseness. Jason was still floating with the whole idea of her being there alongside him. They both drank a little too much and he took the risk of driving even though he was over the limit. They sat in the car in front of her place but he could not remember what they talked about. An hour later she said it was time to go in because of the working day ahead. She placed a honey warm lingering kiss on his lips. He was too overwhelmed to do anything more than return the pressure of her beautiful lips. He knew she was the one.

The first few times they went out to restaurants and pubs. Several weeks later she invited him in to her place. They had sex like he had never experienced. He was so shell shocked that someone so incredibly beautiful could be interested in him. Then he got it. She was as infatuated with him as he was with her. He quickly began to see it as one of those things that are simply meant to be. They were made for each other.

∞

Familiarity carried him along on a cloud until two months later when something did not seem right. They were together at dinner; she kept looking at another table, two men and a woman. A couple of nights later, at her place the phone rang. She was in the shower; he answered the call, they hung up.

Another night out when they were with John and Kirsty, she took several calls on her mobile, tried to sound noncommittal, talking business at 9.30 at night? *Guilty eyes?* The cruncher came late Saturday afternoon. He rang her.

She seemed distant, 'Look Jace,' her voice was dreamy, 'I'm a bit tired. How about in a day or two? I've had a big week.' She finished with a sigh.

Jason had thought it all through; he did not want to give any more away than her. 'Yeah, right, we'll get together soon, eh?' He tried to sound normal. The phone was moist in his hand. The click at the other end had monumental meaning for both of them.

∞

He stood behind the lillypilly hedge; there was a gap between the curtains and the soft lighting was just good enough. He could see her clear silhouette. She laughed and paraded around the room. She discarded her negligee like a stripper. The bloke in the picture gently pushed her back on to the bed. He was starkers too.

Jason's head boiled. He had to see her, talk to her; surely, there was some sort of mistake. She was the one he loved. He had chosen her, after all she had walked up to him in a room full of people. *She had fucking-well-chosen him as well. You can't just forget about that! No, you can't just forget about that.*

'Hi Jody, it's me, I'd really like to see you, can I pick you up from work ... today?'

'What? Umm, well I ... yeah, sure, I suppose ...'

'What time?'

They arrived at the botanical gardens, just before dark.

'Let's go for a walk, I need to talk to you.'

She replied, 'Umm ... could we talk here?'

Clearly, she had things to say to him too.

'I need to stroll, just a walk, we do need to talk.'

'Yeah, okay.' She flicked her pony tail.

From a distance, this young couple could just be observed, tangled in an apparent embrace, at the edge of the tropical forest section. A lover's pash, a smooch-up.

But there, in that huddle, she finally realised what true love can mean to someone.

His fingers tightened around her throat. So quick, her shock escalated, no chance to struggle, she could not scream. He glared not really seeing her. The intensity melted but the anger in his face was crimson. He looked through her and slowly crushed out her life.

The End

Some people dodge bullets

Others walk into the line of sight -

There is no way of knowing

Up Ahead

The elderly man shuffled towards Fiona. Main Western Line, the 6.09a.m. train from Mount Victoria to Sydney was packed, and few seats remained in any of the carriages. The doors whooshed and the jerk of the train nudged him into the seat alongside her. He did not appear to acknowledge her as he wriggled and placed the briefcase on his knees, knocking her in the process.

Fiona was boxed in, but still, what did she expect? She should have stood up earlier and then slipped into a seat in the aisle. The old man sniffed a couple of times. He smelled like wet dog. *Pig she thought, use your bloody hankie.*

He fidgeted with something in his top pocket, and finally pulled out a pen. The next station was announced over the loudspeakers.

More commuters crammed in; all the seats were taken. The train jerked away, clickety clack, past level crossings, cars lined up, boom gates and flashing lights. Fiona looked out the smoky glass window at weeds and rusting steel, old car bodies, broken wire fences, grubby block walls, piles of junk in properties, ripping past like a black and white 16mm movie.

The man sniffed again. *Bad breath. Disgusting.* He opened the briefcase and rummaged around. *Bloody old bastard, keep still, will you?*

He pulled out a piece of paper from a plastic bag. None of her business but he almost made it so. She stole a glance. *Plastic bag. Ah, money.* She could not help noticing a wad of big notes – the colour of fifties and hundreds. He closed the briefcase.

Next stop announced and the train concertinas to a halt. More sardines into the tin. Whoosh and clunk. Train accelerated, swaying, less graceful than a waltz. She clocked him doing some arithmetic. He seemed satisfied and put the paper and pen in the briefcase. Click. A rich, deep sniff this time. *Bloody filthy pig.* He put the briefcase on the floor, once again knocking her. She glared; he did not register. She turned and looked out, the world still zipping by. Graffiti that could be colourful and beautiful, negated by hate and grime. *Nazi power, White Straya, Slopes in ya boat – back where you came from, Communists out.*

Fiona felt the old man's head on her shoulder. *Hang on, mate, piss off!* She shoved him upright and his head lolled back.

Next stop. Cannot fit any more into the carriage. *Wake up old man. Bugger is snoring.* Whoosh, the doors close, train on the move again, clickety clack, sway, creak, and groan. Fiona looks out again, overgrown weeds, litter, dirty walls, broken fences, piles of sleepers, railway workers pretending to be busy. *Not much longer, Fiona.* She detested the train ride, every bloody workday into Sydney. Her friend in Newcastle had been urging her to get out of the greyness, the hustle, and the crime.

Old man's head slowly rolled against her again. *Bloody hell.*

Next station announced as the train pulled into the station with a jolt. Old-timer snorts loudly and jerks awake. *His stop!* She could smell and feel his panic. He grabbed the safety rail on the seat in front and pulled himself to the doors as quickly as his arthritic legs would allow. He just got out as the doors whooshed and squeezed shut. He turned in alarm, just then realising he had left his briefcase under the seat. He clawed at the doors, but the train was all-powerful. He was nudged back by the rush of air and his pleading face tried to lock on to Fiona through the grubby window as the train accelerated. She looked through him pretending he was not there. He waved wildly and pointed as the train sped up, people on the platform with dead faces, not wishing to interfere with a madman. There were plenty of them around.

A young business-type, reeking of aftershave, sat down alongside her and opened the newspaper. She gently dragged the briefcase closer to her knees. A natural reaction, no one noticed anything. Everyone was too absorbed in their own paradigm of existence. She slid the case on to her knees and gently opened it a crack. A quick glance confirmed that Mister Business-type was too absorbed reading about when Malcolm Fraser was going to call an election for a second term. She felt around inside, eased out the plastic bag and slid it down into her shoulder bag on the other side.

How easy was that? Fiona smiled. The train rumbled on.

Fiona barely heard the mumbled announcement over the loudspeaker, 'Next stop Granville.'

Granville train disaster, January the 18th, 1977. The packed 6.09am train from Mt. Victoria to Sydney derailed and crashed into a bridge as it approached Granville station about 8.10am.

83 people died and 210 people were injured.

The End

Some people like

To push boundaries -

Everyone gets hurt

Cry Wolf

'We need to talk,' said Zoe, trying to instigate eye contact. 'What about?' grumbled Logan, pretending everything was alright.

'Let's sit down.'

He went to the kitchen and she knew he was using a delaying tactic. She pushed. 'Please, Logan, we need to talk.'

He came back and sat down opposite and took a slug of wine. He would not look at her.

Thanks for offering me one. 'I think we need some time, you know, on our own for a while.'

'What? Why?'

Zoe had practiced at home. 'Because it's not working out.' *Because we have nothing in common anymore.*

'Are you seeing someone else?' Sullen question.

'No.'

'You are a fucking liar!'

'Logan ... I'm not ...'

'I saw someone's car parked in the driveway at your place last night.'

She sat upright. 'What?'

Silence.

'Have you been spying on me again?'

Logan still could not look at her. He fixed his gaze on a spot slightly left of her head. He took a gulp of wine. 'I just happened to be in the area. You said you were going to see your mother. She hadn't seen you ... by nine o'clock anyway.'

'Logan,' she tried again, as if talking to a child. 'I didn't go to mum's but I was home all night. Did you ring my mum?'

'Whose car, was it?'

'Roslyn, Roz Jones ...'

'Who's she?' His voice had ramped up and his face became flushed.

'Logan! Stop it. She's from my yoga class, look, we need to take some time apart, I need some space.'

'You said that last time, and the time before and we always got back together.'

Zoe tried not to sigh too loudly. At that moment she wondered what in the hell she saw in him. Jealous, possessive, moody. 'I know, but you are, too ...'

'Too fucking what?' He leant forward, glared at her, and downed the rest of his wine.

'Too smothering, Logan, I don't seem to have a life for myself, you are always ... um ringing me, checking up on me, wanting to get mar... I just need some time, that's all.' *Don't back down, Zoe.*

Logan started sobbing. 'I'm going to kill myself!'

'Logan,' her voice softened, 'You won't, everything will turn out alright, you'll see, it's just, we need to take a bit of time off.' *Don't say it, Zoe, don't say it.* 'Please Logan, just a ... just a few days.' She stood up. *You shouldn't have pleaded, Zoe.*

'I *will* do it this time; I can't bear to be without you.' He grabbed her shoulders, 'I mean it, I'm going to ...'

She screeched, 'Stop it!' Zoe shook herself free, grabbed her shoulder bag and hurried to the lifts.

She ran out of the building and crossed the road. A massive thump from behind jolted her. She felt a vacuum of freefall in her soul as she turned.

Someone screamed, 'He jumped ...'

Someone else pointed, 'From up there ...'

Zoe put a shaking hand across her face. A melee had gathered around a body on the footpath.

The End

Karma

Sometimes works in this lifetime -

Sometimes not

Work Exchange

The barrow hovered. A wet mix crept to one side like lava. Billy had no choice but to watch it all. His hands were full so he stuck a foot out. At the same time the shovel, which had initially stood upright, slowly fell, and nudged the top rock almost off its balance point.

All in slow motion. One hand fended off a precarious wall and the other arm to wedge the spirit level against the rock in limbo. Skin and bone, Billy Henderson, spread-eagled, the whole show slowly slipping in micro seconds. It was impossible to do anything but to watch it all. He took a drag on his soggy rollie. That kicked off the cough, he could not help it. Then everything collapsed around and on top of him. Concrete, rocks, barrow, and tools in a dishevelled heap with Billy on the bottom.

'Bugger me senseless!' he screeched with a frantic edge as the feature rock teetered and landed on his knee. It then rolled on to his foot. That last action toppled a bucket of freezing cold water, with rags and scrubbing brushes, onto his mid-section.

'Shit a fuckin' brick! Shit – a – fucking – brick. There's got to be an easier way to do this,' growled Billy as he dragged himself clear.

He stooped, massaged his knee, not being game to inspect his big toe. The catastrophe decorated the area. Overturned barrow, dented brand new spirit level, mortar everywhere and a badly damaged rock wall.

'Fuck this,' he spat, turned, and headed for the house to roll a joint. Plenty to think about, trying to build a rock wall by himself and poorly planned was idiotic. The evidence screamed it out but he was not keen on admitting it. If he had not had that joint before starting the job everything may have been alright. He was prepared to go that far because the blame focused on the dope rather than him. Some strong stuff was doing the rounds these days and it was easy to get a bit bamboozled after a puff.

He wrenched off his wet shirt and pulled on a jumper. The toe began to ache more than the knee as he gently eased down in a squatter's chair on the verandah overlooking his small property. After a quick toe inspection, he rolled a joint. The first lung full brought on a cough. There are coughs and coughs, but Billy's cough was a land mark - loud, phlegmy, rich with depth that rose from deep down inside. Billy's neighbours always knew if he was home by the racking, guttural bark that bellowed through the trees. One of his neighbours, Gary Giles, a workaholic known more as a working alcoholic down the pub, was thankful for Billy's cough. He often joked it acted as a very efficient bird scaring device. Farmer Giles' favourite story credited the cough scaring parrots and crows away from his lychee trees. In the early morning, when the sun filtered through the trees and turned dew into diamonds, everyone within a kilometre could hear the cough. Vigorous throat clearing followed and then rich spitting hawks finished off the ritual.

Billy Henderson was a generally aware sort of person about most aspects of life but he was remarkably unaware about one thing. He could not and simply would not admit that his gravy rich, phlegmy cough could have anything to do with the cigarettes he had smoked every day for twenty or more years. Nor the number of joints he puffed almost as frequently.

After Billy had turned his lungs inside out and had had time to examine his injuries, he mumbled to the world again, 'There must be a better way.'

He did not have enough money to employ anyone and obviously no-one was silly enough to work for nothing. A light went on in his brain. Work exchange. In minutes it all came together like a puzzle ring.

Just as he was applying paw-paw cream to his now swollen foot, Bertrand Barrett burbled up on his Chopper. Bertrand, commonly known as B Squared, or just plain Squared, was a fearsome looking character even for a bikie. He rarely combed his hair and washed his clothes less often. Other bikies never bothered him because he was two axe handles across the shoulders. It was common knowledge around the traps that he had scooted out of New Zealand after a clash with one of the major bikie mobs. Even though he looked tough he seemed a good-natured fellow and was well liked. He did not need to act tough.

Billy had bought some dope off him about a year ago and had also seen him at the pub regularly.

'Hell's it heng'n, Hendo? Thought I'd drup in ta see if ya hed eny pot in quantity fur sale,' he mouthed, guiding his bulk into a chair. He pulled a rolled cigarette from behind his ear.

'What? You're asking me?' They both laughed. After a second or two Billy continued, 'How much were ya after, mate?'

'A pound should do ut,' smiled Squared cupping his paws and lighting the cigarette. 'Why do things by half.' Smoke billowed out.

Billy scratched behind his ear, thinking the while. 'Er, well yeah, I should be able to help you out.' Billy's head was working overtime. 'Hey, look why don't you put a smoke together, I've just had one, while I go for a walk.' He winked at the big fellow and handed over some cigarette papers plus a good-sized head.

'Sounds OK by me,' replied Squared, relaxing back in the groaning cane chair.

Billy had a couple of pounds buried in the back yard and was keen to move one of them on because it was getting near its use by date. 'Here, may as well use this to roll it on, eh,' and he gave the big Maori a Black Label Penthouse magazine. He knew that would keep the mammoth occupied whilst he dug up the dope which was buried out the back.

'Back in a mo'.' Billy stood with difficulty and nodded, 'Slight accident mate, nothin' to worry about though,' and he hobbled off the verandah heading into the bush, only to double back when out of sight. He knew he could not be too careful where dope was concerned. There was no need to worry as Squared was basically lazy and was eyes wide on the Penthouse magazine.

Billy dug up both pounds, stashed one by the back door and hobbled out on to the front verandah.

'I only get them for the articles, mate,' he said pointing to the nude woman evident on Squared's lap.

The big bikie laughed and took a hit on the joint.

'Here we are, a pretty good pound, weighs a bit more to allow for sticks and the odd seed, you know.' He gave it to the big man who dug in, loosely examined a few heads, and nodded. 'This what I'm smokin' here nowra?'

'Yep, same stuff.'

'What sort of menny are we talkin' belt, Hendo?

They discussed money, did a little haggling, and agreed on a price.

Billy had a plan. 'Here, I'll stick this in a rubbish bag,' and he hobbled quickly inside and re-appeared. 'There we are, nice and neat.' That action increased the pain Billy had to endure as his knee and foot were aching like mad. Squared peeled out the notes from down the front of his jeans. Billy was more than happy to put up with the urea aroma of the money.

'Great, want a puff on thus?' Squared handed over the joint that was nearing the end. Billy took a couple of decent tugs and then the coughing began again.

Squared seemed a little embarrassed, not sure whether to joke or say something serious about the cough. Fortunately, it eased and the big fellow took that as an opportunity to go.

'OK mate, I'm off nowra like a harlot's undies in the sun.' He stood, grabbed the bag, nodded, and ambled down to his bike.

Billy did not rise, he simply said, 'Righto mate, my knee's killing me, don't mind if I don't get up ...'

'She's right mate, take ut easy, right?'

Billy took a toke on the joint. His coughing was drowned out by the roar of the Harley Davidson heading out the driveway. He quickly returned to his earlier thoughts and decided to talk to a few other blokes he knew about forming a work cooperative, or as he would like to call it, work exchange.

∞

First on the list was a bloke called Braddo who he saw at the pub from time to time and lived not very far away. Kenneth, Braddo's dog, gave a signal bark, no real commitment but just enough to alert his master who was cleaning up the empties from the night before.

'G'day Hendo, what brings you 'round 'ere?'

'Well mate, I've got a bit of an idea about how we can all get some work done around the place. I help you; you help me sort of thing … work exchange.'

'Mmm … yeah … maybe,' stammered Braddo. He did not know Billy that well and was aware he had a bit of a reputation at the pub for disappearing when it was his round. 'When did you have in mind?'

'Well, straight away, or soon anyway.'

'Er … sorry mate. I'm working at the moment,' blurted Braddo. He made it sound as if he was disappointed. 'Yeah, I'm working full time at the moment with Tint Tyson, only have weekends off and I need that time to catch up with things around here.'

'That's too bad mate, anyway godda go, I'm on a bit of a mish, see ya!' Billy lit a smoke and headed off coughing.

Kenneth, Braddo's faithful dog growled and looked guardedly in the direction of the departing man. His ancestry allowed him to point a bit. He did not usually growl unless there was a reason.

'You don't trust him, eh?' enquired Braddoh.

Kenneth continued to look on sternly, ears up. No tail movement. He was quite happy that his *dad* had acknowledged his perceptive qualities.

∞

Billy ground out his cigarette and knocked on the door of his indirect mate Dudley Wattmore, who lived not so far away either. He hoped sincerely that Dudley's defacto, Cathy, did not answer the door as she disliked him with a passion. She was a force to be reckoned with and not just at home. Cathy was president of the local progress association and had put many people's noses out of whack by her bombastic behaviour. Fortunately for Billy, Dudley answered the door.

'Aaah, Dudders, how's it goin' mate, thought I'd drop in and see how ya gettin' on,' projected Billy smoothly.

Dudley, who was from the UK acted like a person of impeccable breeding and was not only a muso, but a founding member of the local Theatrical Society. He usually answered the door with a misquote from a play.

'Harken who visiteth upon my hearth? Oh, it's you youthful Billyald, welcome to my humble abode.'

He put his index finger to his lips, slowly leaned back and appeared to be listening to sounds in the distance. There was an almighty bang, the slamming of a car door, and within seconds their family car snaked out of the driveway, narrowly missing Billy's rust bucket. Billy's car had personality and gave off the vibe that *if you hit me, you'll regret it, 'cos I've got no insurance.*

Dudley put his hands up to his face for a couple of seconds, 'Oh well, beloved bride hath departed, alas only momentarily, but we may be gifted with a few short hours of temporary respite!' He ushered Billy inside and exclaimed. 'Cup of char?'

'Thanks mate, tea would do nicely,' declared Billy. He knew better than to say anything about Cathy, so he continued. 'Heard you were needin' the gutters replaced around the homestead 'ere mate, eh?'

Dudley stroked his beard. 'Don't know where you heard that old chum but, yes as it happens, I do have the odd thing to do around here. Er why?'

'Here, let's have a puff,' cooed Billy, pulling out a bag of dope and some papers.

'Grand, haven't had a smoke in a while. She won't let me; reckons we can't afford it. Hell, she's making my life miserable at the moment. 'Why don't you get a job, why don't you fix the gutters, why don't you take some sort of responsibility for your actions', all that tommy rot. I can't do anything right.' He poured hot water into two mugs and dropped a tea bag in each. 'Milk and sugar?'

'Bang on mate. Here, light this up.'

Billy handed over a joint and Dudley lit up.

'So, what do ya think, eh?' continued Billy. 'We get together and do a bit of work exchange? Ya know, I could give you a hand to do ya gutters, an' you could give me a hand to do a coupla things at my place.'

'Work exchange, eh? Yeah, I suppose it would be a way of getting a few things sorted around here. My sweet wife has a list a mile long. Yeah, could work out. It would be good to have someone else as well, don't you think?'

'Took the words right out of my mouth, mate. I had been thinking about that very thing on the way, three of us, would get more done that's for sure. I've got someone in mind,' said Billy.

'Who's that?'

'Good ol' Lucy.'

'Why him, he's always so damn busy,' replied Dudley, with concentrated glance.

'He'd be interested I reckon, heard him mention somethin' about a tank of his needin' cementin', or something like that, anyway.'

He had also settled on Lucy because he had a handyman business and had all the tools.

'Oh goodo. Never know Cathy might even be pleased,' offered Dudley although he was thinking that she would be as pleased as receiving a piece of dog shit in the mail. No two ways about it, she did not like Dudley to have anything to do with Billy.

'Yeah. Point out to her the advantages of being able to get things done around here. After all, you're not really a practical bloke, are you?'

'Not a practical?'

'No, sorry what I meant was you are more of an academic, sort of thing.' Billy lit up a cigarette and coughed.

'Yeah, I suppose I do have trouble working out which end of the hammer to grab.'

'But you are still able to do other sorts of things. Anyway, mind if I make a call?' Billy did not mind using other people's phones, particularly if he was ringing mobiles. He had left his in the car.

'Help yourself.'

Billy went into the kitchen, pulled out a piece of paper and dialled a number.

'Mr. Kerzac here,' came the answer.

'Hey Lucy, how ya goin'? What's with the mister bit?'

'Aaaah Hendo, ya clot. I say Mr Kerzac, sometimes Mr Lucifer Kerzac and when they hear me speak, they can't believe a bloke with a name like that can speak proper Ozzie. Also, a sheila's name like Lucy throws them a bit. Anyrate, makes me sound important. I'm pretty busy at the moment, better make it sharp. What's goin' on?'

'Ya gunna be home over the next hour?'

'Should be home in about half an hour, on a job at the mo. Anyway, what's up?'

'Me and Dudders are on our way, tell ya then. Is ya fridge full?' That was a standing joke between them because Lucy was as thrifty as Billy was tight and they always kept count as to who owed who what.

'Hey, it's your round, mate, remember? I ...'

'Just kidding Lucy, I'll pick up a couple on the way.'

'Right, see ya soon. Time's money.'

They jumped into the rust bucket, well Billy did but Dudley had to push the seat back to be able to manoeuvre his bulk into the passenger's side. They careered off in the direction of Lucy's place, via the pub. Billy figured a few beers were worth investing in such an important project.

∞

Lucy's place was a neat little cottage nestled quietly into the bush. Everything was in its place at Lucy's, especially his hair. Many said that if ever anyone had undergone extensive potty training whilst a toddler, it was him. In his life, everything had a place and everything was in its place and if it was not, Lucy would get agitated.

They pulled up at the front, alongside Lucy's prized 1956 Chevvy ute. Lucy, whose parents came from Dubrovnik in Yugoslavia, lived up to his role in life very well. The Chevvy was his prized possession. It was not pink as many of his friends thought it should be. It was black, with an iridescent yellow lightning stripe down the side and a fox-tail on the aerial. Two oversized black and white foam dice hung from the rear vision mirror. He had to sit on a cushion to see over the dashboard. His faithful, useless, lazy dog, Dogsick, was asleep in the back with his head hanging over the side. Dogsick was as useless as a dog could be. Lucy procured him at the local market to act as a deterrent to people nicking his tools, which he kept in the back. But, alas, the dog was not very good at that, as on several occasions tools had gone missing. After losing his nail-bag and hammer and then a brand-new spirit-level, a mate of Lucy's happened to mention that he saw Dogsick trotting down the main street of the local town with a level in his mouth. In Dogsick's favour was the fact that he was big and covered in scars. Although he loved humans, he loved a scrap with other dogs even more which gave him a street fighter look. His brick head sported many livid, pinkie-white, meaty scars.

Lucy came bounding out of the house. 'How's it garn, fellas, where's the bush fire?'

'No rush mate, just thought we'd pop over for a chat, and a beer of course. Here,' offered Billy sticking a stubby in Lucy's hand.

'Cheers,' said Lucy and had a swig. 'Now what's it all about, Alfy? You don't go around chucking beers out and about for no reason, now do ya?'

'Well, I came up with a good idea, we all need to get things done around our places, you know, working together, sort of work exchange, you know.'

'If I did know I wouldn't of arkst, would I? Work exchange?'

Dudley butted in, realizing that Billy hadn't explained things very well. 'Well Lucy, we all have things that need doing and if we all go to each other's places we can get heaps done, we help you, you help us.'

'Work exchange. Mmm. Correct me if I'm wrong, but it'd be even money we go to your place first. Right? Then when we come to my place you aren't available. Right?' Lucy smoothed back his already immaculate black hair and pulled his earlobe.

'Naaah,' countered Billy quickly. 'No, that's not it, we haven't even talked about it. I'd be happy to do something here first if you don't trust us.' He used the plural us because Dudley had a reputation for being reliable, even if he was not. Look it all depends on who's got what to do. You mentioned the other day that you had a tank that needs cementing, Dudders has some guttering and downpipes to fix and I'm doing a rock wall. Nearly finished but I guess I could use a bit of a hand. What do ya reckon?'

'Mmm. Yeah, ya might have something there,' said Lucy in measured words and pulled his ear again, which was a nervous habit he had but he would have been devastated if he had been aware of doing it. 'I priced a new tank. Bloody expensive but, got a shock! Anyway, I'm pretty busy workwise at the moment tho' fellas, time's money.'

Just at that second the mobile phone on his hip began an intrusion on their most important conference.

'Well answer the bloody thing,' suggested Billy, 'then we can draw some mud maps.'

Lucy, who was a carpenter by trade was always rushing around. He never seemed to stay in one spot very long. He had the phone call out of the way quickly. The others witnessed a couple of 'Rightos, yep and mmm's and then he dismissed the caller with a curt, 'OK see ya' at the end, time being money.

Billy was keen to get down to it. 'So, are you in?' he addressed Lucy.

Lucy took a moment to answer. 'Mmmm, maybe.'

Billy could see that Lucy was sceptical. 'Why don't we toss for who goes first?'

'Nah, she's right, no need,' said Lucy.

'No, I insist. Dudders and me will toss first.' He pulled a 50-cent coin out of his pocket. 'Tails it's him firsts, heads me.'

He flicked the coin. 'Oh, bad luck, Dudders, it's heads.'

Lucy chipped in. 'Look I trust yas, orright? I'm in. I won't be ready to do my tank for at least 2 weeks so I don't mind you blokes going before me.'

'As I said, fellers, I have a small job on the go but I guess it would be the way to go to get it out of the way,' expressed Billy, hands out in an almost reluctant fashion.

'I'm busy for the rest of the week but next week I can free up a couple of days,' said Lucy nodding, almost enthusiastically.

'What about you, Dudders?'

'Oh, I'm as free as the wind, except Cathy watches my every move.'

'Well then, my place Monday morning. Let's have another beer to celebrate,' pronounced Billy gathering the flock and lighting a cigarette. His cough started up again. The others watched.

Lucy said, 'You should do something about that cough of yours, mate otherwise you'll be dead before we get to your place.'

'Just have a bit of a cold. Should clear up soon.'

Lucy pulled his ear. 'Right, exactly what are we doing at your place, Hendo?'

'Finishing off a rock wall, pretty easy stuff really. Oh, by the way, can you bring your mixer?'

'Hang on,' queried Lucy

Billy jumped in quickly which caused him to cough a couple more of times. 'Look mate, we can work out giving you extra time for the use of whoever provides tools and all that, no worries, easy to sort out.'

'I'd go along with that, too,' replied Dudley. They took off. 'You should do something about that cough of yours though, mate.'

'Jess said, I've got a bit of a cold at the moment. Anyway, Monday at my place. Bring your lunch too.'

A short time later, Billy dropped off Dudley and headed home to put his feet up and have joint, after all, in his eyes he had really pulled off a major operation.

∞

The big day came around and Billy was more than ready. He not only had all the rocks and associated material waiting, he had a couple of other jobs lined up, just in case the rock wall was finished and the boys wanted to build up credit.

Dudley and Lucy arrived at almost the same time but in different styles. Dudley was happy to wear being called slovenly, slack, untidy and irresponsible, because he saw himself as an artist. He came drifting around the corner on his motor scooter in a cloud of dust. The helmet on him looked like a tea cup on a medicine ball.

Lucy arrived at a sensible speed and backed up to the job to unload the mixer. Dogsick was howling and carrying on as he usually did when the big straight six was running. As soon as the motor was turned off, he shut up, much to Billy's relief.

'All set ta go fellas?' enquired Billy, smiling.

'Thought you said you only had a small job?' Enquired Lucy when he jumped out.

'Oh well, it grew a bit. I thought we may as well do as much as possible,' explained Billy, hands out.

'Suppose that makes sense,' said Lucy untying the mixer. 'No point in standing around like stale bottles, eh? Let's dive in.'

The others agreed and Lucy was designated mixer duties and Dudley to the barrowing and movement of rocks as he was not very practical. This was a cunning move on Billy's part as those jobs were hard going. That is not to say that his job of the actual construction of the wall was easy, it just required more thinking.

Lucy made several constructional and engineering type of suggestions that Billy took on board. Day one worked well, other than Lucy had to be asked to switch off his mobile. They were all tired at knockoff. The wall was almost finished but Billy wanted to keep the pressure up and get as much done as was humanly possible, so he laid on a few beers after work. The other two had a couple and headed off home. Billy put his feet up, rolled a joint, took a deep toke and coughed richly for a minute or two, pleased with the progress.

Next morning Lucy was on time but Dudley was a few minutes late. When he finally arrived, he was grumpy. The other two teased him and eventually he confided that Cathy was not pleased with him having to do such heavy manual work as he was an artist. By lunch time they had completed the second wall.

Billy suggested, 'I've got a couple of other projects we could carry on with, just to pad the day out, I mean as you are here, you can build up credit.'

Lucy agreed. 'May's well, seeinz we're here, tennyrate.'

The afternoon proceeded well and they made it to knockoff. Billy was very happy with the results, two rock walls, a section of fence and most of his orchard mulched.

Lucy could not stay because his mobile rang three times in a row and as time is money as far as he was concerned, he had to excuse himself to go and give a quote.

As he left, he said, 'Let us know about your gutters Dudders, as my tank can wait for a while. I must say this work exchange aint a bad idea. Right then, see yas later.'

He jumped into his prize Chevvy, hit the starter, Dogsick commenced howling and they left in a cloud of dust and a throaty burble.

∞

A week later the work exchange venue was at Dudley Wattmore's place. Fortunately for him, Cathy had gone to Brisbane for a Government seminar on Fire and Rural Transport, F.A.R.T. he called it, as she was very much involved in community issues like that. At 7.30a.m. Lucy arrived in a gentle cloud of dust and the terrible howling accompaniment of Dogsick. Lucy had the tools and the know-how so they started on the gutters. Billy had not yet arrived.

'Where the hell's that bloody Billy?' exclaimed Lucy at around 9:00 a.m.

'I rang him yesterday and he said he'd be in full attendance,' explained Dudley.

Lucy then did an exceptional thing. He used his mobile to ring Billy and he did not suggest that Dudley go halves in the cost of the call. There was no answer.

'Maybe there's something wrong, I guess we'll find out soon enough.'

At about smoko, when the other two were wondering with irritation what had happened to Billy, the man in question rolled up.

'Er, sorry fellas, family crisis,' he mumbled. He looked stoned. Nothing more was said and Billy was given the benefit of the doubt. However, throughout the day the others were given the impression that he did not want to be there as he was keen to roll cigarettes and the tasks allocated to him were not executed with any real enthusiasm. The day passed and all agreed on an early start for the next day.

Lucy, being the sort of person who could not keep his mouth shut, exclaimed with a whetted edge, 'Have an early night, eh Billy, it'd be good to see you put in a decent day.'

Dudley looked on, nodding. 'We've got a bit to do tomorrow, old chum.'

Billy put his hands up, 'Look I said sorry, family stuff, you know.'

'No, not really,' expressed Lucy out of earshot.

Next morning the same thing happened but Billy arrived, coughing, even later. He looked and acted stoned. Both Lucy and Dudley gave him a serve.

Dudley was usually easy going but today he had to chip in. 'You could have let us know.'

'Get off me back! I've had a few problems. Family issues, also I don't feel that well, got a cold.' He kept rubbing his forehead and giving the impression he was worn out.

'Right, well let's get on with it, Billy,' said Lucy with an edge.

Dudley gave him some easy work to do but it was carried out without any great enthusiasm.

At the end of the day, Dudley was overall pleased with the results, but he was more than aware that if it had not been for Lucy, the job would have been a shambles. Lucy was pleased that Dudley was pleased but he was less pleased at the prospect of Billy not pulling his weight when it came to cementing his tank.

Dudley brought out a few beers and the thick air subsided a little but returned when Lucy said, 'Listen here, Billy, I reckon you owe both me and Dudders the time you weren't here. What do you reckon?'

'Why, I was only a bit late, I mean ...'

'Bit late? Bit late? You were three hours late on day one, and four hours late day two. By my calculation you owe each of us three point five hours. Each. Eh?'

'Look, get off me back, I've had a lot to deal with lately, but okay, yep, I'll pay you back, no worries.'

'You'd better old son,' warned Lucy pulling his right ear, 'My tank is on next week.'

'Yeah, no worries, mate, I'll be there.'

Lucy spelt it out. 'Right then friends and Billy, next Monday it is. Okay? Now Billy, how's about you lay off the dope and be there on time.'

'Alright, you've made your point. He lit a cigarette and coughed loudly.

Dudley said as Lucy walked away, 'Look, thanks China, I mean without you, you know ...'

'Don't mention it mate, at least you've lived up to your responsibilities, not like some people. See ya Monday, 7.30, that's AM for your benefit', he said looking directly at Billy.

Billy nodded and coughed.

The following Sunday, Lucy rang the boys and was reassured of a 100% rollup the next morning. On the day, Dudley was there on time but no Billy. Lucy rang him a couple of times to no avail. 'Shit, that low down bastard,' mumbled Lucy.

They started the job anyway. Dudley was on the mixer, after a sheep-shit mix and a porridge-mix, he got the technique right and seemed to rather enjoy the job, showing almost a flair.

Lucy jumped inside and cleaned the tank. Dudders was a bit too chubby to squeeze through the opening, so Lucy mumbled and grumbled through the plastering. He had counted on Billy because he was thin enough to jump inside.

By lunchtime the first coat was finished and the boys were worn out. Billy still was not there.

'He's a mongrel! I should have known,' spat Lucy as he dialled Billy's number for the nth time.

'Yes, how true, me old China,' replied Dudley, 'But I am surprised as he was so keen on the idea.'

'I'm not bloody surprised!' screamed Lucy, 'I'm not gunna forget this. The bloody lazy, scheming, good for nothing, gutter sniping mongrel! Talking of that particular bastard, guess who's here?'

Just then Billy arrived looking considerably stoned and instantly burst into a racking, rich coughing fit.

'I'm late fellas, but I've been a bit crook. My cold's playing up.'

'You're a mongrel Hendo! We bloody well helped you but you don't seem too happy to help us!' boiled Lucy with clenched fists.

'Aaaaaaah, get off me back,' whined Billy, 'I'm here, aren't I?'

They went on with a couple of other jobs that were just fill-ins because the real work had been done.

At the end of the day Lucy pointed at Billy. 'Now listen here, Mr Henderson, how's about you do the right thing and be here at 7.30 in the morning, right?'

'Yeah, look I, er haven't been well, cold is playing ...'

'Listen here, I don't give a flying root, we helped you, how's about doing the right thing?'

'Look, I'll be here on time.'

'And, Hendo, you owe Dudders and me another 2 hours each, understand?'

'Two hours?'

'Yep, but that will come later. Alls I want is for you to be here on time. OK? 'Cos plastering is a bastard of a job on my own and we have to do the second coat. Right?'

'I told you I would.'

'Right.'

The next morning was a repeat performance, although Billy arrived about 8.30 and did jump into the tank to help Lucy. Lucy remained irritated by Billy's attitude and by the fact that he kept wanting to smoke in the tank. It became unbearable, particularly when Billy went into coughing fits. The second coat took longer than the first but eventually it was finished.

'Hell, I am I glad that's over,' commented Billy. 'Makes me want to cough in there 'cos of the thin air.'

'You can't be half as glad as I am that it's finished, Hendo.'

They filled in the afternoon once again with a small cementing job.

At the end of the day Billy commented almost enthusiastically, 'Well, we got that out of the way, no worries. This work exchange is a good idea, eh? What say we start at my place next week, I've got ...'

'Pig shit!' Exclaimed Lucy, standing up to his full five foot six in work boots. Before we do any fucking thing, you have to pay us back five and a half hours each.'

'Five and ...? I will of course but the whole idea of this is that it all works out in the soup, know what I mean?'

Both Dudley and Lucy chorused, 'No, we don't'

Over the next two weeks Billy did honour those extra hours but the work was carried out unenthusiastically and was hardly worth it. Lucy received no extra from Billy, although it was promised, for the use of his tools but Dudley gave him a few hours to compensate.

∞

About a month later Billy was setting up to pour a slab for his new shed at his place and he had liaised closely with the others to use the work exchange idea. At first Lucy carried on like a scrub turkey but reluctantly agreed.

On the day of the pour, the truck arrived but the other two did not. Billy was left with 6 cubic metres of concrete to deal with. The job turned out to be a disaster because the truck driver had to dump the load and go to another job, nor could he help. Billy was at best a handyman and although able to stack a few rocks on top of each other with a blob of mortar, had never poured any slabs. Consequently, the surface was not finished very well because the concrete had begun the drying process and the levels were all over the place.

It was only later that afternoon when he stood sore and coughing looking at the mess that he recalled that Lucy changed his mind quickly from refusing to help to saying yes. He sat exhausted on the step, and rolled a smoke. What a mess. He could not even contemplate how he was going to fix it.

Just then he heard the unmistakable rumble of a Harley Davidson as it spluttered into the driveway. It could only be Squared.

Billy started shaking and almost began to cry. He realized with a fright that he should not have switched half that good dope for the seedy stuff. Also came the realisation that the lucky two headed fifty cent coin in his pocket was not going to get him out of this one.

Billy Henderson began to cough, it escalated rapidly, startling the lorikeets in the gum trees.

The End

Leaders are among us -

For the right

And wrong reasons

No Limits

The clunk of a metal door, far off, clear. Blake shivered. The screws made sure you suffered for as much of your stay as possible. Baldy, the resident biggest swinging unit of the cell block sneered two words a few minutes ago, on his way back to his own cell. *You're next.*

Words had more impact than the cold. Blake glared at the wall, which helped quell his fear. Baldly was a mean bastard alright. The young man knew he was going to cop it, get bashed or cop it up the dot. Getting bashed usually meant getting very badly bashed; some people died in this place.

He shook his head; he should not have made that smart arse wise crack yesterday, in the yard, 'Hey man, why don't you get a haircut.'

Three years earlier.

'Blake, out of bed,' yelled his mother from the kitchen, 'brekkies ready.'

'Gedda life,' he mumbled and rolled over.

10 minutes later.

'Blake, you've got to go to school.'

'No!' His voice was like a rusty can.

'Listen, you lazy little bastard, you've got to go to school, you have to get some sort of edjacation,' she challenged, lighting up another cigarette.

10 minutes later.

'Blake, come on, up! You'll end up a bloody no-hoper just like that bastard, yer old man.'

'Piss off!' he spat with teenage victimised anger.

'Listen here, you little prick, don't you speak to me like that, you hear?' His mother closed the door more than firmly.

He had become more objectionable lately. She could not do a thing with him. What in the hell could she do, his father had left years ago and her boyfriend was away at the mines.

Inside.

'Hey Blakey, you're next, beautiful boy!'

He clenched his fist and did his best to glare at Baldy, who smirked and winked, on his way down the two-tone pea soup green corridor. The muscle, Bolt and Stumpy, a couple of violent clowns, burst out laughing, so did the uniformed guard, who leaned against the centre pillar.

The young man knew there was going to be a showdown. Things were going to get ugly; Baldy had mates, big, strong, nasty bastards.

Three years earlier.

'Blake, you've got to go to bloody school or get a job.' One last try as she negotiated her way through the things on the floor and tried to touch him.

'Piss off!'

She baulked, aware of how far she could go. He was now much bigger than her. She knew men. Her tone softened slightly. 'Listen, you've got to get some sort of edjacation, or you won't be able to get a job, hear me?'

'Go away!' he spat.

He dressed in a pouty rage and slammed the door on his way out. Down at the shopping centre, Doghead and Squint were sitting on the edge of a flower bed ashtray. Gooby was doing a few tricks on a skateboard they pinched from the kids at the beach on the weekend.

'How you doin', Snakey-Blakey?' babbled Doghead in a half-man, half-child voice, a teenage creaking gate.

'Get a life, Doghead, layoff, man. That old lady of mine, she's got her head up her arse, do this, do that, get a job, go to fucking school, all that shit.'

'Hey,' interrupted Squint, 'Let's go down the pub tonight, big night, man, I've got a mate that can get us somethin' ta drink, no questions – I've got bucks too, bud.'

'Where'd you get money?' enquired Gooby.

'Let's just say I found it lying on the road.'

That brought raucous laughter.

Inside.

'Hey Blakey, we got to get together, it's gunna be tonight.'

Baldy stood in front of where Blake was eating. Trying to eat was not easy, sweat hovered. A bead trickled down his back, he was glad it had not trickled down his face. That would be losing face.

The young man looked up; he knew he had to show a distinct lack of fear to survive. Baldy looked left and right as if he was about to cross a road. The place fell silent. In the fraction of a second it took for his smile to click to evil; his ham sized fist came down with a bang on the laminex table. Plates, plastic cutlery and a nest of salt and pepper condiments jumped.

His look was cold but his eyes boiled, 'Yes, you little shit, tonight is it.'

Three years earlier.

Music thumped; the whole place rocked. Patrons lined up outside were slowly admitted to replace the noisy people that ambled out. The door staff was busy. A big night, alright.

'Hey, Snake, here, bud.' Squint laughed and opened his hand showing four small pills.

Ecstasy eased in about half an hour and three beers later. Then a big rush. Their eyes bulged.

Doghead shoved a bottle of bourbon in his hand. 'Hey buddy, drink that, nothin' takes away ya problems like a quiet drink with ya mates, right?'

A hand came over a shoulder with a joint; someone handed it to him. The music got louder, or Blake thought it did. Someone gave him a line of speed. Either way, what a night.

The crowd grew and the party poured into the street. Some young females, off their faces, keen to whip off items of clothing, some blokes did the same, others yelled and encouraged. The street scene bordered on … out of hand.

Someone rang the police. Two carloads of cops, no sirens, arrived in quick time and did their best to ease in and take control without inflaming the situation. Difficult at best, no two ways about it, young people are not keen on authority. A young female constable marched up to Blake's mob and asked them to move on.

Gooby, from somewhere inside the crowd yelled, 'Get a life, sow!'

Many laughed, none were appalled. A more senior police officer stormed over, with a tensioned forearm ready to belt someone. 'Hey, you, over 'ere!'

Gooby ducked and moved further into the mob. Someone else yelled, 'Let's get the mongrels, this is the Eureka stockade; we don't like cops, we have to stand up for our rights. Yeah, fucking well yeah!'

Someone whistled, the yelling increased. The mob switched to ugly. A flitter in time things hovered in the balance, the snap of a twig later, out-of-control. Another cop grabbed Blake.

'Hey pig, what are ya doin'?'

'Come on pal, you've had enough now, let's go!'

'What? What the fuck for!' he screamed with explosive anger and burst free of the police officer's grasp.

Someone in the crowd aggressively and viciously pushed the cop, who tumbled backwards. The other police did not notice; they were engaged with problems of their own. The mob screamed and yelled abuse.

'Let's get the prick!' screamed Gooby.

Blake bellowed, 'Yeah!' and sank his boot into the policeman, who was trying to get up off the ground. 'Yeah!' he screeched again and kicked harder. And harder.

The crowd yah-hoo-ed. The more the crowd yelled, the more he kicked, and the harder … he was on a high. Blake could not remember how long he had been kicking the cop in the head. A vice-like grip crushed his neck and he was mauled into a paddy wagon.

Inside.

'Hey, Blakey boy, you're in a man's world. I'm coming to get ya.'

Blake knew all about a man's world alright. He would never forget the constant bashings from his father and the sexual and physical abuse of his stepfather. His mother had never stepped in. He had already experienced three years in juvenile detention. These places were violent. The bastards, they were all the same to him; guardians, cops, crims, screws, all the bloody same. He knew he had to establish control; this was the big boys' place; he was in for several years. This little plot was his.

He was not going to muck around; Blake *was* going to be the head man. Moving into the adult world, well, he knew how to handle Baldy. He had slipped Stumpy and Bolt a couple of pills each, he knew they would back him up. He knew how to manoeuvre idiots like them. And that jagged piece of concrete in his pocket was about to be buried in the side of Baldy's head. He had sorted out Blubberneck, the jailer man who was always keen to inadvertently be unavailable when needed. Trading happened between social classes. A few bucks fixed him.

Yeah! No worries, there were no limits alright.

The End

Others can dictate our path

Without knowing it -

Timing is everything

Flat Out

'It's not really out of your way.' Her words pulsed in his head.
'Sure it aint,' growled Harvey, 'only by about two hours.'

The crawl through town was worse than trying to find a park at the football. Angry shouts from knuckle-draggers, aggressive honking horns, gnarled fists out of car windows, all tangled up in exhaust fumes. The air-conditioning in the car did not work. He eventually snaffled a park. A tight manoeuvre over a pile of rubble. The sign said, *Building Site – Hard hats must be worn.*

'Bloody safety gone stupid,' he grumbled, stumbling into the pedestrian mass. A stick-thin street kid tried to sell him a badge.

He stepped progressive jive, dodging cruising Generation X and Y *gotta have it now types* with their brains plugged into MP5s.

'Hell, I should have told her to go and take a flying jump,' he said. Fair enough, it was for their daughter Jasmine's school play, but his wife had mouthed off about how she was going to organise it all. Same thing every bloody time. The *Enter-Stage-Left - Everything for the Theatre* shop loomed ahead.

Whoomp! The heavy door made his ears pop at the same insecure second a Dracula dummy swinging from the ceiling made him warm in his pants. He manoeuvred through clutter to the counter.

'My name's Harvey Blinman, come to collect a fairy godmother outfit.'

'Fairy godmother?' The guy sported an inverted, polished, pear-shaped head with half a dozen corkscrew hairs sticking straight up in the middle. 'For whom did you say?'

'Jasmine, my daughter, same name as me, Blinman,' muttered Harvey, rolling his eyes.

'Obviously, I'm not stupid, you know.' A limp wristed gesture located a tattered ledger.

'Yeah, sure. Look, I'm in a hurry, I'm creatively parked up the …'

Pearhead frowned, 'No need to be huffy, I know my job.' He lifted one eyebrow as if wearing a monocle and returned to the ledger. 'Harvey, you say?'

'Mister! That's my first name, okay? My surname's Blinman and the costume is for Jasmine Blinman. Dig it?'

'Hummmph.' The monocle thing happened again. 'Jasmine, you say? Fairy godmother costume? Ah, yes right here, the special, right?'

'Umm. Dunno …'

'You don't know? That's what was ordered, see?'

'Umm, okay, yeah. Look, I'm in a bit of a …'

'You've said that. Now, there is a hundred dollars still owing.' His nostrils went horsey.

'Hundred bucks?'

'I can't let it go without payment, *obviously*.' An outwardly rolled hand.

Harvey's memories scrolled. Yes, he recalled something about money owing.

'Yeah, oh-bloody-kay, here we go,' he grunted and pulled out a hundred. 'I want a receipt for that, right?'

Pearhead sighed, purple lips formed a prune and he fingered a gold chain caught around the top button on his Carnival Ware silk shirt. 'Naturally. I'll get *that* for you, *and* the costume. I shan't be long.'

'I won't be going … never mind.'

Harvey glanced around at the Halloween masks, Superman and milkmaid costumes, papier-mâché props, cardboard swords, and cannons. A dog's black head hung on a wire. Some Roman torches that looked like vibrators stuck out from the wall. He whispered, 'Hurry up, you bloody …'

'Sir! There we are, all packed up, *no* extra charge for the wrapping, *and* your receipt.'

Harvey closed his eyes, so he could roll them inside his head. 'Right, gotta go … er …' He squeezed out, 'Grrrrr … thanks.'

'Not a problem, all in a day's service, *sir*.' He blinked with his monocle eye.

Harvey reached the door.

Pearhead gushed, 'Um wait, there's a note attached. The pumpkin is here.'

'Pumpkin?'

'A cardboard pumpkin someone forgot to pick up with the stage set yesterday.'

'Aaah hell. I haven't got any more money to …'

'*Oh no*, it has already been paid for.'

'Okay, but I …'

'One moment, it's out the back.'

'Christ Almighty,' mumbled Harvey as Pearhead presented a one cubic foot cardboard box.

'There we are, *sir*.'

Harvey manhandled the heavy door with testy token help and staggered into the street. The footpath punters gave no quarter, but he struggled on.

A micro second vacuum of sharp eerie light riveted his feet. Focus registered just in time to see a massive concrete slab accelerate from the heavens and crush his car to a pappadum. Time hovered, waiting for the dust and rubble to work out gravity. Harvey stood there quivering like junket. The thundering noise seemed to continue rumbling and tried to bust his head open. Then people began to scream.

The End

Not everything

Can be explained -

Especially acts of God

God Will Provide

'Eeeek!' yelled Rylee as a tame ripple washed over the rock.

'The water's not, like, *that* cold,' retorted Skyler, absentmindedly toeing a small shell.

'Beautiful day. Do you ever wonder why the sky is blue? Skye, what's wrong?'

'What? Oh, nothing.' She was thinking about the slap her mother gave her this morning.

'Lovely blue Skyler, get it?'

'Ha ha. Don't get your school uniform wet, Babe.'

'Hey Skye, we went to this church thing, you know, and like wow, we all sang and waved our hands above our heads, it was like really cool and we could feel God's vibe.'

'What?'

She scrolled to herself, *Mum said if I said anything like that again she would throw me out. Said I was jealous of her happiness. Like hell! Said that Gav would not try to put his hand in my panties, but he keeps trying all the time, even when Mum's in the next room. Bastard.'* She picked up a curly shell.

'Yeah, Skye and we, like, hold our hands above our heads and do this, see? Mexican wave, but it's not really that, it's like, you know, tuning into God who is … up there.'

'Um … right …' Thoughts again of home.

Mum threatened to put me into foster care if I ever did that again, scratching Gav's face, like for no reason. Prick grabbed my tits from behind. Took me an ice age to tell Mum, I was so freaked out and depressed. The guy is an arsehole. She asked him in front of me. Hell-bloody-low! What is he going to say, eh? Admit it? Ya dopey, skanky Ho why don't you believe me? She covered her ear with the shell. Her eyes glassed. The sound of the sea, a fizzy distant roar.

'… And we go to church, as a family and the pastor is God's, like man here on earth, bit like Jesus. Pastor is this guy who hugs you and touches you and he's a bit creepy at first but he's a bit dishy too, says it is really Jesus who is, like touching you, makes you feel really chosen. He says if we accept Him into our hearts, God will provide for us. Hey Skye?'

'Er … yeah?' Skye slipped back into her own thoughts.

Mum says to stop being a slut and leading males on. And to stop making up stories. Bloody hell, everything I told her was true! Why won't she believe me?

She took the shell away from her ear.

'You should, like come along with us, God will provide, forgive us of all our sins.' Rylee put her arms out in an all-embracing gesture.

'Last church I went to was when Father Fatso, like, tried to rub himself against me. There is no God, Rye, at least not round here.'

'Oh Skye, there is, our pastor tells us God will look after us, no matter what … hey Skye, isn't it heaps cool, the water is flowing out really, like fast …'

Skyler had been looking down and now noted the water receding quickly. She became aware of an eerie light and a roar. The shell was not against her ear as she looked up.

The white water of the tsunami blotted out the horizon.

The End

To save face -

Be generous

To others in advance

Green Light

'You idiot, Nelson, why don't you use your bloody initiative, eh?' The young mechanic looked nervously from under the dashboard. 'Um, no I mean yes, I am using my initiative, I'm following the instruction manual ...'

'You've got the wires the wrong way round.'

'No, Strap, the wiring diagram says ...'

'Wiring diagram? Christ, son, use your brains, that wire should go *there*.' He pointed and a gold bracelet slid down to his wrist.

'But ... if I do that the system could short out if you use any of the accessory functions ... it would overload the system.' Nelson seemed to wince at the proximity of Strap and his fancy aftershave.

'You bloody galah, the way you got it, it will start a fire.'

Nelson, clearly not happy with the way he was being addressed, tried again. 'But Strap, the wiring diagram for *this* radio shows *that* wire goes *there*.' Sweat beaded on the young man's forehead.

'For Christ's sake go and put your tools away and you can sign off.' Strap Fraser, head salesman, was managing the business for the next couple of weeks because the owner, Ernie Hutt, was in hospital having an ingrown toenail removed. 'I'll sort out this mess you've made. We might have to ... oh never mind.'

He was about to say *let you go.* He did not like Nelson, probably because he was young and had only been employed there for two months. There had been regular altercations between them. Strap

Fraser had suggested to the boss a number of times to get rid of him but Ernie wouldn't hear of it.

Strap nipped the ends off the wires, tightened the screws and turned the radio on. 'See there you go, you lazy little prick, works like a charm.'

Because it was Friday, and with the boss out of the picture, Strap decided to borrow the BMW ragtop for the weekend. He smiled, convinced Ernie would not find out because he would have it back well before anyone arrived at work on Monday. He washed his hands, ran manicured fingers through his trendy, red, spikey hair, waved to Celia the secretary as she breezed out, checked that Nelson and Desmond, the two mechanics, had signed off and locked up. He saw them drive out and he was on his own. He secured the trade plates on the Beamer, started it up and eased out of the yard, making sure the automatic mesh security gates closed behind him.

Rag top down, Strap accelerated down the hill to the traffic lights. The BMW engine burbled with balanced precision as it tamed to an idle. Strap was thinking of how impressed Isabella was going to be when he pulled up in front of her place.

Lights on red. He picked a house music station, cranked up the radio to force pedestrians to frantically glance in all directions for the origins of the whoomp whoomp whoomp, and stuck a Marlborough in his mouth. *How cool can a person get?* He chuckled as he pressed in the lighter.

'Come on, you dick-head lights.' Strap drummed his fingers on the steering wheel, admiring his gold bracelet.

Lost in self-gratification it took him a moment to realise smoke was drifting out from under the dash.

'Aaaaaaah!' he yelled and plunged his hand under and burnt his fingers. *'Fuck me d...'* he screeched as thick smoke billowed out.

∞

'It was a terrible accident, officer,' said a male witness.

'You saw it all?' Sergeant Bowden had already directed the paramedics and was checking witnesses with his partner who was on the other side of the intersection.

'Yeah, mate ... er I mean officer, smoke seemed to be coming from under the dash and he, the driver sticks his head under to try to do something, an' then, an' then, the car lurches forward, like he maybe hit the exzellerata and the car is in drive position, see?'

'We will determine that, sir,' added the policeman with a frown, trying to wrestle back control from a creative witness. 'Now, the truck?'

'Yeah, anyrate like I was telling ya, he, that's the BMW bloke takes orf like a rocket, see, into the path of this tip truck coming across from there, see, and he, the truck, has the right of way, obviously cos he's got a green light ... but then he cleans up the BMW, whack! Right amidships. The BMW driver got bloody well lunched, mate, sir, he would have to be cactus ...'

'Okay, sir, right, that will do for ...'

'... And the poor truckie, he'd be feelin' it, poor bastard, I can tell you that,' and he pointed towards the truck driver sitting on the curb at the rear of the ambulance with his head in his hands.

∞

Nelson and Desmond leaned against the front bar.

Desmond said, 'What's up, mate?'

'Aaaaah, that mongrel Strap, always riding me.'

'Try to ignore him, that's what I do. I've been there longer than him. I mean salesmen, they are all arseholes, dime a dozen, liars the lot of em, he'll be gone in a few months, you wait and see, they move around.'

'Yeah, I guess so but if he's there Monday then I'll hand in my notice,' said Nelson with purpose.

The End

Some people

Who should not be -

Cannot be humoured

NTBR

'See that spot there, that's where he landed,' said Jeremy, eyes wide and staring.

The newspaper clipping sat on the table between them. Shards of sunlight through the bars divided the table surface.

'You seem almost proud of yourself.'

'Not a matter of pride, Doc, it's a matter of someone had to stop him from doing it to others and I was appointed.'

'Appointed by whom?'

Jeremy's body began to tremble and he looked up at the ceiling. 'God.'

'It's alright Jeremy, relax, we have time.' Doc leaned back; arms folded. 'Do you recall exactly what happened?'

'Like it was yesterday. He, not God, right, was standing there just straight out denying it. Lying arsehole. I knew Nelly and him had been having it off.' Jeremy's body continued to shimmer.

'What did you do?'

'I launched myself at him, grabbed him by the throat and threw him through the window – four floors to the ground.' He tapped his finger on the newspaper at the dark stain on the pavement in the photo. He stopped shaking for a moment and laughed. 'I showed the bastard that you don't mess around with my woman.'

Doc said calmly, 'It's okay, just relax, no need to distress yourself. Where is Nelly now?'

'She's in heaven with God.'

Doc raised an eyebrow. 'Did you tell the police this?'

'Yep. The lying pricks said they found her chopped to pieces in a bag under the house. She went to heaven, I know that; I held her hand and gave her to God.'

'Mm, what about here and now?'

'You're onto it Doc, that was the old me. All that shit happened over five years ago. Nothing wrong with me now, I'm ready to go out into the world.'

Jeremy's eyes closed for a second and then opened wide. The shadow of the bars had lengthened in the afternoon sun.

'Right mate, I think we can leave it there for the moment.'

'Doc, are you going to recommend my release?' Jeremy leant forward; eyes sparkling.

'Let's just have a think about it and we'll talk again soon, how does that sound?'

'You fucking well said that last time …' Jeremy's voice rose a notch.

'Ease up mate, we have to be sure that you are … ready, I mean it's a complex world out …'

'Whaaaaaaaat? You're all the fucking same, you *bastards* …'

The last word was screeched as Jeremy leapt out of his seat and just managed to grab Doc's arm. Doc pressed the buzzer and a male nurse dashed in and grabbed the patient's shoulders. Another staffer entered quickly and jabbed Jeremy with a needle.

The nurse smiled as they dragged Jeremy out. 'Just as well we had one of his hands cuffed to the desk, Doc.'

'Yeah, you are right, look, thanks for …'

'No prob, Doc that's what we are here for.'

Doc mopped his forehead and scribbled, NTBR - Not To Be Released.

'Should be never,' he mumbled as the others left the room.

The End

Think of others

In the cold of Winter

Be gracious

Paved with Gold

Translated from the Ukrainian to English.

Then - Eastern Europe - February 2017 – late wintertime.

I was twenty-one years old when I said a sad farewell to my parents at the old family farm near a tiny village named Vokapova, just north of the Ukrainian Romanian border. I was going to the United Kingdom to work and hopefully send money back home, and with luck perhaps bring members of my family over later when I was settled.

My family was very poor but we managed to sell off whatever items of value we still possessed, so that I would have enough money to pay my way and to secure accommodation when I arrived there. A friend of ours who had a cousin in London once had advised that I carry only a few euros and keep a credit card well-hidden on my person in case of misadventure or robbery.

I had heard from other acquaintances that there was plenty of work to be had in the UK and becoming a citizen was relatively easy because the authorities were reluctant to send anyone back to their country of origin. The only hurdle was, of course, a traveller had to get there first.

I was unable to secure a passport because if the authorities knew I was going away they would perhaps detain me for questioning, or maybe something more stringent. Fortunately, I had a working permit to work in Romania as a labourer in a power plant just over the border in case I needed it.

I then planned to cross Romania, which was part of the European Economic Union, into Bulgaria, without the Ukrainian authorities knowing and from then on, I was told, these papers would identify me and on arrival in the UK easily I would be able claim asylum.

Now - Calais France - June 2017 - early summer.

Me and my new friend, Vinny, were all set to go. Yesterday the gendarmes had taken a group of asylum seekers to a detention centre. No one knew what happened to those people but it was told that they were processed and deported. When the numbers got too big the authorities rounded them up and took them away. We did not want that so when roundup time came, we remained mostly hidden. The French seemed to have a relaxed attitude, turning a blind eye even though they must have known that some managed to get onto some lorries. They were more than happy to move them on but every few days, because there were so many immigrants, from Africa as well as Eastern Europe and because the world was watching, they had to be seen to be doing something. The French government had been taking people from their own old colonies and the country could no longer offer the hand of help. Move them on, like all the other places they had been through.

Vinny and I had been waiting behind the warehouses at the port for two days and we could see a line-up of lorries. It had cost each of us thirty euros for the services of a Nigerian, Segun, who was the expert with the lead seal crimper tool. Segun was making a good business, he would snip the seal with delicate wire cutters, and open the steel door to the back of the container lorry, thus enabling seekers to jump into a moving lorry. He had a lookout guy who had some feathers on a long stick who would wave them in front of the security camera for 15 seconds, thus confusing the camera. Segun then he would close the door, reseal, and the customs and immigration officials would be none the wiser. Segun had applied for asylum in France and he was helping others in their quest to escape unsavoury regimes or poverty. They had been told that the officials only inspected every tenth lorry, and they always waved through the ones with seals intact.

Then -

I made my way across Romanian - Bulgarian border at night through a loosely patrolled stretch of fence. The night was freezing and snow had fallen during the day. I caught a bus, pretending to be a local and no one paid me any attention because, after all, I looked like everyone else.

I had heard that railway stations were the best places to head for because they had toilets and I could stowaway on a train, or walk the tracks to the next town. That plan turned out to be no good because I quickly became aware that the police always moved you on and by the time I passed into Bulgaria, I was surprised to see there were many others like me, all men. Sometimes people took pity on us and gave us food and sometimes a bottle of grappa.

A month or so later I crossed into Greece with a growing group of young men, all doing the same thing, going to the UK. I hoped to get a ferry to Italy but by the time I arrived in Corfu I was getting through my money. I believed the money I had originally budgeted would be adequate and I managed to keep a few hundred Euros in my sock. We had heard of fishermen, not sure what nationality they were but there were seats available to cross to Italy overnight and I booked a seat. I slept with a dozen others under a tourist shelter, not used until summertime.

That night in darkness I was bashed and robbed. I was lucky they did not find the credit card because I had placed that in my underpants but they tore off my shoes. Another man helped and chased off the robbers so I managed to retrieve my bag but not the money.

This person was a Serbian, Vynnyski Joksmovic, and we quickly became friends. Vinny was a big, strong young man who had worked in a railway yard, had a mobile phone, and from then on other opportunist guys showed us a degree of respect. We found my shoes in the morning.

Friendly people, under the watchful eyes of the police, gave us food and bottles of water as we departed Greece to Italy on a small, barely seaworthy boat and we arrived at a rocky, pebbly inlet, someone said was somewhere north of Oranto. The sea was choppy but luckily not a big swell and we nearly froze to death but we wrapped ourselves in canvas and endured the trip.

Now -

Vinny and I had snuck back to the huge parking area, further down from the container port where fork lifts and cranes loaded container vessels. Segun beckoned us into the part of the port where hundreds of lorries, all set to depart that night were parked, nose to tail and at various angles. The area was mostly well lit but Segun, as part of the fee, would inform us of the lorries that were not guarded, with no driver or official behind who could see.

There was a special spot where trees hung over the vehicles and it was relatively easy to sneak through the fence unseen. The drivers were either standing around chatting in groups or having refreshments at the various food and drink cafes around the edges. I knew that the drivers were aware refugees and people wanting a ride were hanging about but they also knew that the gendarmes would demand to see passports and ID papers as the vehicles went through the gates.

From the gates the lorries would move slowly, one by one through the port area and then past another check of papers. The officials at this point examined, often not very seriously, the lead seals on the locking mechanisms on the back of the container. Then, up the ramp onto the passenger and vehicle ferries that were moored in such a way that vehicles could be directed to the appropriate section of the craft to maximise space.

Some passengers paid the lorry drivers to have transport after landing in the UK, some were taken pity on and were allowed to ride with the driver but when on the boat they had to leave the cab anyway because no one was allowed to be inside the vehicles for safety reasons for the crossing and had to sit in the lounges or on deck for the two-hour trip across the Channel to Dover, England.

The drivers always insisted to see the passenger's papers but also because the officials checked them before going up the ramp anyway, there was supposedly no way anyone could illegally get on board without being caught, or without a ticket.

The French police and other port officials didn't really seem to pay too much attention because the unwritten rule was, *move them on!* and even if one or two snuck through, too bad, make these refugees the problem for the receiving country.

Then -

We slowly made our way up through Italy, being moved on at regular intervals. The Italian Officials made us pay for rail or bus fares or we were simply run out of towns and railway stations regularly. I wondered why they were so aggressive towards the always at least ten or twenty people like me, trying to get to the UK.

One night we were brutally beaten with sticks, it was obvious the locals did not want us there. We did not understand the language very well but the message was more than clear. We were at least thankful that the perpetrators did not rob us, they just wanted us gone.

Vinny and me kept walking because we could not afford to pay fares and it took over two months to get into France and another three weeks to get to Calais. The weather was, in the main, very cold and keeping warm was a major concern. Most of the time, since arriving in the EEC, we had been met in equal measure with cruelty and/or great kindness by citizens of the country. Most officials, police and military had been reasonable, making us move on but at times police did beat us with sticks.

Citizens mostly were kind to us, giving food, fruit, water, whatever they could or would spare because often they did not have much themselves, but some people made it plain that refugees were not welcome and we should go back to where we came from.

We were good at locating places to sleep and when on the road word always got around as to where one could stay. At most of these places some refugees like them had gathered firewood and made the best of a camp that they could. The groups varied in size, were still mostly men, and new faces appeared and disappeared in equal measure. Sometimes we stayed for a week or more. At one camp most of the travellers were from Africa, Chad, Somalia, Nigeria,

Ethiopia, Libya. However, most of those from Africa seemed to be trying to gain asylum in France, due to many of those places previously being French colonies.

Even though we were into spring, the weather was cripplingly cold. Before I left home, I had tried to gather as much information as possible and I was convinced that by the time I reached the UK summer would be ahead and a bright future would bless me.

Now -

It was a freezing night, so cold it seemed as if it might even snow and the wind off the Strait of Dover made our teeth chatter. We had Hoodies as well as scarves wrapped around our faces. We had selected a lorry that looked as if it would do, so we prepared ourselves for the journey which would take several hours of rocking in a steel container in the boat as well as dealing with poor ventilation. Segun had established that the vehicle was supposed to be freighting timber beds and side tables in boxes that people assembled themselves. Loading vehicles onto the ferries would be happening soon as had been established by previous knowledge. Vinny and I drank some water, not too much in case of having to toilet ourselves in the container; we ate some food and awaited the signal from Segun. It was a dark night as well as being poorly lit which suited us. The noise of the lorries drowned everything else out and his spies gave the all clear and he snipped the lead seal.

Then -

One freezing night after everyone, some dozen people like us, had dropped off to sleep, I could feel Vinny shaking, worse than just shaking with cold. We were sheltered partly by an old rusty lean-to that was part of a deserted railway packing shed. I realised Vinny was sobbing.

Embarrassed that he had been discovered by me, Vinny tried to explain his predicament. He confessed that he had lied about his papers and he was very scared that he would be found out and deported when he arrived in the UK. He had stolen the identity of someone in his village who had died. He knew that the deceased person looked like him and had only died a few weeks previously.

It did not make any difference to me who considered Vinny to be a friend and I tried to convince him that it didn't matter at all. Everything would be good after we arrived in the UK because the English were sympathetic to the way Russia had tried to annexe other countries and redraw borders after the Second World War.

Vinny was miserable for a while and considered burning his papers and pleading that they were stolen on his journey. Eventually he was convinced by me that he should keep the papers and none of this would matter. Once the UK authorities realised he was a refugee everything would be alright.

Next day we were moved on by the Bordeaux gendarmes. It rained for two days as we trudged along the railway tracks.

Now -

Segun swung open the big steel door, Vinny and I shoved a large box further in, we leapt up into the lorry and the steel door slammed shut behind us. It was pitch dark inside the belly of the container. We both loosened our face coverings at the same time. Vinny screamed as he opened his mobile phone torch.

The stench was unbearable. The container had bodies lying everywhere. It looked like they were all dead.

We banged on the sides of the container but obviously no one heard us with the noise as the lorries began to move. Seems as if we were waved through by the authorities as we did not stop and the lorries reached full speed very quickly.

After some time we stopped and continued to bang on the container and yell. The doors were opened and we jumped out, glad to be free but both of us shaken and traumatised.

However, we were only free from the horrendous scene inside the truck, but were not as free as we thought because we were escorted under guard to a police station and questioned stringently, firstly thinking we were partly responsible for the dead bodies.

We have now been taken to a refugee station and are now awaiting our fate. I feel great fear about my future.

The End

Think you are ahead of the game?

Luck will run out -

One day

One Step Ahead

I did not really want to move but I had a feeling they were closing in on me. It is just a feeling, but I have a good sense of things because I know myself well. The feelings and sounds become more regular, and I know the sickness is there. Hovering. How can a sickness sound or feel like something? Well, the only way to explain is to liken it to something you could relate to. The sickness sounds something like running your fingernail down the steel base string of a guitar. I bet you have never felt all that, but I do. It seems to ball up inside me from time to time, then more regularly. And then ... That is why it was time to move on.

What better way to get rid of things than a garage sale? Surprising how much stuff you accumulate after about four years. The rental house came with some iffy furniture and I had to buy some stuff too. I am pretty good at garage sales because I have had plenty. The idea appeals to me because you get to see a range of scrubbers. I like to be able to size people up. I can do it easily because most people warm to me. Especially young women.

Anyway, moving on, I like to leave a place and arrive at my new destination, free of any baggage. I do a few different things workwise, but no dole office, no government stuff. No need to be clocked, never anywhere long, no one gets to really know me. Get it? Almost like a new life at each new place.

There are a few things I have that might bring in a few dollars and what did not sell could just be put out by the front gate and the punters can help themselves. Meaning they cannot help themselves pinching things. I know the types, there is a lousiness about them. Some things always got pinched, but mostly it was rubbish. Yeah, I know the types. They have a certain smell to me, a reek.

Garage sale, then if anything was left after being pecked over by dickhead tight arses for half a day, I'd just take it to the dump. How easy is that? A snack.

∞

Saturday morning, steamy already, condensation still on the grass, I painted three signs. They looked rough on bits of jagged tin, but people sort of expect that. One at each end of my street. Funny how little things interest me. Why it was called a street because it really should have been an avenue, coconut palms leaning in like guards of honour. The third sign was wired to the front fence. I opened the roller door and carried things out as the sun started to take charge of the day. Long fingers of sun probed the front lawn. The wheelbarrow was handy to transport a whole heap of small junk from the kitchen to a spot near the gate. There were cardboard boxes, plates and cutlery and some electrical items. The toaster only did one side of the bread - no one knew that but at eight bucks, who would grizzle? The driveway and along the front filled up as the shed emptied. No worries.

By then it was 6:30 a.m., so I made some coffee and had a hit of vodka. The ice-cold slug felt like sun-up again. It is not good manners breathing over people - they do not like it. That is why I drink vodka. It was easy to get nervous with people around. I shnozzed a line of speed to get me going – it makes me really friendly. When I'm on the *Speedy Gonzales* I'm much more outgoing. But when I run out, well you'd better watch out.

The first thing to go, believe it or not, was the toaster. A tall thirty-ish bean-pole spinster in a green sack fossicked through pretty well everything, and then came to the wheelbarrow.

'How much ya want for the toaster?' she snapped. It sounded a bit rude. Usually, women are real friendly towards me, they can't help it. This one was a tangent.

'Well, price is on it, eight bucks.'

'How about I give you a fiver, and I take the corkscrew as well, eh?'

I felt like hitting her with the shovel. Tight arse mongrel.

'Yeah, alright.'

She gave me a twenty. Bitch.

'Haven't got anything smaller, have you?' I did not want to get rid of all my change in the first sale. I waited her out. Watched her tap her sack dress pockets and fart around in her shoulder bag, made a big deal of it. She wanted me to say, 'Look no worries, she's right, er … just a handful of change, no big deal.' They were around those sorts of bastards, I know that.

'There, we're in luck,' she said, almost friendly.

No, harlot you're the one in luck. If you didn't have the five bucks, I'd find out where you lived. I'd come round and then you'd know how I really felt. I might even get a bit angrier if I wanted to and do other things if I wanted to.

She wandered off. People like her don't realise how lucky they are. Just as well she isn't my type. When I have to, I see to people like that. Cocky bastards, full of how important they think they are.

Well, back at the sale, I don't really need to tell you about the other customers, they are not important in this yarn but things slowly sold. There wasn't much of a price on items, I was just happy to move things along, help people out, you know what I mean?

Nearing mid-day, after another line and a slug of vodka, this young couple wandered in.

A blonde headed surfy-type guy said, 'G'day. We just moved in, one street over.'

I nodded. I was aware of her. She had long blonde hair also, a tiny figure, gentle swell of bum, short light-coloured dress, black leather stud belt. Tits pushed against a T-shirt showing a nice chest. She smiled a greeting in my direction. Most young women seem to find me attractive. I have been told it is the shape of my mouth, seems as if I am smiling. And with my dark eyes they somehow can't resist engaging with me. She smiled again. I shot her a glance. I didn't notice him much. Cock-head.

There were not many things left. They picked through a few items and all they came up with was a box of screws he wanted and believe it or not, a bag of plastic bags she held up. He handed over two dollars for the screws.

'You can have the plastic bags, on the house,' I said to her, because she was so beautiful.

He wandered out to have a look at the stuff in the wheelbarrow. She smiled at me again and wandered over to the large wooden packing crate with handles at each end. I didn't really want to sell it because I needed it to throw my few possessions in later on. She examined the lines and leant over to lift the lid. Her short cotton dress rode up. Her panties were not much more than a G string. Hungry bum. Cheeks soft, pink, and grabbable in the light from the spider-webbed window. She turned. I was more experienced at this than she could ever realise. I appeared to be rearranging some odds and ends in a cardboard carton.

'How much do you want for the wooden box?' I could tell her eyes were blue, even from a distance away.

'Well, it's not really for sale. I need it to put things in, but if I had to sell it, I'd want at least a hundred and fifty.'

'Would you take an even hundred?'

I pretended to consider for a moment. 'No, I'm sorry.'

Her schoolgirl tits looked like small lemons pressing out behind a white T-shirt. No bra. She threw her head back sending long blonde hair behind her glint, studded ears. 'That's okay,' she said and smiled again, narrowing her eyes this time.

They wandered down the driveway towards the front gate. My eyes were glued to her shapely little bum, a ripe peach almost below the dress line.

Several other people came and went over the next hour or so but by midday there was very little worth anything. Just rubbish, I had done well.

I knew roughly where she lived.

∞

On Sunday morning I stuck the two remaining rickety chairs outside the gate with a *Free* sign and before the ute was loaded, they were gone. Same old, same-ol', people can't help themselves, too stingy to pay a couple of bucks, would wait another day to get it for nothing. They wanted something for less than nothing. I drove to the dump with the rest and returned home, did a line of speed and swept the back path. There was a noise, gravel crunching. She stood at the side gate. I knew I'd see her again.

She ran a delicate silver ringed hand over her head, front to back. 'Oh, I was hoping you'd be here. Did you sell that box?'

'No.'

Bright red fingernails gently spidered the strap on her shoulder bag, eyes lowered but moving. 'Could I er … please have another look at it?'

'Yeah, no worries,' I said and pointed inside the shed through the side door. The front roller door was closed. I followed her in. She leant over the box and lifted the lid. The thumbnail down the bass string became louder. I couldn't look away. I could feel the sickness coming on. My face became hot.

She turned around. 'Would you take … umm a hundred and forty?' She trusted me. She wanted me.

I smiled and moved slowly towards her pretending to consider the offer. I slapped her hard. Her eyes nearly exploded, no time to scream. A quivering hand moved towards the welt. I punched her as hard as I could in the guts. She lifted off the ground and the shoulder bag hit the floor. The noise of the rake down the bass string hurt my head. A pick down a base string. She was just like the rest of them. My hand shot out and I grabbed her by the hair and smashed her pretty head against the bench in almost one action. I tore her panties off and I had her right there. Boiling tears and sweat streamed down my face; I knew I was noisy; I knew I needed to look at that in future. It all happened so quickly, the sickness, the down elevator on the base string. A force just steered me. It was her fault; she came here for it. She was chosen. That's the way it always happens. I can't be held responsible. I'm sure people would understand that.

I stood there panting and almost sobbing, like hyperventilating, for about five minutes. I did it to her again, but she was dead, I could tell. She wasn't breathing, there was no heartbeat. Her body was somewhere else. Yeah, I could tell.

I washed my hands and had a long guzzle of vodka. At least the thumbnail noise on the bass string had gone away, a violin seemed to be there. Hell, it was all really deafening just a few minutes ago, always is. Things needed to be brought back on track.

'Fuck,' I said. Funny how you remember things like that. Just a swear word but some things mean a lot at the time, and later, too when I click into that headspace.

I wrapped a towel around her head to soak up the blood and then crammed her into the box. I sat down on an oil drum for a minute and had another drink of vodka but decided against a line of speed. There was a real need to concentrate hard, critical moments. Not much cleaning up to do. The rag, her shoulder bag and ripped panties went into the box. The lid closed, all neat, easy as. I backed the ute in, slid the box into the tray, tied it down and dribbled down the driveway.

Just as I crawled through the gates, he nearly walked into me.

'G'day, man, how ya doing?' he said, surfy-bullshit-American-guy blab. 'Get rid of everything?'

A jolt of shock. 'Er ... yeah, pretty much anyway.' My recovery was quick though. 'Sold the box last thing, delivering it now.'

'That's a pity; my girlfriend was really interested in that. She wanted to put all her personal stuff in there. You know how babes are, eh, dude?'

'Yeah, I sure do,' I said in an agreeable way.

'Righto buddy, see ya.' He gave a lopsided grin and kept going.

I knew a place where it was thick with crocs. Perfect spot, no one went there. They hadn't discovered the other two, never would. I'd smash the box up and chuck it in as well further downstream. It was definitely time to move on to the next place though. Never good to get cocky. They were closing in on me, but I had a knack for keeping at least one step ahead.

The End

Sometimes the obvious

Is not as it seems -

Consider the plural

Little Boys Lost

With a burst of diesel fumes, the last bus trundled out of the station. The passengers had been interviewed and the police had come up with nothing, and to avoid a riot the police were compelled to let them all go. Inspector Roland Atwood shuffled uneasily on his feet. He was well aware that if they did not find the perpetrator within a few hours they would have no hope. He needed a cigarette.

Sergeant Sue Piper walked over. 'Sir? Had a good chat with the mother, a Mrs Candice Roberts. She's obviously upset, says she only took a few steps away to check the bus code, when she turned, he was gone. Young Alex is only five, poor little bugger.'

'She would say that, Sue, wouldn't she?' The inspector was mindful that some people did not take the responsibility of looking after their children as seriously as they should. 'Christ. No one saw any bloody thing. How can that be.' It was not a question.

Sergeant Piper continued. 'She seems to think her ex is the one who snatched him. I've instigated an alert, we've combed the area as best we can, and we have interviewed everyone within coo-ee of the bus station. As well as everyone who was here at the time ready to get on either of the three buses.'

'Wish we could smoke on the job, I'm dying for one, can't think like a cop without the nicotine.'

'Sir, it's bad for you and it's not a good look for the public either.'

'I don't need your scolding, sergeant. I get enough of that from the missus. Anyway, bag that up, it probably won't tell us anything, don't even know whose it is.' He pointed to the spilt, crushed drink container lying solo on the massive expanse of the deserted bus station.

Just then one of the constables signalled them over. 'We've picked up the ex, seems he's in the clear, was underneath a four-wheel drive doing mechanical work, others have verified it. Also, his workplace is nearly an hour from here.'

'Shit,' mumbled the inspector. 'He could have arranged for someone else to snatch the kid for him so bring him in anyway and continue to question him, and keep at the other workmates, orright? Right, the rest of yas, spread out again and check everywhere particularly small hiding places. Sergeant, let's you and I talk to the mother again.'

Mrs Candice Roberts was sobbing into an already wet handkerchief. Inspector Atwood nodded towards Sergeant Piper, who had beat him to it, and somehow commandeered a wad of paper from somewhere, probably the toilets.

As they approached, Mrs Roberts looked up, red eyes boiling water. 'Have you found him yet?'

'We are doing all we can,' replied Inspector Atwood, grateful that his sergeant had put her arm around the distraught woman but realising the words he used were totally inadequate.

He asked a few more of those stock standard questions, hoping to pry some usable information but the police seemed to be no closer to a solution than they were a couple of hours ago. The inspector nodded towards the sergeant who heeded his meaning and continued to comfort Mrs Roberts. He stood up and wandered towards the now abandoned ticket office and leaned against the doorframe. A slight movement to his right, inside the office, caught his attention. The cupboard door behind the desk moved. He was sure of it. He tried the office door, which was locked, so he headed towards the main entrance where a cleaner was sitting on and upturned bucket.

'Do you have a key to the office?' Inspector Atwood pointed.

'Um, yeah, no worries,' said the man, fiddling with a bunch of jailers' keys as he walked towards the door.

Inspector Atwood gently opened the door. 'You can come out now,' he said kindly.

The cupboard door slowly moved. 'I'm scared,' said a small voice.

'It's alright, son, I'll protect you.' He turned and waved towards Sergeant Piper.

A young boy gingerly stuck his head out and looked around, eyes wide.

'Your mum has been worried about you,' said the inspector, thinking to himself in jest *and we have been farting around here wasting our bloody time looking for you too, you know.*

He gently allowed the boy to grab his hand. 'I was scared,' said the little man. 'God was yelling at me.'

'God?'

'Yes,' said the boy seriously, 'God was yelling at me through those things.' He pointed at the loudspeakers overhead.

Mrs Roberts was in full sprint. 'You found him, you found ... what? That's not my son! That's not Alexander ... where is my...?' She burst out in a fresh gush of water works.

Just then a flustered, hippy looking woman came running into the bus station.

'There you are you little ... where the hell have you been hiding?'

Inspector Roland Atwood looked at Sergeant Sue Piper.

She whispered, 'Um, we still have a missing child then, sir, don't we?'

He felt a very strong urge for a cigarette at that point in time. 'Christ.'

The End

Things may not be as they appear -

Just be there -

Kindness can be a reward

Grey Man

'Yes, I'm sorry Sweetheart, I'll be over to pick you up as soon as Damian condescends to privilege me with his attendance to take over the job he is paid to perform.' Flanagan continued his eye rolling as he looked at the customer. He mouthed, *the missus.* As if that would explain everything and he held out his hand to take money for the paper.

Whilst sorting through piles of Courier Mails and Weekend Australians, he heard the agency door open and a dishevelled man rushed up to him. Flanagan recoiled slightly from the man, who initially appeared to be quite old and looked as if he was a down and outer. The man was intense, sad, confused and gave the impression he would smell – but surprisingly he did not.

The man's gaze zipped around the room like a terrier looking for a rat, as he pulled back his hood displaying a knitted woolly beanie. 'I'm sorry, you must help me,' he half whispered.

'Um, yes, of course …'

'I missed the bus … Mum's in Saint Margaret's Hospital, she's very old you know … and I have to visit her.' His frantic manner seemed to abate a little towards the last part of the sentence.

Flanagan realised the bloke was not a *down and outer,* just a man maybe down on his luck. The man had a grey pallor about him. He played with his beard which looked clean, but his hammered face and complexion made it look unkempt.

'I managed to finally get a day off work so I could see her. Oh, dear. You don't know when the next bus is? I just moved in down the road a few days ago.'

Flanagan wondered what the initial urgency was because the man seemed calm now. 'Next bus isn't until mid-morning, far as I know.'

'God, I said I would be in there early ... she gets into an anxiety state very easily, you know. I can't afford a taxi.'

Flanagan could not help examining the man's face. Full of fine, spider web wrinkles, skin like old, grey carpet. He felt kinship, a sense of duty. 'Look, mate, my wife works near the hospital in a coffee shop - morning shift - and I will be going in that direction to pick her up soon.'

The man put his hand in a curious way against his beard and his fingers began a gentle tattoo against his cheek. 'Oh, I couldn't put you to that trouble ...'

'It's no trouble but we have to wait for Damian to take over ... he's my son, who is supposed to be here by now, you know how kids are,' he smiled sarcastically, fully aware that his son was nearly thirty and as lazy as a lump of mud. 'Speak of the devil, here he is, only half an hour late.' He mumbled, 'Bit of a line up at the Employment Office, was there, mate?'

∞

Ten minutes later they were in Flanagan's delivery van on their way to the hospital.

'I'll drop you at the front ramp if you like. Just go to the reception and they should be able to tell you what ward she's in.'

As they pulled up in front of the hospital, the dishevelled grey man looked at him with sad eyes. 'I don't know how to thank you, Mr ...?

'Flanagan, just Flanagan, that's what everyone calls me, and you are?'

'Oh yes, Cormac.' His brow bunched into extreme worry lines.

Flanagan wondered why he said that and as he was about to pull away, he said, 'I can pick you up on the way home if you like, my wife and I have to do a bit of shopping first.'

The man floundered, 'I don't really know what to do, I ... I don't know what room she's in ...'

Flanagan, realising the man's distress, offered, 'Hang on, I'll park, and we can go in together.'

'Thanks, I don't know how to thank you,' said the man and smiled in a spacey way.

∞

Flanagan gently directed the grey man to take a seat. He stood at the counter in front of the administrative person, who pretended to be extremely busy, for several minutes. A shock jock commercial radio station hammered out racist and Nazi propaganda in the background. It was clear she had an empire to defend.

She looked up in a way that was intended to make Flanagan feel subservient. 'Can I help you?' she snapped.

Flanagan was not going to bite. He was experienced. His wife was in her middle years as well and he had, for some time now, started each of his sentences with, 'I'm sorry, Dear ... but...'. He knew he could easily come off second best with this health professional woman if he did not take the right approach.

'Good morning, umm I have a ... er friend here wishing to visit his mother. The name is, Cormac.'

'What is she in for?'

'Um, don't know.' He looked around and noticed the grey man was not there. 'Hang on, he's shot through.'

The woman glared in annoyance at him and then looked back at her important work, ignoring, and dismissing him. Flanagan finally caught Cormac two corridors away.

The grey man stroked his beard. 'I can't find her ...'

'It's okay, mate, let's go back to reception and they can look up her room number.'

Back at reception the woman continued to ignore the two men. Flanagan did not have all day and did not like the idea of someone getting the better of him.

'Hey, excuse me, I could start my sentence with sorry but I'm not prepared to do that, can you tell me what room Mrs Cormac is in?' He deliberately did not use the word, please.

'What's she in for?'

'Does it matter?'

'God some people are rude,' the woman mumbled towards another staff member who had just put down the phone. 'Cormac. We have no one of that name here.' She looked up aggressively.

The grey man said in a shaky voice. 'No, that's *my* name, Cormac, Cormac McGinty. Look, I feel a little dizzy, I have to sit down.'

Flanagan rolled his eyes as he turned to the woman. 'Mrs McGinty, I believe the person's name is.'

'Do you think I have a hearing problem? I heard.'

Just then, the other staff member came over and whispered, 'Cormac McGinty?' She put her hand to her mouth. 'He's from Harmony Nursing Home – that's a place for people with,' she whispered more softly, 'dementia. They have been looking for him all morning. He keeps trying to visit his mother, who died many years ago. This is the first time he has ever managed to sneak out.'

The End

Life is meant to be lived

Make the most of it -

It belongs to you

Last Hurrah

Claire sorted the mail, opened them all, wrote a few cheques, read the letter again and threw it to the middle of the table. She made a decision.

∞

Later that day.

'You are going to do what?'

'A skydive.'

Her daughter, Laura, removed her sunglasses and stared. 'A what?'

'I'm not the only one going deaf around here,' said Claire, laughing.

'But Mum ...'

Claire had thought this through; it was one of the things she had always wanted to do; a skydive. Some people wanted more grandchildren, some people wanted to see the pyramids. She wanted to do a skydive. 'It's a called a tandem jump, love.'

'But ... but you're 81 years old?'

'So what, it's one of the things that has always been on my list. My arthritis isn't too bad at the moment, and I can hobble around alright.'

'But ... what if the parachute didn't open and you died?' Laura shook her head in frustration, her mother was worse than a child and she had wondered what had got into her recently.

Claire explained that if the parachute didn't open, she wouldn't have time to worry about dying - whenever that might be.

'What if the person you are strapped to wants to commit suicide?'

'Now why would they want to do that and take someone with them? That's silly logic. Anyway, I've researched the skydiving school, and all the instructors have to do 100 dives before they get their licence to do tandems. Anyway, love, what's the problem? I'm the one doing the skydive not you.'

Laura shook her head. 'I rest my case, I think you probably need to see a psychiatrist, I think you're going crazy.'

'I'm not crazy, Laura, I've got my doctor's okay.'

'Gawd. When do you intend to do this silly thing?'

'Probably next week, dear.'

∞

At Gungdoola Sky Diving School, 178 kilometres west of the Sunshine Coast, Laura pulled up in a cloud of dust beside an old shipping container with *Office* painted on the door. She figured she might have been able to talk her mother out of the silly venture on the way, if she was to drive her there. No show.

She had arrived early at her mother's place and a quick recap confirmed that her mother had not changed her mind. Not one to give up she figured there was still a chance.

'Right let's go then.'

So, on the trip out nothing had changed. Her mother was committed to do the jump. Laura sighed a few times as she helped her mother waddle into the office where some paperwork was dealt with, and money paid.

The young woman on the counter smiled and said, 'You will enjoy this, Claire, we get many older folks who wish to do a sky dive as an experience in their later lives. Not that you are that old, we've had several ninety plus year olds recently.'

Laura, still worrying for her mother, said, 'What's your safety record?'

'One hundred percent. No accidents since we started several years ago. Everything gets checked, double checked and then checked again in the plane. Don't worry, it's all good.'

Laura was about to say something. Claire turned to her daughter. 'Stop it. I've made the decision, it's my life, leave me alone.' She winked at the woman behind the counter.

With that Laura clammed up, in a huff. 'Alright, if that's what you want well so be it,' and she walked outside.

Claire rolled her eyes, 'Don't worry about her, dear, she's just concerned for my wellbeing. I don't have any qualms about doing a sky dive, always wanted to give it a go.'

She was taken over to an aircraft hangar and they passed a group of unruly young men who were being pushed out by one of the staff. She was shown the equipment, and the process was explained. Laura remained in the car.

There was one other person due to jump with her on the early dive.

'G'day, I'm Ron.' The young man explained he was on a dare. He'd had a skin full one night not long ago and was silly enough to tell everyone he was going to do a sky dive for his 21st. He pointed to a group of young men pushing and shoving each other out near the runway. 'They're making sure I'm a man of my word.'

'Twenty-one today?' enquired Claire.

'No, was two days ago but I'm keen. I have to do what I said I was going to do, don't I?' He rolled his eyes and they both laughed. 'What about you?' He frowned, clearly intrigued as to why an ancient person like her was doing an adrenalin rush activity like a sky dive.

'Let's just say I'm having a second lease on life, and I've always wanted to do this. When you get to my age, every day is a bonus. I cheated God this morning by seeing the sunrise.'

Just then, the two instructors, dressed in lightweight jumpsuits wandered in.

'Right, my name is Craig,' said the taller one of the two. 'This is Lukic, he's from Croatia. Call him Luke, alright?'

Just then Laura barged in. 'If you don't mind me asking, how many jumps has Luke done? Eh?' She said, almost aggressively.

Both the instructors started laughing.

Graig put his hands out in front, stop signs. 'You have no need to worry, Luke has a number of awards to his credit and has done over six hundred jumps here, not counting hundreds in Europe.'

'How come he's wearing sandshoes?' She continued, frowning.

'He plays tennis, he's a champ at that, too.'

Claire said, with shaky bravado, 'Can I partner with Luke? I like the element of danger, what do you reckon, Laura?'

Luke smiled.

Laura shook her head and went over under the trees near the landing target.

'Right, lets saddle up.' Craig began to run through the details and safety aspects of the exercise. 'Now, the aircraft is a Cessna 182 …'

∞

Claire had to be assisted on her journey out to the small aircraft that had taxied up to the entrance of the hangar. The jumpsuit was restrictive, and her stiff limbs made it awkward to move freely. Ron's complexion had taken on a pale, waxy look.

'Don't worry, Pet, things will turn out alright. If you like, I'll go first,' said Claire in a voice meant to be brave but containing a slight tremor.

They both laughed.

The aircraft had no door, just an opening obviously designed for easy departure when the time was right up at the correct altitude. There was only canvas padding on the deck. Ron climbed in first and was instructed to clip himself to a D bolt on the floor. Craig jumped in and positioned himself alongside him.

Luke helped Claire in, placing a foam padded canvas cushion, which he secured to the deck under her. He then climbed over, clipping himself to her as well as the floor.

The noise of the small aircraft was deafening, even with earmuffs, and became more so as they taxied out onto the runway. Big noise, speed increase and then up and away into the sky. The concrete runway became smaller as Claire glanced down; her heart raced in time with the shuddering deck as the aircraft did a big loop around the township.

It was too noisy in the cabin to talk and the hand signals they had practised earlier were used. The tiny Cessna continued to swing in ever widening circles as it made its way upwards. With every loop it became colder, and Claire was glad of the jumpsuit she was wearing. She had a padded helmet which kept her head warm, and the goggles kept the cold air away from her eyes.

When they reached the given height of 12,000 feet the aircraft levelled off. Luke tapped her on the shoulder as he re-checked the attachments and connections. He leant around slightly to her side and winked at her. She noticed that he was not wearing goggles. Or a helmet. He smiled. She thought about his sandshoes without socks.

He held his hand out in front of her and counted off the fingers 5-4-3-2-1-go.

Bingo! They rolled out of the plane. The rushing wind tried to tear off her goggles instantly and get inside her helmet as they free fell for what seemed like minutes. The earth looked such a long way down, the houses and the roads looked like a child's play village. The ground did not seem to be getting any closer, but she did wonder when Luke was going to pull the ripcord. The rushing wind tugged at her clothing and safety gear, but she was mindful of the fact the instructors had tightened things up and made it clear that things would not be torn off, and she would be safe.

Suddenly, it seemed like suddenly anyway, to Claire, the ground seemed to hurtle towards them and houses, cars, and everything else became rapidly bigger. She could feel her heart banging against her rib cage.

Claire did not have an opportunity to panic because Luke pulled the ripcord. She now knew why it was called a ripcord because it nearly ripped her shoulders out, even though the parachute was more connected to Luke than her.

With the fever pitch excitement of the freefall Claire realised how calm and peaceful the last part of the skydive was. Luke was obviously skilled at controlling the parachute and managed to glide almost at the same level for some time and other times he made the parachute duck and weave and drop.

They came into the target area at what she thought was very fast and her insides jumped but at the last moment Luke managed to keep the parachute on a glide as they came in and gently landed right in the middle of the target.

It took Claire a few moments to be able to stand on her jelly legs and to talk, she was so excited and high. Luke unhooked her and helped to move away from the landing zone so that Craig and Ron could land safely.

She felt so good, she was 21 again, even though her joints were sore and her shoulders a little bruised from the straps.

She turned and gave Luke a big hug. 'Thank you dear that was the most wonderful experience of my life.'

They watched Craig and Ron land safely.

Ron let out a whoooooooooooop! much to the delight of his mates who continued to rabble him as they came over.

They headed over to the hangar to strip off their safety gear.

Ron was almost beside himself with joy.

Laura came in and stood with arms folded. 'Well, that's a landing you walked away from, Mum. I hope you've now got this silliness out of your mind.'

Craig said, 'Maybe you should try it, too.'

They all laughed at that. The other lads could see that Laura was not pleased about the whole thing.

∞

On the way back to the coast Laura seemed to have calmed down somewhat.

'Why did you decide to do a skydive, Mum?'

'Can't you just leave it, dear. It's just something I wanted to do, alright? I'm still smiling, it was a wonderful experience. That was so good, I think I'd like to do it again.'

'What?' Laura realised that her mother was joking - or was she?

They pulled into the driveway at Claire's place. 'Would you like to come in for a cuppa, dear?'

'No thanks, Mum I have to do some shopping, so I'll see you at the weekend for lunch on Sunday, at our place alright?

∞

Sometime later, with a cup of tea in front of her Claire picked up the letter from the specialist and read it again.

The End

Acknowledgements

There are many people I have met and learned from on my writing journey over several decades, and I sincerely thank everyone who has helped me over the years.

I have listed below the key people who have been influential in guiding me throughout my writing journey and I would like to acknowledge them in alphabetical order.

Ian Austin
Jan Bentley
Beryl Corris
Bronwyn Cozens
Michael Doneman
Bob Goodwin
Pam Hardgrave
Laurie Keim
Rosemary Laver
Morgana McCloud
Denise Miller
Beryl Muspratt
Brian Purdey
Alison Quigley
Andrea Rankin
Steve Reilly
Robin Storey

Thanks also to my friends in the many writing groups I have been privileged to be a member of, especially the haiku and writers at Noosa Arts and Crafts.

Special thanks to Jan Forbes for her amazing cover designs for all of my books. The cover design incorporates a photo of the landscape at Farina in the far north of South Australia. Once a thriving town it was abandoned in the 1950's when the railway closed. Some of the descendants and friends of the pioneer families have returned to Farina to rebuild some of the buildings to create a living historical museum.

On the cover is a single spinner 1954 Ford Customline that has seen better days. Look for *Wheel Bearing* Richards hidden away in the vista.

Without the support and encouragement from my extended family and friends I would not have made it to publication. Finally, special thanks to Denise Miller for the many hours of editing and proof reading to get the book to the publication stage.

ABOUT THE AUTHOR

Ian Laver is a well-travelled fiction writer living in south east Queensland. His first novel, CRUCIAL STEP, was published in 2021. His second novel, UNEASY, was published in 2022, followed by the publication of a short story collection, DEADLY SINS, in 2024. He enjoys writing short stories, and many of these stories have been published in anthologies and magazines. HARD HITS is his second collection of short stories and he is currently writing COMEBACK, the sequel to UNEASY, which continues the adventures and investigations of Queensland detective Rodney FitzMichael.

Ian was editor of a small country association magazine and had a regular column in an on-line publication. He was President of the Sunshine Coast Literary Association, has been active in writing organisations and is at present involved in a Haiku poetry group. Two Henry Lawson Emerging Writer and a Tom Howard Short Story Award are listed among his more than a dozen writing awards.

You can discover more about Ian's writing at-
Facebook: https://www.facebook.com/ian.laver.18
Facebook author page: Ian Laver | Facebook
Website: https://www.ianlaver.net
Instagram: https://www.instagram.com/iwlaver